A Matchmaking Mother

by

Jann Rowland

One Good Sonnet Publishing
Publishers of Fine Romance
and Fantasy Fiction

By Jann Rowland

Published by One Good Sonnet Publishing:

PRIDE AND PREJUDICE VARIATIONS

Acting on Faith
A Life from the Ashes (Sequel to *Acting on Faith*)
Open Your Eyes
Implacable Resentment
An Unlikely Friendship
Bound by Love
Cassandra
Obsession
Shadows Over Longbourn
The Mistress of Longbourn
My Brother's Keeper
Coincidence
The Angel of Longbourn
Chaos Comes to Kent
In the Wilds of Derbyshire
The Companion
Out of Obscurity
What Comes Between Cousins
A Tale of Two Courtships
Murder at Netherfield
Whispers of the Heart
A Gift for Elizabeth
Mr. Bennet Takes Charge
The Impulse of the Moment
The Challenge of Entail
A Matchmaking Mother

COURAGE ALWAYS RISES: THE BENNET SAGA

The Heir's Disgrace

Co-Authored with Lelia Eye

WAITING FOR AN ECHO

Waiting for an Echo Volume One: Words in the Darkness
Waiting for an Echo Volume Two: Echoes at Dawn

A Summer in Brighton
A Bevy of Suitors
Love and Laughter: A Pride and Prejudice Short Stories Anthology

This is a work of fiction based on the works of Jane Austen. All the characters and events portrayed in this novel are products of Jane Austen's original novel or the authors' imaginations.

A MATCHMAKING MOTHER

To my family who have, as always, shown
their unconditional love and encouragement.

PROLOGUE

*F*ew amusements could capture the imagination of a young lady of a certain age more completely than an evening of dancing.

The sisters residing at Longbourn estate in Hertfordshire were as susceptible to the thought of such delights as any other. The ball at Netherfield Park, having been announced the previous week, was a source of much delight and anticipation, and even more so when the preceding four days had been dreary, the skies opening up and rendering them bound to their home as the earth about them became a sodden mass not fit for man nor beast.

Of the ball, much has been said, and it behooves the author to avoid repetition and focus on other matters, such as might surprise the reader and lead to a tale yet untold. As the Bennet carriage pulled up to the door of the estate that evening, Elizabeth's mind was filled with thoughts of the charming Mr. Wickham, of the dances she meant to share with him. Of less interest to her was the presence of Mr. Darcy, the man she had learned to detest, a man she meant to ignore and avoid as much as possible. But fate, it seemed, was destined to interfere with such plans in a manner Elizabeth could never have expected.

The news that Mr. Wickham was not present for the evening's entertainment, Elizabeth met with annoyance, but the absence of Mr.

Darcy as a target of her ire was also denied her. Instead, Elizabeth stood speaking with her friend, Charlotte Lucas, for some time, exasperating herself against Mr. Darcy and Mr. Collins—her father's ridiculous cousin, who was set on giving her the unwanted distinction of becoming the companion of his future life—in equal measure. The only consolation was that Mr. Darcy appeared to have avoided the evening, and thus he would not intrude on her peace of mind. And while the thought of his attending a ball, a pastime he did not enjoy and would consider a punishment, had its appeal, Elizabeth could not find it in herself to repine his absence.

Jane danced the first with Mr. Bingley—and a handsome couple they were—while Elizabeth endured Mr. Collins's inept attentions, longing for the end of the sets promised to him, which would allow her to seek other, more agreeable partners. When she finally made her escape, Elizabeth found her attention caught by a pair of women she had never met.

It was obvious upon a cursory glance that the two ladies were related, likely a mother and daughter, given their respective ages. Both were passing tall, blonde of hair and fair of face, the elder carrying herself with dignity and the posture of a woman of some quality, while the younger was smiling and happy, full of youthful life and hope. Elizabeth put the age of the elder at between five and forty and fifty years, the younger, perhaps eighteen.

Of further interest was the appearance, at last, of the man she detested. Mr. Darcy was standing nearby, speaking to the two ladies—it seemed to Elizabeth he was giving them an account of the principal figures present in the room. Then their eyes fell on Elizabeth herself, and Elizabeth received a shock when the elder woman gestured to her, and Mr. Darcy, though not eager, if Elizabeth was any judge, led them to her.

"Miss Elizabeth," said he, executing a perfect bow, "my mother has requested an introduction to you if you will be so kind as to allow it."

The news that this was his mother—and likely his sister—was not so much of a surprise as that they would request an introduction. With her usual composure, Elizabeth gave her consent, curious about these ladies who claimed such a close connection to the ever-detestable Mr. Darcy.

"Mother, Georgiana, I present Miss Elizabeth Bennet, the second of the Bennet sisters of the nearby estate of Longbourn. Miss Elizabeth, this is my mother, Lady Anne Darcy, and my sister, Miss Georgiana Darcy."

The ladies curtseyed to one another, and Lady Anne spoke in a tone at once kind and cultured. "Miss Elizabeth. My daughter and I are pleased to make your acquaintance. You must excuse the suddenness of the application, for our decision to accept Mr. Bingley's longstanding invitation was made only a few days ago."

"It seems it was," replied Elizabeth, responding with pleasure, instinctively knowing this woman was not at all like her insufferable son, "for we had no word of your coming. Given as I am to understand that you are the daughter of an earl, I might have thought the news would be all over Meryton within minutes of its being announced." Elizabeth grinned at the ladies. "Surely the visit of the daughter of a peer is not so inconsequential to Miss Bingley that she would neglect to mention it to anyone."

The ladies laughed at her jest, and Miss Darcy exclaimed: "I might have expected Miss Bingley to be the main bearer of such tales!"

While Mr. Darcy shot his sister a quelling look, Lady Anne only shook her head with fond amusement at her daughter's words. It seemed neither lady had missed the inference in Elizabeth's statement.

"It is for that reason we did not wish the Bingleys to announce our coming," said Lady Anne. "Though I *am* the daughter of an earl, I am more particularly pleased to be known as the mother of my two children and another in a long line of wives who have helped make my son's estate what it is today."

"I can see where such attention might become tiresome," said Elizabeth, attempting a diplomatic approach, yet pleased the lady seemed so humble.

For the next several moments the ladies continued to speak, Mr. Darcy remaining silent, like a sentinel standing guard over them. The conversation of the two Darcy women was interesting and enjoyable, though it contrasted with the silence of the gentleman, rendering Elizabeth confused as to how they could be members of the same family. Within a few moments, Elizabeth realized she appreciated these ladies very much and hoped she would be in a position to call them friends before long.

Soon, however, the social demands of the evening took precedence, and Elizabeth's partner for the next sets arrived to claim her hand. If she thought, however, that would be the end of her congress with the Darcy women for the rest of the evening, she soon learned her mistake, for the ladies approached her several more times before the dinner hour, engaging her again in their interrupted conversation. From what Elizabeth could determine, they were willing to be introduced to all and sundry, even speaking with Sir William for almost ten minutes. It also did not miss her notice that it was to her they returned repeatedly.

As the supper hour edged closer, Elizabeth noted as she danced that the three stood together, again in earnest conversation, with Mr. Darcy shaking his head while the women seemed to be exhorting. Then, soon after the exchange, the dance ended, and Mr. Darcy approached her.

"Miss Elizabeth," said he with his usual proper bow, "might I solicit your next sets if you are not engaged?"

Surprise did not even begin to cover Elizabeth's reaction as the implications made themselves known to her. Knowing, however, she would appear a simpleton if she stood and stared at him, she answered, though with more composure than coherence, her willingness to stand up with him. If he noted her discomposure, Mr. Darcy said nothing of it, merely expressing his anticipation and then leaving her for the moment.

"Did Mr. Darcy just ask you to dance?"

"It seems he did, though I would never have credited the possibility," replied Elizabeth, turning to Charlotte, who had approached her.

Charlotte fixed Elizabeth with a pointed look in response. "You would not? Did you not inform me—with a certain amount of glee, I might add—of your refusal of Mr. Darcy's offer at my father's party in October?"

"But he only did so at your father's urging!" exclaimed Elizabeth.

"Had he not been willing, he might have ignored Papa," rejoined Charlotte. "I love my father, but I am aware he is pompous at times. I dare say many others have acted the same in the past."

While Elizabeth opened her mouth to respond, the memory of Mr. Darcy suggesting they dance a jig at Netherfield filled her mind, and she found she could not respond. Though she had thought at the time it was nothing more than an idle comment—and she still felt that way—the thought crossed her mind that it may have been something more. The very thought of Mr. Darcy having any interest in her, considering his words at the assembly, brought Elizabeth back to her senses, and she made a jesting comment back to Charlotte, one which seemed to satisfy her friend.

Had Elizabeth any expectation of Mr. Darcy's interest, it would have been dashed by his behavior during their sets, which turned out to be the dances preceding supper. For the entire first dance, the man remained silent and grave, immune to her attempts to prompt him to speak, his gaze often fixed on her in earnest contemplation, which was not at all new, though there was nothing in it that Elizabeth could interpret. When Sir William stopped them during the second dance, referring to his expectation of Jane's imminent change in status, Mr. Darcy's eyes were on the couple for the rest of the dance, and his look was not at all friendly. Thus, when the music faded away and the time came to escort her to dinner, Elizabeth wished to be away from his company, lest she say something in her annoyance which would be both pointed and caustic.

"I am happy you shall sit with us for dinner," said Miss Darcy when Elizabeth arrived with her escort to the supper room. "Did you enjoy your dance with my brother?"

Though Elizabeth had rarely found anything more disagreeable, she could hardly say so to the man's sister. "Mr. Darcy is an excellent dancer," said she, using every measure of diplomacy honed by living her life as Mrs. Margaret Bennet's daughter.

"He ought to be," said Lady Anne, shooting a mirthful glance at her stoic son. "His father and I devoted much attention to his education in ensuring he knows the steps, so this evidence of his diligence is welcome."

"It is evidence I do not believe you lacked before," replied Mr. Darcy. In his manner, Elizabeth found a warmth she had not thought he possessed, so cold had he always been to every one of her acquaintance.

As they sat together and continued to speak, Elizabeth was interested to witness Mr. Darcy's interactions with his mother and sister and contrast them with his occasional comments to Elizabeth herself. While he was much as he ever was, reserved and restrained, there was an undercurrent of affection in his eyes, his words almost gentle, particularly when addressing his sister. Clearly, he adored her and would do anything for her.

His mother, on the other hand, provoked a degree of deference Elizabeth would not have thought possible in such a prepossessed man. When Lady Anne spoke, Mr. Darcy remained silent and attentive, and when he responded, his arrogant tone was softened. Not that he always agreed with her. In fact, they disagreed on more than one occasion and were both intent upon defending their positions. But whereas Elizabeth had never experienced the gentleman's interest or respect for her own opinion, he gave it to his mother and sister without thought.

After some time of sitting together, in which Elizabeth found herself unaware of what was passing in the room around them, Jane happened to pass close by, and as Lady Anne indicated she had not yet made Jane's acquaintance, Elizabeth beckoned her sister closer. The two ladies stood to greet Elizabeth's sister, and the introduction was thus performed. Jane, as was her wont, greeted the new acquaintances with her usual serenity.

"I am pleased to make your acquaintance," said Jane. "Do you mean to stay in the area long?"

Elizabeth did not miss the glance shared between Miss Darcy and her mother, though she was not as adept in understanding its meaning. "At present, I do not think we mean to depart," said Lady Anne. "But it is possible our plans might change."

"Then I hope you enjoy your time in Hertfordshire. Though I have heard others speak of Mr. Darcy's estate in glowing terms, and understand Derbyshire to be more picturesque than Hertfordshire, I believe we have some beauties to tempt you."

Lady Anne laughed and pressed Jane's hands. "I believe you do. This is a worthy part of the kingdom, Miss Bennet, and I assure you we are in no hurry to leave it."

With Jane added to their little group, the dynamic changed ever so slightly. Now there was someone else to share in the attention which they had lavished on Elizabeth herself, and she was able to witness a little more and consider the actions of those around her. For Elizabeth, character study had always been a favorite pastime, and she used the opportunity to determine further the characters of the two ladies. She was not disappointed.

"Do you play, Miss Bennet, Miss Elizabeth?" asked Miss Darcy after a time of talking with them.

"Lizzy does," replied Jane. "I only play a very little, but Lizzy is skilled."

"Do not speak so!" exclaimed Elizabeth. "When they learn the truth, it will only be that much more disappointing!"

Lady Anne and Miss Darcy laughed, though Jane only looked with mild amusement at her sister. The most surprising response came from Mr. Darcy.

"On the contrary, Miss Elizabeth, I have rarely heard anything which gave me more pleasure than when you played at Lucas Lodge."

At first, Elizabeth thought to tease the man back for making such a caustic observation concerning her playing. Then she reconsidered, for she realized Mr. Darcy was entirely serious. Mr. Darcy praising her! In Elizabeth's wildest dreams, she never would have thought such a thing possible.

"It is inevitable my daughter will turn the conversation to music," said Lady Anne, caressing Miss Darcy's cheek with affection. "And my son has excellent taste, so I hope you will forgive me, Miss Elizabeth, if I believe his account rather than your attempt at modesty."

The comments put Elizabeth off balance such that she was unable to respond. Then the opportunity was lost, for an interruption came from a most unwelcome source.

"Cousin Elizabeth," came the pompous voice of Mr. Collins, "I hope you will attribute my intrusion, not to any unseemly motive, but to the discovery of an astonishing discovery, the likes of which I never would have thought to make. It has come to my attention that not only is Mr. Darcy, Lady Catherine de Bourgh's nephew in attendance tonight, but that only today, Lady Anne Darcy and Miss Darcy have come to Netherfield!"

"And who are you, sir?" demanded Mr. Darcy, clearly annoyed with the parson for speaking to them without an introduction.

"My name is William Collins," said Mr. Collins with a bow so low Elizabeth thought his head might touch the floor. "I have the great pleasure and honor of being your aunt's parson. I am also in the happy position of informing you that Lady Catherine and her excellent daughter were in the best of health only eight days ago!"

Though Elizabeth thought Mr. Darcy prepared to say something caustic in reply, Lady Anne interrupted him, saying: "It is my thought my sister mentioned you to me in a letter, Mr. Collins. It was last spring she installed you in the parsonage, is it not?"

"You are correct," replied Mr. Collins, his homely face lighting up in pleasure at the notice he was receiving from his patroness's sister. "Just after Easter I received my ordination and was in the happy position of coming to Lady Catherine's notice."

Then Mr. Collins turned to Elizabeth and stated, in a voice so syrupy sweet as to cause Elizabeth to gag: "You have been fortunate to receive the attention of so great personages as these, Cousin. I dare say it will bode well for the future to be recognized with so little effort on your part."

Elizabeth wished to sink into the floor in mortification. Whatever friendship she had attained from these ladies, it was clearly gone with Mr. Collins's stupidity. What she would not give for his immediate absence!

The evening could not have proceeded better, in Lady Anne's opinion.

At least it was perfect until Mr. Collins appeared. A perceptive woman, Lady Anne did not miss the man's interest in Miss Elizabeth, nor had the accounts she had heard of his first sets with the girl given her any reason to suppose his words were motivated by anything less than an intention of making her an offer.

Though Miss Elizabeth was humiliated, Lady Anne left her daughter to raise the girl's spirits, for if this opportunity was not to be lost to them, she knew she must divert Mr. Collins from his path. When supper ended and the dancing once again began, she moved back to the ballroom with the rest of the company, her eyes open for a chance to speak with the parson. Such an opportunity presented itself shortly thereafter.

"Mr. Collins," said she in greeting. "If I might have your attention, there is a matter of which I would speak with you."

The parson gaped at her in surprise, as she intended—if she allowed him to speak first, Anne knew it may be thirty minutes or more before she could turn the conversation to where she desired it to go. It was best to state her case at once, for the man was as much of a dullard as any man she had ever met.

"Thank you," said Anne, not waiting for him to gather what there was of his wits. "It has come to my attention that you have singled out Miss Elizabeth Bennet. Might I surmise you have come to Hertfordshire intending to make her an offer?"

The man's face lit up, and his eyes darted to where the young woman was dancing with a man of the neighborhood. It seemed Miss Elizabeth had not missed his sudden scrutiny, for as she passed nearby, there appeared on her cheeks a hint of a stain of embarrassment. Anne determined to ensure Mr. Collins would never provoke such a reaction again.

"I should have known you would understand all within a moment, for you are very like your sister," said Mr. Collins, preening in his self-satisfaction. To Lady Anne Darcy, being compared to Lady Catherine de Bourgh was not so much of a compliment as the man wished to pay. But instead of allowing him to ramble on about the perfections of Miss Elizabeth Bennet, Anne interrupted him.

"Then I should advise you, Mr. Collins, in the most strenuous means possible, to rethink such a strategy, for I assure you my sister would *not* approve of Miss Elizabeth."

The silly man stopped and gaped at her, no light of comprehension in his eyes. Then the inevitable sputtering began.

"But . . . but . . . Lady Anne! I have the highest confidence in my cousin's abilities and in her suitability for the position of mistress of the parsonage. There can be no other interpretation on the matter, I am certain!"

"No, of her capabilities, there is no question," replied Anne, amused Mr. Collins had forgotten himself enough to contradict the sister of his patroness. "But if you persist in considering Miss Elizabeth suitable, I must question if you have ever met my sister."

Mr. Collins paused when he appeared likely to further protest. Then he asked, and in a voice more subdued than Anne thought him capable, on what she based her opinion.

"Does my sister ask for your opinion, or does she direct, Mr. Collins?"

"Lady Catherine is the noblest, the most rational and knowledgeable person in the land!" exclaimed Mr. Collins. Anne thought it was more than a little overdone, even for one of Catherine's toadies. "Surely she knows best in any situation—one cannot go wrong in following her wise counsel to the letter!"

"I am interested to hear you say that, Mr. Collins. If that is so, tell me what you know of your cousin. Does she seem to be the kind of woman to allow another to direct her in *anything*? Or is she more likely to state her opinions without disguise and follow her own counsel?"

Mr. Collins's eyes widened in comprehension. "But the respect Lady Catherine commands would induce her to silence, respect, and obedience."

"It is not my purpose to cast aspersions on your cousin's character, Mr. Collins. However, it is clear to me there are few adjectives one could use which would be less efficacious in describing your cousin. Quite the contrary, in fact.

"Perhaps another choice would be best? I understand Miss Elizabeth's sister, Miss Mary, is knowledgeable of religion and pious besides. Does she not sound like the perfect wife for a parson?"

Confident she had made her case, which Mr. Collins would take to heart, Anne left him to his own devices which comprised standing by the side of the dance floor, studying Miss Elizabeth, peering at her as if trying to make her out. Then later when his attention turned to Miss Mary, Anne noted it, confident her point had been made and received.

"Might I assume Mr. Collins will now desist?" asked Georgiana when she joined her a few moments later.

"I have every confidence he has seen the sense in my advice," replied Anne. "Even if he had proposed, I doubt Miss Elizabeth would have accepted him."

"Do you not think her father would have insisted on it? Given what we have heard of the family, a marriage to Mr. Collins would secure their future."

"It is possible," conceded Anne, "but I do not believe Mr. Bennet would have prevailed on her to accept."

Nodding, Georgiana drew in closer. "She is wonderful, is she not?"

"With that, I cannot disagree," replied Anne, watching the vibrant young lady as her current partner whisked her around the room. Further down the line, Anne noted her son also watching her, laughing at his earnest look, one she had not been certain she would ever see, given his lack of interest in any young woman.

"I knew it," added Georgiana, the smugness clear in her voice. "William never speaks of *any* young woman. To have mentioned her as often as he did was akin to him shouting his interest from the rooftops."

"Perhaps it was," said Anne. "But we must tread lightly, for you know your brother will dig in his heels if he feels he is being led. We must allow him to come to his own realization of her qualifications."

"Given what I am seeing, that will not be difficult," replied Georgiana. "He seems half in love with her now."

"I agree. But his sense of duty and honor are not allowing him to consider her as he ought."

"Then we must help him to come to the proper conclusion."

With an absence of mind, Anne nodded to her daughter's words. There were several possibilities, she thought, though she knew not which one would work. It was best to consider the matter for several more days while observing her son and the young woman who had caught his interest. Lady Anne Darcy had one motive in mind, which was to see to her son's happiness, which was not at all assured, given the present circumstance. But he was stubborn and not easily led. It would be a monumental task.

CHAPTER I

*H*ad Darcy considered the matter in advance, he might have predicted what would ensue next. Unfortunately, he had spent the previous day consumed with surprise for his mother and sister's sudden appearance and most of the evening considering Bingley's predicament with Miss Bennet. While he did not wish to ponder it to any great extent, Darcy was also honest enough to confess that he had thought much of Miss Elizabeth Bennet the previous evening.

Whatever had prompted his distraction, he was soon required to put such matters to the side in favor of the current situation. Miss Bingley had his agreement in her opinion of Miss Bennet, but for different reasons. Darcy was concerned for the girl's standing in society, family, and lack of dowry, yes, but of greater concern was her lack of any interest in his friend. In Miss Bingley's eyes, their standing in society must disqualify Miss Bennet, for her suitability to become Darcy's wife in her eyes must take a serious blow if her brother lost himself enough to propose to Miss Bennet. In short, Darcy could have forgiven the woman's unfortunate circumstances if she cared for Bingley, while Miss Bingley would do everything in her power to prevent her brother from offering for her, regardless of the girl's feelings. Had Darcy any evidence of such regard, he might have thought their actions unwarranted and officious.

The morning after the ball offered Miss Bingley the opportunity to press forward with her plans, for Bingley departed early for London.

"I will not be long," said he in a cheerful tone that morning at the breakfast table. "No more than two or three days, I should think. The timing is poor, for I have little desire to leave Hertfordshire at present, but at least I shall be comforted in my quick return."

Darcy made no returning comment, for the inference of Bingley's intentions with respect to Miss Bennet filled him with disquiet and he had known of Bingley's return to town for some time. When the man rose to depart, Darcy considered his options, and in so doing found a willing and expected ally, and a most unexpected foe.

"I am concerned for Charles," said Miss Bingley, making her move while the company was in the sitting-room. The sisters had made their appearance far earlier than was their custom that morning, a testament to their determination.

"This attention he is paying to Miss Bennet can only end badly, and as you know, I will do anything to spare my brother heartache."

Darcy nodded, though he was aware her words were nothing more than obfuscation of her real motive. She accepted his reply as a sign she should continue.

"As I am certain you already apprehend, Mr. Darcy, Charles's infatuation with Miss Bennet is deeper than I have ever seen before, and I suspect he might actually lose himself and propose to her. It would be nothing less than a disaster for us in society, for the Bennets as relations cannot be contemplated." The woman huffed with disdain. "Imagine having to acknowledge Mrs. Bennet or Miss Lydia as a close relation! It is not to be borne!"

"The Bennets *are* unsuitable," replied Darcy. "The larger concern, however, is Miss Bennet's feelings for Bingley."

"Exactly!" cried Miss Bingley, Mrs. Hurst nodding her head in more restrained agreement. "Mrs. Bennet, as you know, is hunting for wealthy husbands for her insipid daughters. The woman would not hesitate to insist her daughter accept whatever proposals come their way, for if they do not, they shall surely end living in a leaky tenant cottage. Ha! It would surprise me to discover they have the funds for even that!

"My brother, as you know, has departed for London on a matter of business. But Charles loves the delights of town as much as I do myself, and I am convinced we can induce him to stay there, given the right encouragement."

"You mean to follow him to London, then?" asked Darcy.

"That seems the most prudent course, Mr. Darcy," said Mrs. Hurst. "Jane Bennet *is* a lovely girl, and if she had any connections worth considering, I might almost accept her as suitable."

"But she does not, so there is little reason to concern ourselves with what might be," said Miss Bingley, her impatience seeping into her voice. "There is nothing to be done except to travel to London to convince my brother of the folly of considering Miss Bennet a prospective bride. May we have your support, Mr. Darcy?"

"I am happy to be of service to my friend," said Darcy.

What he did not say—though he implied—was that it was his friendship with Bingley that prompted him to act. Whether Miss Bingley understood his meaning, and he doubted she possessed the self-honesty to own to it, the woman seemed content to accept his words at face value. Her effusive thanks wore on his patience, but the need to prepare for their departure soon superseded all other considerations. Then the opposition made itself known.

"You wish to leave Netherfield?" His mother's voice was laden with disbelief, but knowing her as he did, Darcy thought it was calculated. Instantly on his guard, Darcy witnessed the ensuing conversation with growing confusion.

"We do," was Miss Bingley's firm reply. "Tomorrow, we are determined to leave this place and return to town."

"That *is* a surprise. I had thought you meant to stay at least until the New Year, and possibly until the season. Netherfield is a lovely estate and there is nothing in town at present, as the little season is over. I find it curious that you are wild to be away from here, and this only a day after hosting a late event for all the neighborhood."

Miss Bingley's confusion was etched upon her brow, but the woman did not lack ability to respond. "There is no need to be diplomatic, Lady Anne, for I have no illusions as to the estate or the neighborhood. Netherfield is in every way inadequate, not only in the house, but also the location, the décor, and the servants, who should be put out without reference.

"And the society!" cried Miss Bingley, her performance needlessly melodramatic, in Darcy's opinion. "I have never met such ill-bred savages in all my life! There is no fashion among them, no sophistication, and only a modicum of acceptable manners. Last night was nothing less than a punishment to any person of any quality. I am certain you must agree."

"Your certainty is misplaced, Miss Bingley." Lady Anne's tone was mild, but Darcy could sense the steely undertone in her voice. "In fact, society here reminds me very much of what we have in Derbyshire, though perhaps there is a preponderance of families of lesser consequence here. I found myself very comfortable last night, and I know Georgiana felt the same."

By her side, Georgiana nodded to agree with her mother, further confusing Miss Bingley. Darcy, however, regarded the two women in his life, a gravity settling over him. There was something at play here, something he did not like. Of what his mother's game consisted he could not be certain, but he was becoming convinced there was a purpose in her assertions.

"Netherfield is an adequate estate," said Darcy before Miss Bingley could muster a reply. The woman shot him a hard glance, but Darcy took no notice. "It is what Bingley required, both from the prospective of learning how to manage an estate and from its proximity to town.

"However, I agree with Miss Bingley. It seems to me we have been here long enough. It would be best if we were to return to town."

"Why do you say that, William?" asked Lady Anne. "Did Mr. Bingley not go away intending to return at the earliest opportunity?"

"He did," replied Miss Bingley. "But we mean to go to town and prevent him from returning."

"I will own I do not understand why. Should a man not return to the estate he leased when he chooses?"

"Because, Mother," said Darcy, "Miss Bingley is concerned her brother means to offer for Miss Bennet and means to dissuade him."

"I see," said Lady Anne, her brow furrowed in thought. "Then, given your support for this scheme, might I conclude you do not approve of Miss Bennet?"

"Approval is not mine to give," replied Darcy.

"And yet you have given your consent to this plan, against your friend's wishes, I might add. Will you not share your reasons?"

"My brother can do better than Miss Bennet," said Miss Bingley.

"He can do better than a gentleman's daughter?"

The question was mild but laced with meaning, most of which Darcy did not even wish to consider. "Yes, she is a gentleman's daughter," said he. "The gentleman, however, is a minor sort of landowner, and the lady has little to offer other than herself. To the best of my knowledge, their connections consist of no one of more note than the obsequious parson we met last night—"

"Do not forget their *tradesman uncle*," interjected Miss Bingley with an unpleasant sneer.

"Of course," said Darcy. "As I was saying, their connections are not sterling, and it is said there is little dowry between the five girls."

"My brother will become responsible for them, should he marry Miss Bennet," said Mrs. Hurst.

"Unless they also marry," was Lady Anne's mild reply.

"There is little enough chance of that," rejoined Miss Bingley.

"And yet Miss Bennet has attracted your brother as a potential suitor, Miss Bingley. There are some who would see their status as daughters of a gentleman as all that is required to make them acceptable wives."

"I doubt anyone of any consequence would do so."

Lady Anne favored Miss Bingley with a serene smile, which seemed to worry her. "I believe they may, in the end, surprise you."

"Your defense of them is admirable, Lady Anne," said Miss Bingley, attempting to take a different tack. "It seemed you became friendly with the eldest daughters last night, and for you to descend to giving consequence to such ladies so beneath you is admirable.

"However, that in no way makes them suitable. Given your focus on Miss Bennet and Miss Elizabeth, I must assume you missed the performance of the other members of the family. The younger girls are wild, flirting with any man wearing a red coat, drinking too much punch, and laughing with raucous abandon, while Miss Mary played very ill, prompting her thuggish father to remove her from the pianoforte most improperly, I might add. And Mrs. Bennet, the crowning bit of glory, crowing to all her friends about how they had captured *my brother*, and how marriage to him with throw the rest of her brood into the paths of other rich men!"

"None of this escaped my notice, Miss Bingley."

It seemed his mother's mild replies were beginning to annoy Miss Bingley. For his part, Darcy reflected that most of what Miss Bingley related had quite escaped *his* notice, though he was not surprised. It was little different from any other evening in company he had experienced with the Bennet family.

"Then this is the manner of family to which you propose my brother connect himself?"

It was, Darcy thought, admirable that his mother ignored the accusatory tone Miss Bingley's frustration was provoking. That did not mean his mother's well of patience was inexhaustible.

"The only thing I propose, Miss Bingley," said she, a hint of hardness in her tone, "is that you allow your brother to make his own decisions without interference. This conversation leads me to believe you think him incapable of directing his own affairs."

"I have often rendered assistance to Bingley," said Darcy, attempting to prevent Miss Bingley from saying something impolitic. "It does not mean he is incapable, but I have often noted he requires a little guidance."

Hurst, who had sat without speaking, indifferent to the discussion, laughed and said: "He is a puppy, with boundless energy and an eagerness to lick the hand of everyone he meets!"

This appeared to be too much, even for Miss Bingley, for her face lit up like a ripe tomato. Mrs. Hurst glared at her husband, who took no notice, while Darcy struggled to refrain from laughing. There was something about Hurst's description of his brother which was nothing less than apropos.

"Then again," said Lady Anne, "I suppose you are determined, so there is nothing else to be done. Since you are abandoning this estate, Georgiana and I cannot stay, though I enjoyed the ball last night. I shall see to our packing."

Miss Bingley did not understand Lady Anne's sudden change of heart, but she was not about to question her good fortune. "It gladdens me you have seen the matter from our perspective, Lady Anne. I anticipate our intimacy in town, for I am certain the lack of society will be no impediment when such good friends are close at hand."

"Indeed," said Lady Anne. "Then we had best be about our business, for we have a busy day. There is not only the packing and closing of the house to see to, but you will, of course, wish to visit some of the principal families of the district and take your leave."

Once again Miss Bingley's countenance fell and she opened her mouth, presumably to disagree. Then she stopped, considered the matter, and let out a sigh of frustration.

"It *would* be the proper thing to do, I suppose."

"It is," replied Lady Anne. "To leave without visiting would be a serious breach of etiquette. It is not necessary to visit *all* the families of the district, but you should visit those with whom you have been friendly. Perhaps the Lucas family and your neighbors to the south?

"And the Bennets," added his mother when Miss Bingley was about to agree. The mention of that family once again brought a frown to her face, but Lady Anne was not finished. "You have become close friends with Miss Bennet, as I understand, so visiting them is imperative."

Miss Bingley straightened her shoulders, as if setting herself to an unpleasant task and said: "Of course. Then let us be about our duties, for I am eager to depart for London."

The morning after the ball, Elizabeth found herself in a state of confusion. Not that it was unwelcome if she was to be honest with herself. After Mr. Collins's arrival, she had done her best to ignore him, not understanding until a few days before that the man had matrimony on his mind and had chosen her as the companion of his future life. From that point it had been her goal to do everything she could to dissuade him from proposing, knowing what uproar would ensue if she was required to reject him.

Until the previous evening, Elizabeth had not thought her efforts were bearing any fruit, as evidenced by her dance with the gentleman and his rather ineffectual attempts at paying court to her. The evening spent in the company of Lady Anne and Miss Darcy skewed her perspective and prevented her from understanding when the man's attentions had cooled. But cooled they had, such that the morning after, as the family rested after their exertions from the previous evening, Mr. Collins held himself aloof from Elizabeth. She thought he was paying more attention to Mary, with whom he had rarely exchanged any words which were not centered on Fordyce.

"Lizzy!" hissed Mrs. Bennet after some time of this. Mr. Collins had left the room and was not likely to overhear, which was an interesting bit of restraint from her often unrestrained mother. "What have you done to Mr. Collins?"

"I am sure I have done nothing," replied Elizabeth. "Why do you ask?"

"Why do I ask?" echoed her mother. "You must have seen the cooling of his ardor. It was my thought he would be persuaded to offer for you today, and yet he has avoided you as if he thought you diseased. You must have done something to push him away!"

In fact, I have spent the last week attempting to do everything in my power to dissuade him, thought Elizabeth to herself, stifling a laugh in response to the thought. Mrs. Bennet would not appreciate that observation, though it was nothing less than the truth.

"I have done nothing," said she aloud. "Mr. Collins danced the first with me last night and stayed close by whenever he was at liberty thereafter. But I did not see much of him after I made the acquaintance of Lady Anne and Miss Darcy."

"Then you must go to him and regain his attention! We must not lose this opportunity, for we must secure Mr. Collins if we are to have a home in the future!"

It was fortunate visitors arrived at that moment, for it saved Elizabeth an argument with her mother she wished to avoid. But the door knocker sounded, ringing throughout the house, and though Mrs. Bennet glared at Elizabeth, as if suspecting she had somehow contrived the interruption to avoid her inquisition, the demands of presenting her daughters to best advantage took precedence. After a few moments, Mrs. Hill led their visitors into the room, surprising them all when it was the Darcys and Hursts, along with Miss Bingley. Of Mr. Bingley, there was no sign.

The newcomers were invited to sit with the family, and when everyone was settled, Miss Bingley took the initiative of addressing the company. "Mrs. Bennet, how . . . fortunate it is to be with you all again. And Miss Bennet," added she, turning to Jane, "I apologize my brother is not here to take his leave, but he went into town very early this morning."

This was a piece of information Elizabeth had not yet heard, but to Jane, it was no surprise. "Mr. Bingley informed me of this himself last night. I also know of his intention to return within three or four days."

"Yes, I can imagine Charles said that!" Miss Bingley's attempt at joviality Elizabeth instantly detected as false. "It is my brother's character, you know, to always be coming and going. When you were at Netherfield, I seem to remember him speaking of his impulsivity and his comfort when in London."

"He also spoke of being happy to be in the country too, Miss Bingley," said Elizabeth.

"That is true," said Miss Bingley. "But when he arrives in town, with all its attendant amusements, I am certain he will be in no hurry to leave it again. Thus, we are all closing the house, intending to join him in London. I hope we will depart by tomorrow morning at the latest!"

Miss Bingley continued to speak at some length, informing them all of her eagerness to return to town, the things they would do and the people they would see. She even hinted, though with an amusing sort of oblique avoidance, of some other attachment she hoped would come to fruition, but though her instantaneous glance at Miss Darcy spoke volumes as to the subject of her hopes, she dared not approach the subject closer with the girl and her mother sitting there. After a moment's consideration, Elizabeth dismissed it as wishful thinking, for Miss Darcy betrayed no particular interest in Mr. Bingley.

Of greater concern was the effect the woman's words were having on Jane—who, though calm to all appearances was showing signs of stress—and Mrs. Bennet—who Elizabeth thought might call for her smelling salts. Mrs. Bennet held on to her composure until Miss Bingley ceased speaking and sat back on the sofa she occupied, a half-smile, self-satisfied and haughty, playing about the corners of her mouth. Had Lady Anne not spoken, Elizabeth was certain her mother would have humiliated them all.

"We are for town also," said the lady. "Georgiana and I anticipated a restful time in the country, but it seems our hosts have their hearts set on Christmas in town, which has its own charms."

"I suppose it does," said Mrs. Bennet with an admirable measure of self-control. "My husband does not like town, and as such, we go but rarely, though my brother lives there. It is unfortunate you shall not meet them."

"It is a *pleasure* we shall have to defer for another day," interposed the insolent Miss Bingley. "As it is, I believe we should depart before long, for we still have much work to do today."

"Miss Bingley speaks the truth," said Lady Anne. "But before we go, it is on my mind that I would like to see more of your excellent daughters, Mrs. Bennet. As such, I would like to invite them to join us in London for the season. Would you be willing to come to us in February?"

"Oh, Lizzy, Jane!" exclaimed Mrs. Bennet, her consternation replaced with elation. "What an honor to receive such favor!"

"Indeed, it is," added Mr. Collins, who had remained silent. "To be preferred by such as Lady Anne Darcy, sister to my patroness, the venerable Lady Catherine de Bourgh, is a privilege few could boast. Why, you might even make Lady Catherine's acquaintance, for she has informed me herself of her intention to travel to London for the season!"

While Mr. Collins lost himself in contemplation of the perfections of Lady Catherine, Elizabeth glanced about the room. It was clear no one—save perhaps Miss Darcy—had known of Lady Anne's intention to invite them to London. Miss Bingley appeared shocked and Mrs. Hurst no less so, while the grim set to Mr. Darcy's mouth indicated dismay and mounting anger. Lady Anne, however, paid none of them any heed, instead looking to Jane and Elizabeth for their answers.

"I believe I speak for my sister," said Jane, "but we would be delighted to accept if it would not be too much trouble."

"If it was too much trouble, my dear Miss Bennet," said Lady Anne, "I assure you I would not have extended the invitation. Georgiana and

I will wait eagerly to resume our acquaintance—there will be so much for us to do in town that I am certain you will be glad you came!"

The arrangements were made, and the approximate dates selected, after which Lady Anne promised to write to them with more information, inviting them to write to her in return. Miss Darcy added her voice to her mother's, shyly requesting leave to also write to Elizabeth and Jane, both of whom accepted with alacrity. Then Miss Bingley rushed the visitors out of the house, seeming annoyed she had not done so before calamity struck.

"We are both thrilled you have accepted," said Lady Anne as they were walking her to the door. "Georgiana will count the days, and I am scarcely less eager. Though it is wonderful to escort my daughter around town, having two additional young ladies will make our party that much more agreeable."

"Thank you, Lady Anne," said Elizabeth. "I believe Jane and I will anticipate our reunion with equal longing."

As the party went away, however, Elizabeth noted that Lady Anne spoke of her and her daughter's anticipation but said nothing of Mr. Darcy's. The gentleman himself did not speak. But Elizabeth was certain he was feeling all the offense at the prospect of hosting two unsuitable ladies in his elegant London home, and she wondered how he would endure. Then she smiled at him as he was going away, wondering what she might do to further tease and exasperate him.

CHAPTER II

A strained silence in the Darcy carriage characterized the return journey to Netherfield. Darcy could only be grateful Miss Bingley was not unleashing the full measure of her disappointment and knew it was nothing more than the presence of his mother which prevented her. The anger she harbored was not hidden in any meaningful way, and Darcy knew she would not remain silent forever. His expectations were realized when the carriage came to a stop in front of the manor and the occupants disembarked from its cramped confines and made their way to the sitting-room.

They spent the first few moments settling in for a little refreshment before the task of preparing for their departure again beckoned, allowing those with an opinion on the subject to marshal their thoughts. Miss Bingley, as mistress of the estate, served them all, as was her right, when the service was delivered, and it was not long after when she began to express her opinion.

"I must confess, Lady Anne," said she, her tone offhand, "I am surprised at your tolerance for those of a lower station." She paused and gave his mother an insincere smile, adding: "Not that I expected you to be anything less than welcoming. Your level of comfort with those beneath you is refreshing, to say the least."

Lady Anne eyed Miss Bingley over her teacup, considering her hostess. "It is interesting to hear you speak so, Miss Bingley, for, by my estimation, we have not been among unsuitable people. Might I ask you to explain your comment?"

Feigning shock—or perhaps it was not feigned—Miss Bingley exclaimed: "I must disagree with you most strenuously! There is no one in this district who may be called suitable, and certainly no one we visited this morning."

"Are the Bennets not landed?" was Lady Anne's mild query. "Do they not obtain their living from the rents received by those who farm the land? Is the family not descended from a long line of gentlemen?"

Miss Bingley opened her mouth to speak, but Darcy's mother precluded her, saying: "I have no intention of debating the circumstances which make a man a gentleman, Miss Bingley, nor do I wish to examine in exacting detail the levels of society gentlemen inhabit. The only thing I shall ask is this: is it not my business whom I invite into my home?"

"Of course, Lady Anne," replied Miss Bingley, backtracking quickly. "It was never my intention to suggest otherwise. If you believe the Bennet sisters to be worth your time, then I must salute your ability to endure the lower classes. I, unfortunately, lack your patience."

"Miss Bingley," said Lady Anne, "I will not say I possess the patience you describe. It is nothing less than the truth that I *am* the daughter of an earl, and thus have the privilege of the title 'lady' before my name. Remember, however, it is a courtesy only, given due to my ancestry. If you consider the matter, my daughter," mother reached out and touched Georgiana's cheek with affection, "is only the daughter of a gentleman. In that context, Georgiana is the equal of the Bennet sisters."

"But Miss Darcy's lineage is much greater," said Miss Bingley, restraining herself from snapping in her frustration. "Who are the Bennets' ancestors? Who are their mother's? In consequence, there can be no comparison."

"By that last measure, you are correct. But remember this, Miss Bingley," added Lady Anne, this time her voice infused with steel, "the Bennets may not have riches untold, but they are of gentle stock, and it has often been said that birth trumps wealth. I should ask you to remember this simple fact. Though our meeting with the Miss Bennets was short, I liked them a great deal, and Georgiana agrees with me. I mean to do everything I can to forward our friendship."

The steady look with which his mother regarded Miss Bingley was enough to convince the woman she was in earnest, not that Darcy thought it had ever been in doubt. While his mother was not a woman to put herself forward at every opportunity, she was a woman who stood by her convictions. Though Darcy had no notion of what she saw in the Bennet sisters, he knew she would not relent. That did not mean Darcy would not attempt to change her mind.

The opportunity presented itself later that afternoon. After partaking of the fortifying tea together, the party separated to attend to their various tasks, which, for the Darcys, meant seeing to their personal effects and the status of the servants who had accompanied them. That was no great task, for Snell—Darcy's manservant—already had matters well in hand, as did Lady Anne and Georgiana's maids. Thus, Darcy knew while his mother and sister would be supervising their maids, he thought they would be available to speak to him. Thus, he made his way to their adjoining rooms, entering when the maid answered his knock.

"Are you ready to depart, William?" asked Lady Anne upon spying him.

"Snell is completing my preparations as we speak," replied Darcy.

"Then he is efficient, as usual. I had thought it would take you at least another half hour before you knocked on our door."

Darcy could not help the smile which crept over the corners of his lips, for he should have known his mother would anticipate him. But the seriousness of the matter he wished to discuss replaced his mirth. Choosing a seat nearby, Darcy turned to his mother, trying to understand her actions.

"I would not presume to question your motives, Mother," said Darcy.

"Yet you are curious why I would invite the daughters of a country squire to be our guests for the season."

Again, Darcy allowed a slight smile. "Yes, that is what I wish to know."

His mother considered him for several moments before she spoke, and when she did, it was with a question he had not expected. "Before I reply, might I know why you object to the Bennet family?"

"Are they not unsuitable?" asked Darcy.

"Do you not know it is impolite to answer a question with a question?"

The impudent response prompted a laugh from Darcy. "I might say the same thing, Mother, for is that not what you just did?"

"As I recall," was his mother's prim reply, "you asked no question.

You confirmed my conjecture, but you did not pose a question."

Shaking his head and still chuckling, Darcy said: "Then let me state my opinion without disguise. Yes, I consider the Bennets unsuitable. The family is uncouth and improper, they have close connections to the tradesman class, and they inhabit a sphere far below our own."

"Fitzwilliam," said Lady Anne in a reproving tone, alerting Darcy to the fact she was disappointed—she did not usually address him using his full name. "It is a rare thing when you speak words which sound like they may have come from my sister, or even from Miss Bingley."

Darcy gaped at his mother, his mouth falling open, only to regain his senses when he heard Georgiana's soft giggles. Then he became displeased. "I do not appreciate the comparison, Mother—though I know you are fond of your sister, I know it was not a compliment, to say nothing of likening me to Miss Bingley, of all people."

"Can you deny it?" said his mother. "Miss Bingley has attempted to make those points ad nauseum since we arrived. Have I missed your meaning?"

"The fact that she spoke similar words does not make them untrue," replied Darcy.

"Then let me enlighten you as to my opinion," said Lady Anne. "Everything you said is true. There is much to be desired in the behavior of certain members of the family—of this, I am well aware. However, I doubt it is anything that cannot be resolved with a firm hand and a little education on the subject of proper behavior. Mrs. Bennet was not, as I understand, raised a gentlewoman. Is that not true?"

"It is," replied Darcy. "But that is the problem. Mrs. Bennet may not have been raised with such advantages, but Mr. Bennet most certainly was, and yet he takes no trouble to correct that which he may influence."

"That is unfortunate, indeed. That does not mean the family as an entity is beyond redemption. And really, William, is there anything you can say against the behavior of the eldest girls?"

"I thought them perfectly lovely," ventured Georgiana.

"Which is what makes the family that much more puzzling. How did Miss Bennet and Miss Elizabeth avoid the weaknesses their younger sisters display?"

"I cannot say," replied Lady Anne. "It may be there was some elder member of the family to guide them—perhaps a grandmother or elderly aunt. In the end, it matters not, for it is the eldest two girls who interest me."

Darcy gazed at his mother, suspicion floating about the edges of his consciousness. Why his mother should take such an interest in those two girls was beyond his understanding. But then she moved to her next point and quite drove the matter from his mind.

"Your next point, I believe, was their connections to tradesmen. To refute that, I need only point to your association with Mr. Bingley, for is he not of that class?"

"Bingley is no longer active in trade," objected Darcy. "This uncle of the Bennets is, by all accounts, proprietor of his own business."

"Perhaps he is," replied his mother. "Until we know more of him, however, I prefer to withhold judgment. If he is an unfortunate relation, what is it to us? It is not as if the Bennets are our family—they are friends, the eldest of whom I have invited to stay with us for a few months. It is on my mind, however, that this uncle may be a good man of business, and as the world is changing, a worthy connection."

"If you think Mrs. Bennet's brother is anything other than coarse and unrefined, I must wonder if you have taken the woman's measure."

"Like I am Catherine's mirror image?"

That was a point Darcy could not refute, nor did he make the attempt. Considering the matter further, Darcy supposed he had made a rash judgment concerning a man of whom he knew nothing based on the behavior of a woman he did not respect.

"Your third point," said his mother, pulling his attention away once more, "is that the Bennets inhabit a sphere far below ours. This point I cannot refute, for it is nothing other than the truth. I do not consider it an impediment, however, for less fortunate members of our society are often sponsored by those of a higher position. Regardless of the family or connections or the state of their father's finances, I am convinced the eldest Bennets are veritable diamonds, ones which require only a little polishing before they will shine. I hope to know them better and assist them in meeting their potential."

Darcy paused and considered his mother, wondering if there was something she was not telling him. Though he could say his mother was of a friendly temperament, he had not seen her take such an interest in any other young ladies who were so wholly unconnected to them. This entire episode was beyond his understanding of her, which made it impossible to fathom her motives.

At the same time, Darcy knew his mother and knew she would not be explicit if she did not wish to be, and in this instance, Darcy could see unmistakable signs of obduracy. Thus, he played the one final card he had at his disposal.

"What of Bingley?"

"Please be more explicit, William, for I do not understand your question."

Convinced his mother knew to what he was referring, Darcy nevertheless explained: "Part of the reason for returning to London at this time was to remove my friend from the influence of Miss Bennet. Yet you propose to bring her into his sphere yet again."

"Why would this be of concern to you?"

"Because Bingley is my friend."

"Miss Bennet is unsuitable?"

"Perhaps, though that is not for me to decide," said Darcy, beginning to feel the first hints of annoyance. "Miss Bingley would consider her so."

"And she would be incorrect," replied his mother with curt words and a frown. "Miss Bennet *is* the daughter of a gentleman and would be a step up for Bingley." Holding out a hand to silence him when Darcy would have spoken, his mother continued: "Yes, William, I understand a woman of greater consequence and position in society would raise his position, something Miss Bennet could not do for him. But consider these two points before you propose to separate them:

"First, would a woman of higher society have your friend? He *is* still connected to trade, and unless he could find some impoverished noble who needs his money, I doubt any such woman will have him.

"Second, should Mr. Bingley not be afforded the opportunity to make his own choice in the matter? And if he chooses Miss Bennet, who can gainsay him?"

"If he chooses her, then there is nothing anyone can do," said Darcy. "But you must consider that in such a situation, he would offer for her, not for those virtues society deems important, but for no other reason than pure inclination."

"Yes, I understand this. What of it?"

"Why, Miss Bennet does not care for my friend, and would accept his proposal only because her mother would not allow her to refuse."

Whatever rebuttal he might have expected, Darcy did not expect his mother and sister to share a look and then bursting into laughter. Feeling a hint of offense, Darcy regarded them, and his clear annoyance only made them laugh harder.

"I must think you a simpleton if you believe Miss Bennet does not care for Mr. Bingley," said Lady Anne at last. "I was in their company for only five minutes when I saw it."

"And yet, I have observed her and have seen no symptoms of particular regard."

"Oh, Fitzwilliam!" exclaimed his mother. "What would you have her do? Should she throw herself at your friend, agree with everything he says, hang off his arm, clutching it in her talons like a hawk?

"She is reticent, my son, much like you, I might add. In company with him, she is perfectly proper, shows the correct degree of interest, and yet is modest and shy, and will not put herself forward. If you watch her when he is speaking, she hangs off every word he says, her regard for him clear in her eyes, her posture, her very being. I have never seen so promising an inclination as that shown by Miss Bennet."

"You should believe us, William," said Georgiana with an impish smile. "Who is better to determine the feelings of a woman other than another woman?"

"Who, indeed?" asked Lady Anne. "In that vein, there is one more point I would like you to consider: would Miss Bingley be so eager to separate her brother from Miss Bennet if the affection between them was not so obvious?"

"Or perhaps she understands Mrs. Bennet as I do," said Darcy. "Do you think Mrs. Bennet would allow her daughter to refuse a proposal of marriage with a man who may be her future salvation?"

"Just as Mr. Bennet would have allowed his wife to force Miss Elizabeth to marry that silly parson of my sister's?"

Darcy started at the suggestion. "Mr. Collins? I saw no reason to suspect he will propose marriage to Miss Elizabeth."

"I begin to wonder if your eyes have been closed your entire time here," replied his mother. "Mr. Collins opened the ball with her and attempted to stay close to her the entire evening, and furthermore, my sister wrote to me boasting of how she had sent her parson to his family to marry one of the daughters. Has he paid enough attention to any of the other girls that may reasonably lead to a proposal to one of them?"

"Then you believe he will offer for her."

It was a statement, not a question, for all that his mother treated it as the latter. "No, I do not believe he will. But if he did, I doubt Miss Elizabeth would accept him. As her father is a man who will not take his family in hand, can you imagine him taking the trouble to force his daughter into a marriage she did not want?"

A tightness in his shoulders eased and departed, leaving Darcy feeling relieved. "No, I cannot imagine he would," said he with an absence of mind. "Particularly when she is his favorite daughter, by all accounts."

"Then you must remember that it is the man who must approve a proposal of marriage," said Lady Anne. "I will own I do not know Mr. Bennet well. However, I will also state that if Miss Elizabeth *is* his favorite daughter *and* Miss Bennet is Miss Elizabeth's favorite sister, can you think he will insist upon her marrying Mr. Bingley if she did not favor him, despite her mother's resolve?"

There was, Darcy decided little to refute in his mother's logic. But his own observation would not be so readily put aside.

"It seems I cannot dissuade you, and as you have already extended the invitation, there is nothing to be done."

"Thank you for seeing it that way."

"Be that as it may," continued Darcy as if his mother had not spoken, "my concerns are still valid. If I am correct about Miss Bennet, then we may be putting Bingley in a situation where he will make a grave mistake."

"If I am incorrect, William, then I will join you in dissuading Mr. Bingley."

Knowing this was the best offer he was to receive from his mother, Darcy nodded his agreement. After a few more moments of speaking of their departure the following morning, Darcy excused himself to see to his own final preparations. The rest of the day, however, he continued to think of what might have been, about the person of Miss Elizabeth, to whom he still felt an intense level of attraction.

She might have married Mr. Collins! The thought beggared the mind, how a bright, intelligent jewel of a woman could find herself shackled to a dullard. Of more concern was the thought that in a few shorts months, Miss Elizabeth would reside in his house, that she would intrude on his notice for more than just those few days at Netherfield. Darcy had no illusions by this time in their acquaintance—he felt more for her than he ought, for she fascinated him like no other woman he had met. The weeks before her coming he must spend preparing himself to resist her allure lest he forget himself and do something rash. Perhaps Anne's presence during the season would protect him—in fact, it might be best to formalize their arrangement before he could contemplate doing something rash with Miss Elizabeth.

When the door closed behind her son, Anne turned to her daughter, her arched eyebrow prompting Georgiana to break into laughter.

Anne joined in, enjoying the close companionship of her daughter, knowing they were quite alike, though Georgiana was a little shyer than Anne. It was good she had such a co-conspirator, for it raised their chances of success.

"Did you see the look on William's face when you told him how Mr. Collins might propose to Miss Elizabeth?" asked Georgiana.

Anne shook her head and laughed harder. "It was priceless, was it not? Though how he missed it, I cannot understand."

"Oh, I think he is so fixed on denying his interest in her that he cannot see anything else."

That sobered Anne. "That is the problem. My son is adept at regulating himself, and while we might have penetrated his defenses, I am not so naïve as to assume we have won the battle."

"It seems to me, we need not do anything to win the battle, Mother. When Miss Elizabeth is before him, I doubt my brother will have anything in mind but his attraction for her."

Anne huffed in annoyance. "I am uncertain you are correct. Even now, he is no doubt attempting to shore up his defenses and considering if he might propose to Anne before Miss Elizabeth comes to London."

"Then make sure to invite her before Aunt Catherine comes to London," replied Georgiana. "You know Lady Catherine orders matters exactly as she wishes — she will come to London at the time of her choosing and will not come early for any reason."

"Unless she suspects she might lose my son to a country miss."

"William will not take any action to inform her. Unless I miss my guess, he does not wish to marry Anne — it is only he does not have a woman for whom he feels anything, so he feels it does not matter who he marries. And Anne does have benefits attached to her situation."

Georgiana paused a moment, then she ventured: "The only part of this that concerns me is Miss Elizabeth. Though she has not been open about it, I do not believe she holds my brother in much regard."

"That is possible," said Lady Anne. "It is possible William showed himself in a poor light, as he has done so many times in the past."

Mother and daughter shared a look, one fraught with meaning. It was unfortunate, for he was a good man, but William's manners were such that he was often giving offense when he did not mean it. Others mistook reticence for arrogance, and because of it, his reputation was of a prideful man, disdainful of others. Anne knew her son knew of it, and often used it to his advantage to fend off fortune hunters and those seeking to curry favor.

"But William is a good man," said Anne. "If we can induce him to lower his walls and act as he does with family and close friends, I believe he will win Miss Elizabeth's affection."

"Aye, that will be the trick."

They then set about planning what they would do when the Bennet sisters joined them. Though each was eager to allow Mr. Bingley the ability to choose his own path in life, the greater concern was William and Miss Elizabeth. Anne knew her son, was familiar with his ways and his manner of thinking, and she was becoming more convinced that Miss Elizabeth was exactly what he needed to obtain true happiness. If there was anything she could do to ensure it came about, Anne was determined to do it.

Chapter III

For days after the Netherfield party left, nothing could distract Mrs. Bennet from the honor shown to her two daughters, and by the time a week had gone by, she was convinced this invitation to London would answer all her hopes for salvation. Thus, it was rare even an hour went by when she was not giving both Elizabeth and Jane some instruction concerning how they should conduct themselves when in Mr. Darcy's home. It was unfortunate, but her mother's words were often for Jane, rather than Elizabeth, as the one Mrs. Bennet had always thought would more easily find a marriage partner, and those words were not often to Jane's liking.

"You must only put yourself forward," she would say, "and I am certain you will attract some man of Mr. Darcy's acquaintance. Lady Anne Darcy must know many of high position in society and can do much to promote your interests. Why, it should not surprise me if you were to catch a baron or even an earl!"

Then her eyes would slip to Elizabeth, who was her least understood daughter, and she would add: "And you may attract some gentleman too, Lizzy, for you are pretty enough for any man, though not the equal of your sister. If you will only stem the tide of your words and not rattle on, I am sure Lady Anne may do much for you as well."

Elizabeth cared not for Mrs. Bennet's lowered expectations, and she did not expect that Lady Anne had invited them for the purpose of pairing either off with a duke. It was her mother's constant advice which concerned her, especially given what ensued after Mrs. Bennet began her monologues.

"But, Mama, what of Mr. Bingley?"

"You must forget about Mr. Bingley, my dear, for you will now be put into a position which will see come into the sphere of men of much more consequence."

"Mr. Bingley is the most amiable man of my acquaintance. I need not attract the attention of any other man."

"Now, now, Jane," replied Mrs. Bennet. "There are many amiable men in London, I am sure. Just make certain you find one who possesses a good fortune."

Then Mrs. Bennet continued to speak, imparting other instructions of equal nonsense. It was fortunate to Elizabeth's mind that Mr. Bennet was in the room on this occasion, for his amusement at his wife's excesses was not unexpected, and his words after were welcome.

"Do not concern yourself with your mother, Jane, for if you recall, it is not she who must approve of any suitor. Should you be certain of your regard for Mr. Bingley, you may be assured you will have my blessing, for you do not require my consent."

"Thank you, Papa," said Jane, to which Mr. Bennet grinned and excused himself to return to his study.

Of more importance than Mrs. Bennet's nonsensical ramblings was Jane's opinion of what had kept Mr. Bingley in London when he had informed her of his return. Elizabeth possessed her own opinions on the matter, but she thought to inquire after Jane's.

"There was something in London to keep him there," replied Jane, not bothered about his loss despite her wish for his attentions. "Caroline informed us of the matter before Lady Anne extended the invitation, after all."

"Is that all?" asked Elizabeth. "Do you not think there is something suspicious in all of this?"

Jane shook her head. "If there is, I do not understand what it might be."

"Jane," said Elizabeth, warning in her tone, "perhaps you did not notice the way Miss Bingley delivered her news. Did you not see the way she took great pleasure—dare I say glee—when she informed us there was *nothing* which could draw him back to Hertfordshire?"

Though silent for a moment, Elizabeth thought her sister might finally understand Miss Bingley was not so great a friend as she claimed. "I had wondered on that point," said she, "though I suppose it is not much of a mystery. Caroline has told me several times she prefers London to the country."

"Which makes her determination to capture Mr. Darcy all that much more curious," replied Elizabeth. When Jane directed a questioning look at her, she added: "Mr. Darcy is a country gentleman, which means he must spend half the year or more at his estate.

"But Jane, I would not have you taken in. I know you consider Miss Bingley a friend, and I do not wish to speak out of turn and accuse someone of deception when I have no proof. It is on my mind, however, that she is not as much of a friend of Mr. Bingley's interest in you as you might wish."

When Jane made to speak, Elizabeth held up her hand. "It is not my wish to argue with you—if you consider her a friend, that is enough for me. I would ask you to guard yourself against the possibility she is false. It would not surprise me if she is in London at this very minute attempting to persuade her brother against you."

"If she is, that is her prerogative." Jane paused and smiled. "However, with this visit extended by Lady Anne and Mr. Darcy's close friendship with Mr. Bingley, I expect to see the gentleman again. If he decides he does not wish to pursue me, I shall accept it. But if she wishes to keep him from me forever, she must leave London, at least for those weeks. As she enjoys society, I shall assume I will be in Mr. Bingley's presence again."

"Good for you, dear Sister," replied Elizabeth. "I hope you attain all you desire, for there is no one more deserving. Let us pray that Miss Bingley is your true friend, or that Mr. Bingley is made of stern enough stuff to endure her displeasure if she will be displeased."

"Darcy! I thought we had agreed you would await me in Hertfordshire. What is this I hear of your eagerness to return to town?"

Bingley had entered the room swiftly, his countenance etched with agony, followed by Miss Bingley, who fixed Darcy with a gaze which could only be termed beseeching. At that moment two things flittered across Darcy's mind, the first that it had taken Bingley an hour longer to appear than he might have thought, and second that Miss Bingley had stretched the truth. Not that her stratagem was surprising—the woman knew, though she little liked to confess it, that she did not have as much influence over her brother as she wished. Thus, giving Bingley the impression *Darcy* had instigated their return was the strongest card she could play.

"There must be some mistake, Bingley," said Darcy, ignoring Miss Bingley's frown, "but I was not eager to leave Hertfordshire."

Bingley regarded him with suspicion. "It is clear you little liked the neighborhood."

"That is true, my friend, but I was content to stay until your return. In the end, however, it seemed better to follow you to London."

Miss Bingley latched onto his words and nodded her head with vigor, saying: "It is as I told you, Charles. Netherfield is a quaint little estate, but it is not right for us. We should winter in town and then attempt to find a better estate in a more suitable location. Perhaps Derbyshire?"

"What a quaint notion you have, Miss Bingley," said Darcy's mother, who regarded the proceedings, her mouth curved into a smile. "While I am fond of my home, since both my brother and my son's estates can be found therein, one can find beauties in other parts of the kingdom. I should think Cornwall would be just as suitable as Derbyshire for your brother to settle."

"Cornwall would be much too far distant," said Miss Bingley with what seemed suspiciously like disdain. "I would much prefer the wild and untamed landscapes of Derbyshire."

Darcy dared not look at his mother, for he knew he would burst out laughing. There was but one reason Miss Bingley preferred Derbyshire, and it had nothing to do with beauty. When Miss Bingley visited Pemberley with her brother the previous year, she had ventured no further from the house than the rose garden and had Darcy's mother not been present, there were several instances in which he might have suspected her of trying to direct the servants.

"That is not the point," said Bingley, frustrated with the direction the conversation had taken. "I promised Miss Bennet in the sincerest manner possible that I would return to Netherfield within a few days at most. What will she think of me if I do not return, and all with no word of my change of plans?"

"There is no need to return to Hertfordshire," said Miss Bingley, her voice tinged with desperation, "and Mr. Darcy and Lady Anne agree with me. Is that not so?"

Miss Bingley watched him, almost daring him to disagree, and Bingley turned his attention—approaching anguish in Darcy's estimation—to Darcy also. Given the conversation he had with his mother before leaving Netherfield, Darcy was not of a mind to say anything on the matter, either yea or nay. Unfortunately for Miss

Bingley, his mother was not so circumspect.

"Though I might have preferred to stay in Hertfordshire for a time, perhaps it was best to return to town for Christmas. But all is not lost, Mr. Bingley, for we visited several of your neighbors, including Longbourn, to take our leave. The Bennets knew of our departure and will not question it."

Bingley did not like what he was hearing at all, but his innate sense of good behavior prevented him from responding in a fashion he might have preferred. Behind him, Miss Bingley heaved a sigh of relief, albeit a silent one. Then disaster struck for the woman.

"And it is not adieu to the Bennets forever," added Lady Anne. It was obvious to Darcy his mother enjoyed cutting Miss Bingley's web of untruths and providing comfort to his friend. "The estate will be there whenever you choose to return, Mr. Bingley, and you were so well-liked in the neighborhood, I have no doubt you will be welcome with open arms.

"Oh, and I have invited the eldest Miss Bennets to stay with us during the season."

The final piece of information had been delivered with an offhand casual air, and it arrested Bingley from whatever he was to say next. Instead, he gaped at Lady Anne, unable to comprehend what he was hearing. Miss Bingley was glaring at Lady Anne as if she were a traitor, but Darcy wondered how the woman had meant to keep Miss Bennet's presence a secret. The Bingley schedule of events derived almost exclusively from that of the Darcys' by virtue of her brother's friendship with Darcy himself. Unless she meant to spirit him away to Yorkshire, it seemed impossible to keep it from him.

"You have invited the eldest Miss Bennets to London?"

"I have. My impression of them was so positive and the time to come to know them so short, that Georgiana and I determined at once to host them for the season. It is my thought they shall be welcome by our friends, for they are fine ladies."

Miss Bingley snorted with disdain, but Bingley fixed his gaze on Darcy's mother. "To be clear, you have invited Jane Bennet to London?"

Lady Anne hid a smile behind her hand. "And her sister, Elizabeth. Do not forget her, Mr. Bingley."

For a few moments, Bingley considered this development, and when he spoke, his voice contained the slightest hint of a whine. "It will still be two months or more before I can expect to see her — them — again."

"Perhaps it will be, Mr. Bingley," said Lady Anne. She stepped forward and laid a hand on his arm, saying: "Unless I heard amiss, you were only acquainted with Miss Bennet for a little more than a month. Is that not so?"

"It is," replied Bingley.

"Then perhaps it is best to allow a little time to pass in which you think of what you want for your future. There has been some talk of Miss Bennet's indifference, though I must own I have seen nothing of it. The suspense of a mere two months will do much to inform you of the strength of your feelings. I cannot but think it will do the same for Miss Bennet."

"Yes, I have heard much of indifference," said Bingley, shooting a look at his sister, who returned it with defiance. "You do not think she is indifferent to me?"

"Does my opinion matter?" asked Lady Anne. "It seems to me, Mr. Bingley, that the only opinion that carries any weight is your own."

"You are correct, of course," replied Bingley. "But I would hear your opinion all the same."

"Then my opinion is that a blind man could see Miss Bennet's regard for you." Miss Bingley closed her eyes as if praying for patience, but Darcy's mother took no notice of her. "Do not make your decision based on my opinion, Mr. Bingley. Trust your own."

"I will do that," replied Bingley. He paused for a moment, then he said: "It is quite certain that they will come in the spring."

"They have accepted my invitation. What more is required?"

"And Miss Bennet knows you all followed me to town, and that it was my intention to return."

"She does," said Lady Anne, clearly enjoying the exchange. "But if thee situation still concerns you, you are acquainted with Mr. Bennet, are you not? Write him a letter, explaining your opinion that it is best that you stay in town at present, expressing your anticipation for seeing his daughters when they come."

"Yes," said Bingley to himself. "I will do that. I thank you for your sage advice, Lady Anne, for it is most appreciated."

Then Bingley turned and, without excusing himself, hastened from the room. Miss Bingley possessed a little more prepossession, for she opened her mouth to excuse herself when Bingley's voice commanding her to join him floated back through the door. With a grimace, the woman dropped into a hasty curtsey and fled after her brother.

*   *   *

A few days after the ball at Netherfield, Mr. Collins returned to Kent, on the day that he had intended. Though he had withdrawn his attentions to Elizabeth, his society was still irksome and his words never-ending, and could feel no sorrow at the prospect of his departure. It was impossible, however, for the gentleman to depart without leaving them a veritable cornucopia of words expressing his gratitude and his wish to see them all again—a wish not returned by any of the family that Elizabeth could see. One particular comment caught Elizabeth's attention.

"I hope you will not be made too unhappy to see me go, Cousin Mary, for I assure you I have every intention of returning when I can. Then, I know we shall have happy news to impart to the rest of your family."

There was no need to interpret Mr. Collins's words, for his meaning was without disguise. Mary, however, made little comment at the gentleman's leaving, not that her indifference dimmed his enthusiasm in any way. Though Elizabeth could not determine the state of her sister's feelings, she thought Mary appeared indifferent to him. Then again, Mary was often quiet, little displaying her feelings for anyone to see. For this reason, Elizabeth decided it would be best to allow the matter to rest—she had never been close to Mary and was not certain her advice would be welcome anyway.

The departure of Mr. Collins brought peace back to Longbourn. The family returned to their previous activities, which consisted of the pianoforte and Fordyce for Mary, the officers for Kitty and Lydia, books and walking for Elizabeth—though the season was becoming too cold for walking much—and Jane's sewing and embroidering. Jane and Elizabeth were, as always, in each other's company, sharing confidences, speculation of how their time at Mr. Darcy's house would proceed, and the other matters they regularly discussed. There was not much society in those days—the ball at Netherfield had rendered other amusements tedious affairs—and they spent such much of their time at home.

In this fashion, the month of December passed, and the Christmas season was soon upon them. As was their custom, their Aunt and Uncle Gardiner soon arrived in Hertfordshire for the holidays, to the eager welcome of the family, the Bennets having much to tell them.

The Gardiners, though of the trade class, were possessed of such manners that they could pass for gentlefolk. Between the eldest Bennet daughters and their aunt and uncle existed a deep and abiding affection, and they had often stayed with them in London, partaking of superior society and the gentle and patient tutelage they did not receive at home. Elizabeth was curious to hear Aunt Gardiner's opinion of their upcoming stay in Mr. Darcy's home.

"This business of Lady Anne Darcy inviting you to stay in London is astonishing," said Aunt Gardiner when they sat down to discuss the matter soon after their arrival.

"It was shocking to us too," said Elizabeth, Jane nodding by her side. "We had only just made her acquaintance the day before."

Mrs. Gardiner was still for a moment, regarding Jane and Elizabeth, speculation evident in her gaze. "Perhaps you do not know this, but Lambton, where I was raised, is no more than five miles from Pemberley, the Darcy estate."

"That *is* a coincidence!" exclaimed Elizabeth. "Are you at all acquainted with the family?"

"I have met Lady Anne on occasion, though not for some years," replied Mrs. Gardiner. "I was the daughter of the parson of Lambton parish, and it is possible she may remember me. Lady Anne is, as you must already know, the daughter of an earl, and as the Darcy family is a prestigious and old one, she inhabits a sphere which is the envy of most. If you attend events of the season in Lady Anne's company, you will mingle with the highest of society."

"That is what concerns me," said Elizabeth. "How are we to present ourselves with any level of credit in such a society?"

"You will behave with perfect composure and poise, Elizabeth," said Mrs. Gardiner gently. "There is nothing amiss with your manners, and if there is something you do not know, I am certain Lady Anne will inform you of it."

That was certain to be true, thought Elizabeth, for Lady Anne would not wish her guests to embarrass her in society. Elizabeth felt less intimidated than she had only a moment before.

They continued to speak of what Jane and Elizabeth could expect when in London, and while Aunt Gardiner could not know, not being of that level of society herself, her wise and kind words set many of her nieces' worries to rest. Aunt Gardiner was also adept at calming and distracting their mother, and for a time, they were free of her schemes.

At the Christmas function held at Lucas Lodge every December, a situation arose which prompted Elizabeth to question all she knew of the Darcy family and Mr. Darcy himself. Sir William was a genial man who enjoyed nothing better than to invite everyone in the neighborhood who could fit into his house — and a few who could not—and then mingle among the community dispensing his civility upon all in equal measure. The Gardiners, long known to the neighborhood because of their yearly visits, were also invited, and it was there that Elizabeth introduced Mrs. Gardiner to Mr. Wickham.

Of late, Elizabeth and Jane, having been occupied by other matters, had not been much in company with the officers, though Kitty and Lydia always dispensed the latest news, regardless of whether their sisters wished to hear it. Therefore, Elizabeth had not been in Mr. Wickham's company since the ball. A few moments of conversation revealed the man was eager to inform her of his regrets and lay the cause for his lack of attendance at Mr. Darcy's feet, after which he was much the same as he had ever been. When Elizabeth spied her aunt nearby, she grasped the opportunity to make the introduction.

"Have you returned to Derbyshire of late, Mrs. Gardiner?" asked Mr. Wickham when the pleasantries, including their mutual regard for their home county, had been offered and accepted.

"I have not had that opportunity," replied Mrs. Gardiner. "It is on our minds, however, to visit again, perhaps as soon as next summer."

"Then I shall envy you," replied Mr. Wickham, "for it has been some years since I was last there, and it will be several more before I may see it again."

"It is a longing I well understand, sir, for I have not been since I was a girl." Mrs. Gardiner turned to Elizabeth. "Perhaps you will travel with us, Lizzy, for I had meant to invite you. Then again, perhaps you shall see it before then."

"Ah, yes," said Mr. Wickham before Elizabeth could answer. "Your sisters mentioned something of an invitation offered by Lady Anne."

"Yes, Jane and I have both received an invitation, but it is to town during the season. Lady Anne said nothing of Derbyshire."

"And yet, I must think it a possibility," said Mr. Wickham. The man laughed and then said: "Or perhaps not. In truth, hearing of the lady's invitation to her home in London astonished me, for Lady Anne has ever been a proud woman. Darcy is naught but his mother's son."

Surprised, Elizabeth did not know how to respond. It was fortunate, therefore, that her aunt was not similarly afflicted.

"Lady Anne Darcy a proud woman? Indeed, I have met her many times, Mr. Wickham, and she never struck me as anything other than lovely and amiable."

While one might have expected Mr. Wickham to express surprise at Mrs. Gardiner's rebuttal, it might also be expected he might retreat, take a more conciliatory tone, or even attempt to explain his point of view. Mr. Wickham did none of these; if anything, he showed the arrogance he had accused of Lady Anne.

"Perhaps she is amiable to those of her station, Mrs. Gardiner, but to those who are less than she, I am afraid she is very much like her son—proud, and above her company. It was my great fortune to be the protégé of Mr. Darcy, and he was nothing like his wife, who is, as you must understand, the daughter of an earl."

"And yet, when I met Lady Anne, I was nothing more than a parson's daughter, Mr. Wickham. That can hardly be called an equal to the daughter of an earl."

A slight shrug was Mr. Wickham's response, followed by a simple: "Much more than the son of a steward, I am certain you would agree. Had his son followed Mr. Darcy's wishes, I should have risen to the position held by your father."

For some time after, Mr. Wickham regaled them with tales, his words taking him from the subject of Lady Anne, Miss Darcy, the goodness of the elder Mr. Darcy—whom he seemed to believe was the only member of the family who was worth his time—seasoned with stories of the current Mr. Darcy's offenses against him. By the time they had been standing with him for five minutes, Elizabeth wished him far away. When salvation came in the form of her youngest sister begging him to join her, Elizabeth eagerly relinquished his company.

"You did not inform me of Mr. Wickham's interest in speaking of the Darcy family," said Mrs. Gardiner to Elizabeth.

"Mr. Wickham did not speak of anything other than the present Mr. Darcy previously," replied Elizabeth. "I am as shocked as you."

"What has he said?" asked Mrs. Gardiner.

Elizabeth spoke of her history with Mr. Wickham, including the first meeting and the reactions of Mr. Darcy and Mr. Wickham to each other, his subsequent communications, and the absence of the latter from the ball at Netherfield. Mrs. Gardiner listened, not speaking, and the longer Elizabeth spoke, the more forbidding her aunt's demeanor became.

"Lizzy," said Mrs. Gardiner when Elizabeth had related all there was to tell, her tone chiding, "did it not occur to you to wonder why Mr. Wickham made such a communication to you within a day of making your acquaintance?"

"It did not," replied Elizabeth, "though, in retrospect, I do not know why."

Mrs. Gardiner regarded Elizabeth, her expression remaining severe. "The reason is clear to me. It seems to me your first meeting with Mr. Darcy colored your opinion of him. Furthermore, it is clear to me that Mr. Wickham recognized this and used your existing antipathy for the gentleman to play on your sympathies."

"But why would he do so?" asked Elizabeth, unable to keep a plaintive note from her voice.

When Mrs. Gardiner gave her a significant look, Elizabeth colored, yet defended herself. "I am not in love with Mr. Wickham if that is what you are suggesting. In fact, I do not know him well at all. Since the ball, I have not seen him, nor did I miss his society. Kitty and Lydia have a much closer acquaintance with him."

"That is also a concern," said Mrs. Gardiner, looking over to where Lydia was now dancing with Mr. Wickham. As she watched them, however, she noted that much of Mr. Wickham's attention was to another side of the room, though Elizabeth was uncertain who or what he was watching. When she pointed this out to her aunt, Mrs. Gardiner nodded.

"It may be that my concerns are for naught, but I shall speak to your uncle before we leave — perhaps he can persuade your father to watch your youngest sisters more closely than is his wont. Regardless, I urge you to consider what you know of Lady Anne and Miss Darcy, and contrast it with Mr. Wickham's assertions. If the man is speaking untruths about Mr. Darcy's mother and sister, can he be trusted when speaking of Mr. Darcy?"

"You make a very good point, Aunt," replied Elizabeth. "It is a matter I shall consider with great care."

"Good," replied Mrs. Gardiner.

Elizabeth was not in her aunt's company much the rest of the evening, but her words were her constant attendant. Mr. Wickham approached Elizabeth on several occasions but sought more interesting partners when he found Elizabeth more reserved than she had ever been before. It did not seem to bother him — nothing appeared to bother the man. It was another mark against him.

CHAPTER IV

"*L*izzy may go to London and stay at stuffy Mr. Darcy's house. I shan't envy her a jot, for I would much rather stay in Hertfordshire where I am the center of attention of all the officers."

For a change, Kitty did not respond to her sister's boasting statement, though it was too much to ask that she had grown enough to ignore Lydia's poor manners. To hope for such an improvement would have been foolish, and Kitty proved her continued lack of maturity by rolling her eyes and glaring at her sister.

"It is fortunate you are not to go, then," said Mr. Bennet from behind his morning newspaper. "Though we have given you leave to consider yourself out in Meryton society, in London you would be deemed too young."

Lydia scowled at her father's reference to her still young age, but it was fortunate she said nothing, for Elizabeth did not know if she could avoid snapping in response. As they continued their meal, Elizabeth considered the two girls, giggling and carrying on as they always did. The feeling which had grown since Lydia had come out the year prior—and even before—was becoming ever stronger. Kitty and Lydia, if left unchecked, were on a path to ruin the Bennet family name.

The question was, what to do about the situation. Mrs. Bennet would be no help, for she was not the best behaved herself and encouraged them in their antics. They did not listen to Mary, who, though much better behaved, was not one to provide an example regardless, and the two youngest Bennets ignored their eldest sisters' admonishments—why should they listen when they had their mother's support?

That left Mr. Bennet as the only one who could affect their improvement. Elizabeth loved her father, had always esteemed him as an intelligent man, one whose affection for her had always counteracted Elizabeth's more difficult relationship with her mother. Even so, Elizabeth was not blind to his faults, and the lack of guidance for the youngest girls and his wife was an oversight which had always caused her grief. But Elizabeth could not go to London without making the attempt.

As always, Mr. Bennet listened to her concerns with more gravity than he would if it were any of her sisters. When she completed her recitation, of the evils of allowing the girls to continue unchecked, Mr. Bennet sat back and regarded her.

"Yes, Lizzy, I understand your concerns, though I do not believe the danger as great as you suggest. None of these poor officers will risk their positions, and Lydia cannot be an object of prey, given her lack of a fortune."

"There are other ways for a girl to disgrace her family, Papa. I doubt any of these men would take Lydia, even if she had ten thousand pounds."

"You are hard on your sister, I think."

At Elizabeth's severe look, her father shrugged and said: "I cannot say you are incorrect. Do not concern yourself, Elizabeth, for I shall attempt to limit the amount of damage your sisters can do to the family name."

And with that, Elizabeth was forced to be content, for it was the best she could do. She suspected her father considered the matter a joke. As there was little she could do, Elizabeth decided there was no reason to make herself unhappy, and instead focused her energies on her preparations for her own upcoming amusement.

There was one more event of some import to occur before their departure, for late in January, Mr. Collins returned to Longbourn. Over the past several weeks, Elizabeth had attempted to determine where the gentleman's interest in her had waned. What was certain was that it had happened at the ball, but try as she might, Elizabeth could remember nothing that might have happened to put him off. When she had exhausted her recollections, Elizabeth determined not to think on it. There was little to be gained in considering something which, in her estimation, was in her favor.

Though Mr. Collins's attentions to Mary were unabated, his first duty seemed to consist of speaking of his patroness. "Lady Catherine has, I assure you, heard of your invitation to London, and though she had some concern that you might have imposed upon her sister, I have reassured her, not only of your worthiness but of her sister's immediate liking to you and subsequent invitation."

"That is a great relief, Mr. Collins," said Elizabeth. The parson did not understand the dryness of her tone—though her father snorted in his attempt to refrain from laughing—and nodded in vigorous approval.

"Therefore, as Lady Catherine and her daughter are to attend events of the season, I am certain Lady Anne will introduce you to them. What an honor it shall be for you, my dear cousins, to be so favored by *two* daughters of an earl and their families. With these delights, your sojourn in town will not only be highly enjoyable, but I cannot help but think Lady Anne means to introduce you to men who might suit you. What credit you will be to your dear family should you return to Longbourn engaged!"

Though Elizabeth was not at all certain of Mr. Collins's speculations, there was little reason to debate the matter with him. Along with Jane, Elizabeth thanked him for his words and allowed him to turn his attention back to Mary. Then, within two days of his arrival, Mr. Collins proposed. The result, however, none of them could have predicted.

One day in late January, Henry Bennet was enjoying a morning in his study. The earliest part of his day, he had focused his attention on the estate ledgers, a task he detested and had put off for far too long. As usual, he found upon doing the accounts that his wife had spent more of his income than he wished, necessitating another conversation with her about the need to practice economy. Bennet had little notion *this* time would be any different than the last, but he knew it must be done. But it did not follow that he needed to do it at once, and after a time bemoaning his wife's lack of anything resembling restraint, the lure of his books called, and he yielded with little resistance.

It was some time later when a knock sounded on his door, almost diffident, meaning it was neither Elizabeth—who was much more confident—nor his wife—whose knock sounded like a sledgehammer's blow. Curious as to the identity of his visitor, Bennet set his book down and called out permission to enter. When Mary opened the door and stepped inside, Bennet looked on her with shock, for Mary did not often come into his room.

"Yes, Mary?" asked Bennet when his quietest daughter paused in the open door. "May I help you?"

This seemed to provoke Mary to action, for the girl stepped in and closed the door behind her. "Papa, may I have a moment of your time?"

"Of course, Mary," said Bennet, attempting a smile to set her at ease. It was a miserable failure as evidenced by the girl settling gingerly on a chair, her hands rested on its arms, and then clasped in her lap—though she did not wring them, Bennet thought it was a near thing. It was some few further minutes she sat there saying nothing. Mary not speaking was nothing unusual, but sitting in his study *was*, rendering the situation more curious by the minute.

"Did you have something of which you wished to speak?" Bennet tried after a few more moments of this.

"Mr. Collins proposed to me."

"Ah, then I will own I had some inkling of his intentions," replied Mr. Bennet. Inside he laughed, though he was careful he did not show it to his daughter, for even if she wished to marry his foolish cousin, it was no surprise it would cause any woman to pause and consider what they were about to undertake.

"Then have you come for my blessing?" asked Mr. Bennet. He fixed his daughter with a grin and added: "If so, this is quite unusual, for it is the suitor's duty to approach the father for permission."

That his jest made no impression on Mary was no surprise, but her next words were beyond anything Bennet might have expected. "I do not wish to marry him, Papa."

Bennet gazed at her with unabashed astonishment. "Have I heard you correctly, child? Are you saying you do not wish to marry Mr. Collins?"

Finally, Bennet saw a little spirit, for her gaze hardened, and she glared at him. "I am aware I am not the prettiest of my sisters, and I know my prospects are dim, but I would hope I have the right to expect more than a ridiculous twit for a husband."

"Nor did I say you do not," said Bennet, suppressing a snort of laughter. "My surprise is not because I think you unable to attract the attention of any man other than Mr. Collins, but because you have not given the man any reason to doubt your acceptance."

"Should I have?" asked Mary. "If I had, how do you think Mama would have reacted? Since it was not certain he would propose, I saw no need to create an incident unless it was necessary to do so."

This time Bennet could not suppress the snort of laughter. "Yes, I can well understand your desire to avoid your mother's paroxysms on the subject, though I cannot imagine we will be free of them now."

"Papa," said Mary, her tone as serious as ever, "do you mean to make me accept him?" When Bennet paused in surprise, Mary continued, saying: "I have not given him a response, as I informed him I wished to think on the matter before answering. But I doubt we have long, for I suspect Mama will learn of the matter soon, and when she does, she will consider it a fait accompli unless I refuse him first."

Right on cue, a shriek sounded from somewhere further in the house, and given the clarity with which Bennet heard his wife's outburst through the door, he suspected it must have been deafening. Ignoring that for the moment, Bennet studied his middle daughter, wondering how well he knew her. Mary took his silence as a prompt to speak again.

"I hope you do not make me marry him, Papa, though I shall do so if you require it of me. He is a silly man, with little but his patroness on his mind and entirely too much deference for her opinions. His knowledge of the Bible is sketchy at best, he does not often bathe or wash his hair, and I am certain his attachment to me is imaginary, for all he claims a deep and abiding affection."

"Mary," said Bennet, when he could finally speak over her torrent of words, "why do you think I will force you to marry Mr. Collins?"

"The entail," his daughter said without elaboration.

"The entail is what it is. I would not have forced your sister to marry him if he proposed—why should I force you?"

"Lizzy is your favorite," argued Mary, a statement of fact rather than an accusation.

Bennet smiled, amused the girl was finding reasons for him to insist on her marrying his cousin. "I would not insist on any of you marrying where you do not wish. Surely you have seen the state of my marriage with your mother."

It seemed to Bennet that Mary relaxed ever so slightly, again causing him much amusement. But it was sobering at the same time, for this neglected and overlooked daughter had declared herself willing to sacrifice her future for the family if he required it of her.

Bennet did not think Elizabeth would have been so selfless as this.

"Then you will not make me marry him."

"No, child," said Bennet. "I will not. Whatever you decide, I will support you." Bennet paused and grinned. "Your mother will make a fuss about it, but I am prepared to endure her reproaches. I hope you are similarly resolute."

Mary shook her head. "Why you think Mama's displeasure would affect me, I cannot say. When has she ever paid me the slightest hint of attention? I am sure she will lament my refusal and return to it over the coming months, but I shall soon be out of her thoughts, as I ever am."

The matter of fact words shamed Bennet, for he realized that he was no better than his wife. Kitty was more noticeable than her elder sister, for she attempted to follow Lydia to gain some of the praise her mother lavished on her youngest, but Mary almost never drew attention to herself. She truly was the forgotten Bennet.

The sounds of his wife approaching his sanctum reached Bennet's ears, and he knew he must speak quickly, for he doubted she would remember to knock, though he had instructed her many times over the years. To her credit, Mary did not look concerned in the slightest at the coming confrontation.

"Very well, Mary. I shall speak to your mother and Mr. Collins on the matter, for I know it will be a trial for you. However, if you will . . ." Bennet paused, uncertain how to say what he wished. In the end, he decided it was best to come out with it. "If you are interested, Mary, I should like to discuss . . . whatever it is you are reading at present. I only ask you to leave Fordyce out of it."

Surprised though she was, Mary soon recovered and nodded, favoring him with a shy smile. "I believe I should like that too, Papa."

True to form, the door swung open in that instant, and Mrs. Bennet rushed into the room, her countenance alive with excitement, mixed with puzzlement. "Mr. Bennet, do you know what has happened in our house this morning? Mr. Collins has proposed to our middle daughter. We are saved!"

"If you had allowed me to speak," said Bennet as Mary slipped from the room, as always unnoticed by her mother, "I would have told you I have, indeed, heard this news. There is, however, the necessary conversation Mr. Collins must have with me, and I should be very much obliged if you would call him in and leave us in peace."

Mrs. Bennet responded with a vigorous nod and an excited: "Of course! I would not keep you from it, Mr. Bennet!"

Then she darted from the room, exclaiming as to the family's good fortune and calling for Mr. Collins all at once. Bennet grimaced, not at all eager for the coming discussion with his dullard of a cousin. He had no notion Collins would understand why he was being refused and suspected it would offend him.

"Come in and close the door, Cousin," said Bennet when the man himself appeared. Mr. Collins complied and entered, lowering his heavyset frame into one of the chairs in front of Bennet's desk, causing an alarming creak. Bennet made a mental note to have those chairs replaced before turning his attention to Mr. Collins, who regarded him with a beatific smile as he wallowed in his imaginary regard for Bennet's middle daughter.

"I have spoken to Mary, Mr. Collins," said Bennet, "and she has informed me you have made her an offer."

"I have, and I cannot be happier that this matter has been resolved in a satisfactory fashion for all. As you know, it was the particular advice of my patroness, Lady Catherine de Bourgh, who told me to seek a bride from among your daughters with alacrity. And while I thought to act when last I came, there arose matters . . . Well, let us simply say I cannot be more satisfied with today's events, for I shall obtain my happiness, while this olive branch will strengthen the ties between our families."

Bennet pinched his nose, praying for patience. The man's mention of something presumably stopping him from paying his addresses to Lizzy pricked his interest, but the inexhaustible supply of words soon stretched Bennet's patience, and he wished to end this interview. Thus, he ignored the matter and cut Mr. Collins off as he was drawing breath to continue to speak.

"That is all very interesting, Mr. Collins, but I have one question, for you: did my daughter in actuality give you a reply to your proposal?"

Opening his mouth to speak, Mr. Collins paused before speaking, and his confusion rendered him mute. A moment later he looked across the desk at Bennet and ventured: "As I recall, Miss Mary wished to speak to you first."

"Thank you, Mr. Collins, for taking the time to remember that fact, for it is a most salient point. You see, Mary entered my room after speaking with you and informed me she does not wish to marry you."

A look of utter stupefaction came over his cousin's countenance. "She does not wish to marry me? Why ever would she wish to refuse me? Is she not sensible of the fact that an offer of marriage may never come her way again?"

Though the parson's words were offensive, Bennet sensed he had not intended any insult—it was nothing more than the man's utter lack of tact. It was this insight which prompted Bennet to pause and consider how best to manage the situation. The remembrance of Mary, sitting warily in the very chair Mr. Collins now occupied, clutching the arms in her nervousness, though willing to do whatever required, demanded more from Bennet than to dismiss his cousin's buffoonery with a caustic remark as he wished. Thus, he exerted himself to do whatever he could to smooth her way.

"Tell me, Cousin: would you wish a woman to accept your proposal for no other reason than because she has no other prospects? Is this the basis for a marriage of felicity?"

Mr. Collins frowned. "But it is true, is it not?"

"At present, perhaps it is. But Mary is naught but eighteen years old, and still has many years to attract a husband. More than this, however, it is not tactful to attempt to induce a woman to accept you by reminding her she is not popular with the gentlemen. A woman wishes to hear she is the center of a potential suitor's world—not that she is not capable of attracting another man."

A comical widening of the man's eyes preceded Mr. Collins's exclamation of: "Do you suggest I should have attempted to make love to her?"

"In our society, Mr. Collins," said Bennet, "it is customary for the man to court a woman. Conversations, walks, dances, attending events together—all of these are expected. It is considered gauche for a couple to rush to the altar, for it speaks to possible other reasons for a hasty marriage."

If Bennet thought the man's eyes could not become any larger, his cousin was ready to prove him wrong, for Mr. Collins gaped at him in surprise. Then he shot to his feet and exclaimed: "Then that is what I shall do!"

"Sit, Collins," growled Bennet, surprised when Collins obeyed him, though with clear hesitation. "If you wish to go pay court to some young woman you are welcome to do so. But please refrain from doing so with Mary, for she has already stated her disinterest."

"B-But—" stammered Mr. Collins.

"It is not my purpose to offend or anger you, Cousin," said Bennet. "But it is clear Mary is not an option, nor do I think my elder daughters are likely to accept a proposal from you. Did you wish to consider either of my youngest girls?"

A quickly shaken head was Mr. Collins's response, unsurprising to Bennet. He chuckled and reached over, grasped two glasses, poured a measure of port into each and handed one to his cousin. Mr. Collins accepted it, though appearing uncertain. Bennet raised his glass as if to offer a toast and said:

"To your continued single status, Mr. Collins. In the future, I suggest you take my advice to heart and take the time to come to know a woman, rather than rushing to marry the first woman you can find. Remember, if you choose amiss, your regrets may very well last a lifetime. Please, sir, for my sake and your own—choose wisely."

"I shall do so, Mr. Bennet," said Mr. Collins, sipping from his drink.

For the rest of the time Collins was in his library, they chatted amiably about what he should search for in a wife, his company as tolerable as Bennet had ever experienced with him. It was an unfortunate fact that Bennet doubted his cousin would become a man whose society he could tolerate. But he had high hopes that in this, at least, Mr. Collins would think more than was his wont, and perhaps even make a choice for himself, rather than doing exactly what his patroness told him to do.

It was unfortunate but expected that Mrs. Bennet would not understand, for she was not as inclined as Mr. Collins to listen to Bennet's words of advice. She was also not shy in expressing her opinion.

"I cannot believe you have betrayed me thus, Mr. Bennet!" wailed she for perhaps the tenth time. "You shall not endure the consequences of your refusal to make Mary accept Mr. Collins. *I*, on the other hand, shall be thrown into the hedgerows to starve!"

"There shall be no starving done by any of us, Mrs. Bennet," replied Bennet, refraining from voicing a half a dozen sardonic comments which entered his mind. "All shall be well, I dare say."

"No, it shall not! But let me inform you of this, Husband," exclaimed she, her shrieking giving way to vindictive petulance, "if Mary does not wed Mr. Collins, I shall not have her in whatever reduced circumstances I will find myself when you are gone. She will be required to shift for herself."

"Reduced circumstances it shall be," said Mr. Bennet. "But you will not be in such severe straits as to find yourself in the hedgerows, for I have made some provision for you."

Though she drew breath to wail yet again, Mrs. Bennet paused at his words, puzzlement adorning her features. "Provision? Of what provision do you speak?"

"It was not my intention to inform you until all the particulars had been completed," replied Bennet, for once feeling a hint of pity for this woman. Her fears were real, and he supposed he might have saved her much worry if he had informed her before. "Mr. Gardiner has been taking a portion of our income and investing it, and while it will not be a fortune, it should be enough for you to subsist comfortably in a cottage we shall purchase for your future home."

"I am to have a cottage?" asked Mrs. Bennet.

"You are, Maggie," said Bennet, grasping her hand. "It is not yet done, but it should be soon—in no more than a year or two. Though I do not know where it shall be yet, it will be in the neighborhood. There should be enough to support you and whatever girls remain unmarried, and even a servant or two. You will *not* be homeless should the worst happen."

"But would it not be best to keep Longbourn in the family?"

"That matter has already been decided, Mrs. Bennet," replied Bennet. "If we treat him well now, it is possible Mr. Collins will even be persuaded to help when the time comes. But none of our girls—not even Mary, by her own testimony—would be happy with him, and I dare say Collins would not appreciate any one of them either. Trust me, Maggie—it is for the best."

Though she did not speak for a time and she appeared unable to understand, the news she would not be homeless was enough to distract her. After a few moments of this, she closed her eyes, swallowed, and attempted a watery smile.

"Very well then, Mr. Bennet. I shall trust your judgment."

"Thank you, my dear," said a relieved Bennet. "I shall not fail you."

Mrs. Bennet nodded, though distracted. "If you do not mind, I shall take to my room to rest for a time. This morning has been tiring."

"That is for the best, Mrs. Bennet."

When his wife had departed, Bennet thought back on the morning, satisfied with his endeavors. Perhaps it would have been best had he told his wife of the provision being made for her, but he thought it had worked out in the end. And he may even have gained a replacement companion in Mary when her elder sister went to London.

With that thought, Bennet retrieved his neglected book and immersed himself again in its pages.

CHAPTER V

Winter had never been Elizabeth's favorite season, and while there were mixed emotions concerning the upcoming stay in Mr. Darcy's house, Elizabeth welcomed the waning of February, as it gave way to the marginally warmer weather which characterized March. There was some feeling of disappointment she would not see spring in Hertfordshire, but Elizabeth was philosophical about the near future. Having heard so much of the part of London where Mr. Darcy lived, but not having visited, she was anticipating the sights, especially of famed Hyde Park.

Of the upcoming amusement, Elizabeth had thought much and decided little. With Jane, they had spoken of what they could expect, but neither had come to any conclusions. For Elizabeth's part, she was attempting to reconcile what she knew of Mr. Darcy, contrasted with what Mr. Wickham had said of him, and what she now suspected of the man, revealed in his moment of unguarded conversation with Elizabeth and her aunt.

The officers Elizabeth saw but little, and she did not repine the lack of their society. Mr. Wickham had attempted several times to speak to her and had raised the subject of Mr. Darcy more than once. When Elizabeth did not give him any encouragement, he responded with the equivalent of a shrug—he seemed perfectly content to bestow his attention on those who gave him consequence, and when Elizabeth did not, he did not repine her disinterest. With Kitty and Lydia in residence at Longbourn, reports of the officers were not lacking, for they spoke of the officers more than all other subjects combined. But it was nothing to Elizabeth if Mr. Wickham began lavishing attention on some other young lady of the neighborhood, one with whom Elizabeth was not at all acquainted.

The day arrived for their departure and Elizabeth and her elder sister oversaw the disposition of their trunks before descending to break their fast and farewell their family. It was while they were in the breakfast room that a carriage pulled upon the drive. The sight of the large coach and four pulled them from the house to inspect it, and they were not disappointed. The large springs installed above each of the wheels promised a smooth ride, the panes of glass would prevent most of the dust of the road from entering the compartment, while the plush interior spoke to the comfort the passengers would experience while within. It gleamed and shone in the morning sunlight, the black lacquer of the paint showing nary a blemish, a bright coat of arms had been painted on the back. The four horses drawing it stamped and snorted, the lead left horse whickering its greeting when Elizabeth approached.

"This is Mr. Darcy's carriage?" asked Mrs. Bennet, her voice colored with awe.

"It seems to be so, Mrs. Bennet," said her husband, though it was clear to Elizabeth he was equally impressed. "Our daughters have been favored, indeed."

Mrs. Bennet appeared overwhelmed by what she was seeing and unable to respond, a situation unusual for the voluble woman. As the family watched, the servants loaded their various effects, and then when all was prepared, the family said their farewells. When it came time for Jane and Elizabeth to part with their mother, she bid them adieu in a manner Elizabeth might have predicted in advance.

"Be certain to do your best, girls," said she, peering more at Jane than Elizabeth. "As your father said, Lady Anne has favored you, and if you both make the attempt, I am certain you will return with husbands in tow."

Then she turned and entered the house, leaving Elizabeth and Jane standing, grinning at each other, while their father laughed and wished them a pleasant journey. After receiving the well-wishes of the sisters—Kitty and Lydia finally appeared to understand their good fortune, for they appeared envious—the two eldest Bennet sisters boarded, and the carriage departed.

They spent the first few moments of their journey in silence, but then when the carriage proceeded through Meryton and from thence to the road to London, Jane ventured a comment. "I do not know your feelings, Lizzy, but I will own to some intimidation. We are about to enter a world so unlike that to which we are accustomed, we might as well be on the other side of the world."

"Come now, Jane," said Elizabeth, attempting humor to lighten their spirits, "you know that every attempt to intimidate me causes my courage to rise."

"And yet, I know you well enough to understand your courage is more bravado than true confidence."

"You know me well, indeed, dearest Jane. There is nothing we can do, however, other than to meet this challenge with fortitude."

"If you have some to spare, I should be very much obliged."

Laughter passed between them, which helped to lessen the tension, and the rest of the journey passed swiftly and with much banter between the two girls. Before long, the outskirts of London came into view, and soon they were rattling through the busy streets, the carriage driver weaving his expert way through the congested thoroughfares of the city. Then they passed, as if through some unseen barrier, to a series of quieter streets, the bustle of the business districts being left behind in favor of a series of homes, which grew larger and more impressive the longer they proceeded forward.

At length, the carriage turned onto the drive leading to one house more imposing and larger than the rest, with a large portico with about a dozen steps leading up to a sheltered door. The house was four stories, stood on the corner of the street, with a hint of greenery around the side and the appearance of a large park beyond the end of the road in the distance. The façade was impressive, with stone pillars and a pair of large doors beyond, which stood open, Lady Anne and Miss Darcy standing on about the third step awaiting their arrival.

When the carriage lurched to a halt, Elizabeth and Jane exchanged one last glance for courage and then exited with the help of the waiting footman. Lady Anne and Miss Darcy were quick to greet them and express their pleasure, inviting them inside.

Therein they found another impressive sight of an open entryway, a large curved stairway leading to the second floor, decadence and wealth dripping from every tile set into the floor, every item displayed in a position of honor. For all this, however, there was no sense of overwhelming riches, no sense of display for the sake of informing the visitor of the wealth of the inhabitants. It was a home, and though fine, appeared comfortable and lived in, and not overly ostentatious.

"Here are your rooms," said Lady Anne as she showed them up to their bedchambers, pointing out a few locations of interest along the way. "I have assigned you chambers with an adjoining sitting-room—I hope it meets your approval, for I thought you would be comfortable near to each other. If not, please inform me and I will make other arrangements."

"No, this is lovely," said Jane, echoed by Elizabeth's agreeing nod. "I believe Lizzy and I will find it agreeable to be situated so close to each other."

"Excellent! Then we shall leave you to refresh yourselves."

"Might you also leave us a guide to assist us in reaching the sitting-room?" asked Elizabeth, feeling her courage rise a little with her light-hearted comment. "If you do not, I feel we shall become lost in this intimidating house!"

Their hosts laughed, and Miss Darcy said: "Oh, Miss Elizabeth, Miss Bennet—we shall have so much fun together!"

"Yes, I am certain we shall," said Lady Anne. "If you have any trouble, feel free to ask any of the servants for assistance. Should you wish to rest at present, then we shall see you again for dinner."

"I cannot speak for my sister," said Jane, "but I have no need of rest."

"Then I hope you will join us for refreshments," replied Lady Anne, before leading her daughter from the room.

"Should Mama see us now, she would die of mortification at the sight of your daring, Lizzy," said Jane once they were gone.

"Then it is well she is not here," replied Elizabeth. "It is also well that Lady Anne is of a more relaxed demeanor."

Jane shook her head. "Only you, Lizzy. But I must thank you, for I am more at ease now than I have been since we left Longbourn."

"That is why I said it, Jane," replied Elizabeth, kissing her sister's cheek. "Humor is my defense against intimidation, and I am confident Lady Anne will endeavor to make everything easy for us."

The sisters separated thereafter, going to their rooms to change. In these rooms and the sitting-room outside, Elizabeth discovered her impression of the house was accurate. The chamber which was to be hers while in London was large—perhaps as large as Elizabeth and Jane's rooms at Longbourn together, and the furnishings, while fine, did not leave one with the impression they were to be shown and not used. Elizabeth particularly enjoyed the sight of the bed, which was far larger than anything she had used before. She would sleep well in such comfortable surroundings.

Elizabeth also discovered Lady Anne had assigned her a maid for her stay, a young girl by the name of Lucy, who was already setting about unpacking her effects. Though Elizabeth was uncertain of this development, she greeted the girl with cheer, answered a few questions concerning her preferences, then allowed her to assist when she changed her dress. Within a few moments, they had dispensed the dust of the road, the damage to her hair repaired, and she found herself ready to descend and greet their hosts.

"Well, here we all are now," said Lady Anne when they were seated together. "Georgiana and I have been anticipating your visit, for as my daughter said, I have no doubt we will all enjoy the visit very much.

"Now, I will ask after your preferences, for I wish to construct our activities based on what will give you the most pleasure during your stay."

"Oh, do not concern yourselves for us," protested Jane. "I am certain Lizzy and I shall enjoy whatever activities you believe would be best."

"It is kind of you to say it, Miss Bennet," said Lady Anne, patting Jane's hand, "but we wish to take your preferences into account too. I have had many years in London to attend events, and as such, there is nothing which I particularly wish to do. While we will attend balls, parties, and dinners as expected, there are many more activities in London than those. Do you like plays and the opera, or do your tastes tend more towards exhibits and art?"

For several moments after, they considered what would best suit the tastes of all. As it was, Elizabeth was partial to the theater, while Jane enjoyed opera more, and both sisters were agreeable to any exhibits Lady Anne might recommend. Though it was too early to draw up a schedule, within thirty minutes they had compiled a rough list of amusements they would like, and their plans were loosely set accordingly.

"As newcomers, you will be quite the sensation when we begin to attend balls and parties," said Lady Anne with a smile at the sisters. "And when the gentlemen catch sight of you, you will cut a swath through hearts by force of nothing more than your pretty faces."

Elizabeth felt her cheeks heating and knew that Jane was experiencing an even greater measure of embarrassment. It was fortunate Lady Anne did not notice or affected ignorance to avoid further embarrassing them.

"In that, I am sure we will be doubly grateful for your presence, for it will take some of the attention away from Georgiana. She is not one who enjoys notoriety."

"Not at all," added Miss Darcy. "I appreciate your presence and support."

"Do you have many acquaintances in London?" asked Elizabeth. "And your son—is he here as well?"

Lady Anne seemed pleased that Elizabeth asked after her son. "Yes, William is in town. There were a few matters of business with the bank to which he needed to attend this morning, but I should expect him to return before long. We also have many other acquaintances, though many more than we would call friends. I expect you will meet many more people than you wish."

"And Mr. Bingley and his sisters?" asked Jane, a hint of eagerness in her voice which was not usually present. Jane flushed a little when she realized how excited she had sounded, but Lady Anne smiled and took pity on her.

"Yes, Mr. Bingley is here, though his sister mentioned something of a visit to the north. But Mr. Bingley could not be moved from town at present. In fact, the man determined to camp on my doorstep until you appeared and was only dissuaded when I reminded him about your need to settle in with us. I have invited the Bingleys and Hursts to dine with us tomorrow evening, so you will have the opportunity to renew your acquaintance with them."

"Oh, that is excellent," said Jane, and for the rest of their time in the sitting-room, a slight smile was visible for them all to see. Their hosts possessed the good manners to refrain from mentioning it, though Elizabeth thought Lady Anne was pleased.

"I also remember your cousin was a guest in your house when we were there, so you must have heard of his patroness—who is my sister—Lady Catherine de Bourgh."

"Yes," said Elizabeth, forbearing the mention of Mr. Collins's continual flow of praise for Lady Catherine. "When he visited us again in January, Mr. Collins informed us that your sister is also to come to London."

"That is true, though we do not expect her just yet." Lady Anne paused and smiled. "Catherine sees no reason to come to London early, for she claims the highest tiers of society do not arrive until at least late March. Whether she has the right of it I do not know, but to me, the lack of those of the highest society is no impediment."

The sisters laughed as Lady Anne had intended. "There is also the question of *who* makes up the best of society, and if they decided themselves that they belong within that august group!" exclaimed Elizabeth.

"Exactly!" said Lady Anne. "Events will start slowly but I am sure we shall occupy ourselves in some other manner. Then, when we begin attending some of the more prestigious events, you will have gained a tolerance for them and be at greater ease. I should also like to introduce you to my brother and sister, the Earl and Countess of Matlock, and those of their children who are in town. You will like them very much, for they are not at all given to airs or false superiority."

"If you recommend them so warmly," replied Elizabeth, "I am certain Jane and I shall find them nothing less than amiable."

For some time after they continued to speak of the coming weeks, and Elizabeth, though she participated, was immersed in thoughts of Mr. Wickham. Lady Anne and her daughter's behavior since their arrival, their eagerness to introduce them to family and friends gave the lie to his words, further convincing Elizabeth that Mr. Wickham was adhering to some other agenda when he spoke of them being proud and unapproachable. More than once Elizabeth thought to ask Lady Anne of the officer, but she could not find a good way to raise the subject. In the end, she decided it would be an impertinence and refrained.

Then, after they had been sitting for some time, the one member of the family for whom Elizabeth still possessed doubts entered the room. And she was once again brought face to face with the tall and imposing figure of Mr. Darcy.

As the time of the Bennet sisters' visit grew near, Darcy had grown more pensive, unable to determine the state of his own feelings. The sensation of fascination with the younger sister persisted, even as it had been three months since he had last seen her. That his mother and sister's conversation had often consisted of the upcoming visit was a contributing factor, but Darcy was left uncomfortably aware he would have thought of her regardless.

It was clear he could not with any good conscience consider anything of a more permanent nature with Miss Elizabeth, not that he would have considered such anyway. Beyond his duty to his family name and the future prospects of his sister, any alliance with Miss Elizabeth would bring the Bennet family — especially the mother — into his closer sphere. That was not something Darcy could tolerate. Miss

Elizabeth had nothing of any consequence which would be of benefit to a man in his position, and there *was* Anne to consider.

Thus, when Darcy entered his house that day, knowing they had arrived, he was torn between wishing to avoid them—knowing he could not—and hurrying to greet them. In the end, it was good manners which forced his footsteps toward the sitting-room where the butler told him they were with his mother and sister.

The sight of Miss Elizabeth Bennet was a shock to Darcy, for though she was everything he remembered, in some fashion, she was much, much *more*. From almost the first moments of their acquaintance, Darcy had been attracted to her, had considered her one of the handsomest women of his acquaintance. There was nothing he could see that marked her as changed. But she was more beautiful, livelier, and altogether more desirable than any woman he had ever met.

"Miss Bennet, Miss Elizabeth," said Darcy as the two ladies rose to greet him. "I hope your journey to London was a comfortable one."

"It was, indeed," said Miss Elizabeth. "I believe we have you to thank for sending the carriage to retrieve us."

"It was no bother, Miss Elizabeth," replied Darcy. "It is good to have you with us, for perhaps the season will be enlivened with your presence."

"And you need our presence to make the season any livelier?" asked Miss Elizabeth, arching an eyebrow in an utterly enticing fashion. "From all I have heard, lively events are already plentiful—I do not know what my poor sister and I can do to improve it for you."

"Oh, that is just William's way," said his mother, fixing him with a fond smile. "I declare that if I was not present to insist upon his attendance, he would stay at Pemberley the entire season."

"The season does become tiresome," said Darcy, "and as you have previously said, I am not enamored of society."

"That is understandable, Mr. Darcy," said Miss Elizabeth. "But is not the society of good friends enough to pull you from your estate?"

"Good friends, yes," said Darcy. "However, I bestow my friendship most carefully, and as such, have few acquaintances I would call good friends."

Miss Elizabeth considered Darcy for a moment before turning back to his mother. "Your mention of your estate brings to mind an unknown—and tenuous—connection between us, Lady Anne, for when my aunt visited us at Christmas, I discovered that she has actually met you."

"She has?" asked his mother, curiosity and uncertainty evident. For

Darcy's part, the woman's words were akin to many said to his family over the years by those attempting to curry favor with them. Darcy found himself disappointed, for he had thought Miss Elizabeth was above such blatant machinations.

"My aunt is Madeline Gardiner, who grew up in Lambton, which I believe is very close to Pemberley. Before she was married, she would have been known as Madeline Plumber."

The expression of confusion turned to one of delight. "Little Madeline Plumber is your aunt? Why, I have not seen her since her father resigned his rectorship in Lambton to take a position in the church at Merton College!"

"I believe he has since retired, Lady Anne," said Miss Bennet. "But Aunt Gardiner still speaks often of her years in Derbyshire and of her love of the county."

"And your aunt lives in town?" When the Bennet sisters nodded, his mother said: "Then we must visit her, for I long to see her again. I never would have expected to become reacquainted with a familiar face so long after last seeing her. Do they live nearby?"

"Their residence is on Gracechurch Street, Lady Anne," said Miss Elizabeth.

"Then you must send a note around, for we shall visit as soon as you have settled in."

Lady Anne continued to question the Bennet sisters about their aunt, drawing whatever news she could concerning her old acquaintance while Darcy looked on with dismay. Gracechurch Street was not a neighborhood in London to which he would choose to take his mother and sister, and furthermore, this Mr. Gardiner was the brother of Mrs. Bennet. Though Darcy remembered his mother's words about the difference between siblings, he wondered how much different the brother could be from the odious, scheming mercenary mother in Hertfordshire. Notwithstanding his friendship with Bingley, the connection to a tradesman with the manners of Mrs. Bennet was not one he wished to contemplate.

When the sisters expressed their desire to return to their rooms to rest before dinner, Darcy rose with his mother and sister, Georgiana departing with them to ensure the sisters reached their rooms again without mishap. After the door closed behind them, Darcy turned to his mother, noting she had anticipated him.

"Do you wish to object to our expected visit to Gracechurch Street, William?"

"It is not the best part of town," replied Darcy, cautious because of the knowledge his mother would be disappointed. "I know you hold that Mr. Gardiner's character may differ from his sister's, but I wonder how much similarity there is."

"Madeline Gardiner would not marry a fool," said his mother. "Perhaps you do not recollect her, but I remember her well. She was a lovely young girl and I cannot imagine she will be anything less than a lovely woman. Given the characters of the eldest Bennet sisters and the time they have spent with their aunt and uncle, I suspect their good manners, so much in contrast with the rest of their family, were likely learned at the feet of these Gardiners."

Darcy shrugged, knowing he had lost this skirmish if there had ever been any question of the outcome. "Then I suppose you will visit this aunt of the Bennets."

"Yes, and I should like you to join us. Then you may see for yourself whether the Gardiners are worthy people to know."

For a moment, Darcy thought to object, but he realized there was no good reason to refuse. His dignity could well withstand thirty minutes in a house on Gracechurch Street, even if the family was objectionable.

"Very well. If you inform me when this visit is to take place, I shall ensure my calendar is clear."

"I am happy to hear it, William," said his mother. "Then if you will allow me, I will go speak with the housekeeper about dinner. We would not wish to make a poor impression on our guests by feeding them substandard fare, now would we?"

"You had best not let cook hear you speaking so," jested Darcy. "For if she learns of it, she may quit on the spot!"

"Oh, I should think she could do with a little humbling," replied his mother.

Then with a smile, she excused herself, leaving Darcy alone. The sitting-room, where the Bennet sisters may return at any time, was not conducive to deep thought, so Darcy took himself to his study. In his mind, as he walked, he thought of the sisters and, in particular, the younger, mahogany-haired sprite of a woman. Perhaps this visit would not be too taxing. In, fact, being in Miss Elizabeth's presence once again was invigorating, regardless of the impending visit to the aunt and uncle's. Darcy would keep himself under good regulation — she was only a woman, even if she was one of the most captivating specimens he had ever met. Surely, he could keep the allure of her attractions at bay.

CHAPTER VI

"*S*hopping?" demanded Elizabeth. "Why on earth would we need to go shopping?"

"This is a world with which you are unfamiliar, Elizabeth," said Lady Anne. By now, the four women had agreed to an informal mode of address, though the Bennet sisters had decided it was best to stay with the more formal "Lady Anne" for their hostess. "The clothes you and your sister brought are lovely and of excellent quality — this is easy to see. But there is a certain level of sophistication expected of those who attend the season, particularly at the events we attend. Furthermore, your evening wear is a little out of date, which necessitates a few adjustments in your wardrobe."

"That sounds expensive," said Jane, sounding fretful. "Papa did not give us enough funds to pay for a new wardrobe."

"You do not require a new wardrobe, Jane," replied Lady Anne, favoring Jane with a fond smile. "We shall purchase you some dresses and other accessories for evening wear, but your daywear requires little adjustment, for it is already lovely.

"As for the funds necessary to purchase what you require, that shall be *my* responsibility."

The look Lady Anne wore dared them to protest further, and

Elizabeth was only happy to oblige. "We cannot ask Mr. Darcy to pay for our purchases."

"Nor would I suggest you do," replied Lady Anne. Now she was smiling, perhaps sensing their resistance was crumbling. "Do you suppose I do not possess my own income? *I* shall take responsibility for your purchases, and I shall not hear any further dissension."

"You had best let her have it," chimed Georgiana. "Mother can be quite an ogre when she puts her mind to it."

"That is enough from you," said Lady Anne, though her glare lacked any bite. Then she turned back to her guests. "Well, shall we discuss the matter further? Before you respond, I should inform you my daughter is correct—I am not often inclined to give way when I know I am in the right."

Elizabeth shared a glance with Jane, wondering if further protest would gain them anything. Jane seemed uncomfortable with the situation, and Elizabeth liked it no better than her sister. But Lady Anne, Elizabeth was learning, was a force with which to be reckoned. Given what she had heard of Lady Catherine de Bourgh, Elizabeth wondered how obstinate the woman could be like if she was considered the more determined sister. It was difficult to imagine.

In the end, though neither was comfortable, they were forced to give way, and the ladies prepared to depart. It was then Elizabeth learned there was never any chance to refuse, for Lady Anne informed them she had made an appointment with the modiste for a fitting. Elizabeth decided there was no real reason to protest further, despite what she learned, and the look she received from Lady Anne suggested she made the correct choice.

The shops of Bond Street were no strangers to the Bennet sisters, as they had often visited in the company of their Aunt Gardiner. Uncle Gardiner, whose import business supplied many such industries, usually provided the fabrics for the Bennet ladies' dresses, and Mrs. Gardiner's usual modiste had a shop on Bond Street, though she was not one of the more prestigious dressmakers. On this occasion, their destination was a woman of much renown in London.

"Lady Anne," greeted the modiste when they stepped into the shop. "Welcome back. Are these the ladies of whom you spoke?"

"They are," replied Lady Anne. "This is Miss Jane Bennet, and Miss Elizabeth Bennet, who are my guests in London for the season. Jane, Elizabeth, this is Madame Fournier, the premier modiste of London and creator of the most divine gowns I have ever had the good fortune to wear."

"Thank you, my lady," said Madame Fournier. Elizabeth noted the woman did not claim any false modesty—she had confidence in her prowess and yet did not waste words flaunting or denying it.

Of more interest to the madame was the two sisters, for she stepped close and inspected them, and soon Elizabeth began to feel like a prize stallion on a display. As she studied them, Madame Fournier muttered to herself, a little of which was audible.

"Tall and graceful," said she of Jane. "Beautiful coloring. A light blue would be divine."

Then when she came closer to Elizabeth, she said, "Not so tall as her sister, but beauty seems to run in the family. A green to highlight her eyes and contrast with her hair would be just the thing."

When she had finished, Madame Fournier invited them into a private room and ordered a tea service for their comfort. Elizabeth could not help but feel flattered at being compared favorably to Jane, who was, in Elizabeth's estimation, the most beautiful woman she had ever seen. When they were seated, Madame Fournier promising to return in a few moments to see to their measurements, Georgiana turned to Elizabeth.

"It appears you dislike shopping, Elizabeth. I was under the impression that all ladies loved nothing more than to obtain new and prettier clothes."

"Just because that is what *you* like Georgiana, it is no reason to suppose *all* young ladies are the same," admonished Lady Anne, though with affection for her only daughter.

"I shall tell you," said Jane with a sidelong look at Elizabeth, "since she will not. You see, my mother has definite opinions about fashion, and they do not agree with Lizzy's."

"Too much lace!" cried Elizabeth, much to the amusement of her companions. "Sometimes I think my mother would create a dress in nothing but lace if she thought she could get away with it. For myself, I do not like lace very much. The battles Mother and I have fought on the subject were such that in the past few years, I have purchased gowns when in London with my aunt's help."

"And your mother," said Lady Anne, laughing, "endures it, for you are getting your clothes in London, even if they are not in the styles she prefers."

"That does not mean she will not write to my aunt, beseeching her to make my dresses fancier," replied Elizabeth, making a face. "In the end, however, she decided it was best to ignore it, for I believe she has grown as tired of the dispute as I have."

"A little lace is lovely," said Madame Fournier as she entered the room, overhearing a little of their conversation. "In this instance, however, I must side with you, Miss Elizabeth. An excess of lace only detracts from the natural beauty and youthful appearance of health and vitality.

"Now," added the madame, gesturing to a pair of girls who had followed her into the room, "let us take your measurements. Then you may browse through my fashion magazines to choose what styles you prefer, and we may move on to fabrics and other accessories."

"And do not worry, Elizabeth," said Lady Anne, Elizabeth being well aware her ladyship was still regarding her with amusement, "I shall not attempt to direct you."

"Direct, no," said Madame Fournier, "but I shall guide you. There are styles and colors which would render you both divine and have every man in London begging for an introduction. We shall create the proper effect and make you both the talk of the season!"

While Elizabeth thought the woman was exaggerating in her comments about anyone named Bennet being the talk of the season, the sight of Madame Fournier's fashion gazettes caught her attention. With much conversation between the two sisters, each knowing the other's preferences and what suited them, they began to turn the pages. Lady Anne and her daughter added their comments whenever the opportunity presented itself, but their main contribution was to protest against any attempt at economy.

Two hours later, the foursome left the modiste, all satisfied, especially Lady Anne, who appeared more than a little smug. Then they visited several other shops, spending another hour on the street.

It was not to be supposed that a fashionable shopping district as Bond Street was devoid of other shoppers, nor that those other shoppers would be unknown to the Darcy women. Soon after they left Madame Fournier's shop, a lady of about Lady Anne's age accosted them, accompanied by a younger woman, seemingly a daughter, perhaps two or three years Georgiana's elder.

"Lady Anne," said the woman, an affected lilt in her voice which spoke of pride and conceit. "It is curious to see you here, for the Darcys rarely arrive in London in February."

The look on Lady Anne's face when confronted by her acquaintance spoke to amusement, and perhaps a hint of exasperation. "This year we wintered in London after my son spent some time with a friend in Hertfordshire." The lady wrinkled her nose, indicating she knew the identity of Mr. Darcy's friend. "We also have guests staying with us for the season."

The gimlet eyes of the woman found Elizabeth and Jane, and it was soon clear she was not at all impressed by what she saw. For a moment, Elizabeth thought she might request an introduction if nothing more than to know with whom she was dealing. However, she did not, instead turning back to Lady Anne.

"Perhaps we shall meet again, but for now we must depart."

Then with a nod, the lady turned away, pulling the young girl along with her. They had not been gone but a moment when Lady Anne spoke.

"Insolent woman! She has a much higher opinion of herself than she should, and her ambition of marrying her insipid niece to William will never be realized."

"She seemed like a woman of much standing," said Jane, ever the diplomat.

"You have the right of it, Jane," said Lady Anne, "but it is all in her mind, for she is not highly placed at all."

Elizabeth suppressed a smile, as for all that Lady Anne was not a woman given to excessive pride or a superior manner, she was still the daughter of an earl. It was clear the other woman's obvious self-importance had offended her sensibilities.

"That was Lady Eugenie Clark," offered Georgiana, "and the younger lady was her niece, Miss Yates."

"Lady Eugenie is the daughter of a baronet and the wife of a baron, and her elevation has gone to her head." Lady Anne turned to the sisters and smiled. "We need not concern ourselves for the likes of her. There will be others who are more amiable."

And indeed, there were. In time, Lady Anne introduced them to several others, and most proved to be much more welcoming then Lady Eugenie had been. Though Elizabeth could not remember all the names, nor did she think she would pair what names she did remember with the faces, she was generally well pleased with their reception.

"Do not concern yourself if you need a reminder of whom you have met," said Lady Anne when Elizabeth made this observation. "You shall meet with them all again—and many others besides. We would not wish to overwhelm you."

When they returned at length to the house, Elizabeth found herself fatigued and wishing for a rest in her room, and she knew Jane was no better. They stepped through the doors, the servants on hand to take their outerwear, and then moved further into the house, chatting as they went.

"The Bingleys are not due to arrive for several more hours," said Lady Anne. "If you wish to return to your rooms, there is plenty of time to do so."

"Ladies," came the voice of Mr. Darcy, the gentleman executing a perfect bow at the sight of them. "I hope your day was enjoyable. I had not known you were to go out."

"We went shopping and had so much fun!" exclaimed Georgiana. "Though not all was agreeable, for we encountered Lady Eugenie and Miss Yates. I am certain you have been longing to be in company with your future fiancée."

Georgiana giggled at the expression of utter distaste which came over his countenance, but Elizabeth, who was watching him, thought she detected something else in his manner. It was gone in a moment, but the look he shot at his mother suggested curiosity for their destination and activities. The old feeling of disdain for this gentleman welled up within Elizabeth's breast, though she tamped down on it — had she not made the same objections to the day's activities?

"Come, Elizabeth, Jane," said Georgiana, beckoning to them and making her way to the stairs. "We should sort through your purchases, and I should like a rest before we are forced to endure Miss Bingley this evening."

Not at all averse to finding her way to her room, Elizabeth pushed thoughts of Mr. Darcy to the side and followed Jane up the stairs. Whatever the gentleman thought, she was certain Lady Anne would set him straight.

As it turned out, Elizabeth's guess concerning Mr. Darcy's feelings was accurate, though Darcy had no notion the young lady had seen through his expression. Watching Miss Elizabeth as he was, he noted the easy rapport she had developed with his sister, not that it was at all surprising. During his time observing her in Hertfordshire, Darcy had developed a firm opinion that the woman could charm even the worst curmudgeon and pulling a smile from him.

"What is it, William?" the voice of his mother sounded, drawing his attention back to her.

"I beg your pardon?" asked Darcy, his thoughts jumbled by his observation of Miss Elizabeth.

"It is there is something bothering you. Will you not share it?"

Darcy shook his head. "It nothing more than my thought that it may not be for the best to show so much favor to the Miss Bennets."

"Why?" asked Lady Anne, far blunter than Darcy might have expected. "Are they somehow undeserving of our attention?"

With exasperation, Darcy shook his head. "I have nothing against the Miss Bennets, Mother. However, they are unknown to society, and the mere fact you have seen fit to invite them to stay with us will spawn rumors. Taking them to Bond Street and purchasing new dresses for them will no doubt set tongues to wagging."

"Who is to say they are not purchasing their own gowns?" asked Lady Anne. "I have not made an issue of it, and I know the shopkeepers are discreet enough to avoid spreading rumors, lest they risk losing my custom."

"That will not prevent the rumors," said Darcy. "You know society needs little excuse to gossip."

"Then let them. When it is not confirmed, they will move on to other tittle-tattle, and I am convinced the Bennet sisters will do much to focus the attention on themselves rather than any purchases I have made for them."

Darcy did not respond, the frustration of his mother's continued attention to the two ladies making him more than a little cross. When he did not speak, Lady Anne stepped forward and put a hand on his arm.

"Do not concern yourself, William. There was a simple reason for this morning's excursion—the Bennet sister's evening wear, while the rest of their wardrobe is fine, was not up to the standards of society. Miss Bennet and her sister *are* our guests for the season, and I would like them to make a good impression on society, not only to justify our attention but because they are estimable ladies in their own right."

"I suppose they must reflect well on us," said Darcy, though grudgingly.

"That is exactly it. I have every confidence in their manners and deportment, but I would be a poor hostess if I allowed every supercilious matron and jealous miss to disapprove of them because of the way they dress. Now that we have ensured their evening wear will be of a certain quality, I am certain we will not be required to shop in such a fashion again. Besides, it appears Miss Elizabeth does not have much of a taste for it and would protest if I insisted upon it too often."

The amusement in his mother's voice alerted Darcy to her growing affection for the dark-haired beauty. "I might have thought any young woman would enjoy shopping, not least of all when another was paying for her purchases."

"And you would be incorrect in this instance, and I will thank you not to cast shade on Elizabeth's character."

Noting his mother's severe look, Darcy put out a hand in surrender. She was placated, but only after she indulged in a few more moments of glaring.

"If you have not noticed by now," said Lady Anne, "Elizabeth is a woman of a different stripe from most ladies in society, whether high or low. It was only after much persuasion that we convinced her of the necessity, for she made many of the same objections to our outing as you did yourself.

"The Bennet sisters are not artful, William. They are not grasping, they have no thoughts of climbing the ladder of society, and they certainly do not behave as if they feel the world owes them everything they desire. If I am not very much mistaken, we are to host a young lady tonight who is the very epitome of that description."

"I have no choice but to endure her if I wish to keep Bingley's acquaintance."

"I do not suggest you throw her off, William. My only suggestion is that you watch Miss Bingley's behavior and contrast it with that of the Bennet sisters. If you are honest with yourself, I am certain you will come to the correct conclusion."

Lady Anne patted his arm once again. "For now, I should speak with the housekeeper and the cook to ensure all is ready for tonight. Then, I shall not be averse to seeking my own room for a time."

Darcy bowed and his mother moved away. For a time, Darcy stood in the hall, looking in the direction his mother had disappeared, though seeing nothing of his surroundings. A woman of confidence and intelligence, Darcy knew she would do as she pleased, not that he would attempt to direct her.

That evening went about as well as Lady Anne had any right to hope, and from several perspectives. It began when they were preparing for the evening, and Lady Anne, having readied herself early, went to the Bennet sisters' suite, knowing they were preparing for the evening together with Georgiana. The laughter from the younger sister's room alerted her to their activities, and she walked into the room, noting Georgiana's shining eyes and amusement, confident her daughter's new association with the women was a benefit to her daughter, who had always been of a shy disposition.

"Will you be ready soon?" asked Anne upon entering. "Our guests will arrive before long."

"We will be soon, Mama," replied Georgiana. "We are attempting to determine what Elizabeth should wear tonight."

Anne focused her attention on the younger Bennet. "I was not aware that you were of such a vain disposition that it required you an hour or more to choose which dress will suit you most."

The girl blushed, much to Anne's delight. "I am not, but Jane and Georgiana took issue with that I intended to wear."

An excellent opportunity, thought Anne as she moved toward the closet. As she rummaged through the dresses, she found what she was looking for, an ivory gown the same hue as the one Elizabeth had worn to the Netherfield ball, which had drawn such glances of appreciation from her son. It was not so elaborate or so fine as that dress had been, but Anne thought it would do well for an evening entertaining guests and, more importantly, would provoke William's approval.

When she suggested it, Elizabeth directed a look at her, and Anne wondered for a moment if she suspected ulterior motives. Then Georgiana and Jane exclaimed their approval, and the decision was made. It was all worth it when Elizabeth descended the stairs for supper.

"Did you see the way William almost devoured the sight of Elizabeth?" asked Georgiana with a giggle a short time later.

"I knew how it would be," replied Anne, unable to keep the self-satisfaction from her voice. "Do not forget how he watched her when we were at Netherfield."

"While attempting to give the impression he was not watching her," added Georgiana, allowing her mirth free reign.

As William attempted to avoid the young woman's obvious allure, the Bingley party arrived and were shown into the room. And then it was proven that Elizabeth was not the only Bennet sister in a position to dominate a gentleman's attention. The way Mr. Bingley entered the room, his addresses to all so perfunctory as to be nearly rude, spoke without possibility of another interpretation as to his affections.

"Miss Bennet," said he, stopping to kiss her hand almost reverently. "How wonderful it is to see you again. I hope your journey from Hertfordshire was everything comfortable."

"It was excellent, Mr. Bingley," said Jane, a rosy blush suffusing her cheeks. "Now we are in London. I would not wish to be anywhere else."

"Excellent!" exclaimed Mr. Bingley, a beaming smile covering his face. Taking her hand, he guided her to a nearby sofa and refused to be moved from her side the rest of the evening.

William mustered the will to remove his eyes from Elizabeth to watch the renewal of Mr. Bingley and Jane's acquaintance, and Anne watched as he studied them for several moments. Then he caught Anne's eye, and when she shot him an arched brow, he shrugged and turned away. Though the poor boy thought he did not immediately turn back to his contemplation of Elizabeth, Anne knew better. So did Miss Bingley, it appeared.

"What a fine thing it is to be in such company this evening," said she to nobody in particular. "We are all—or most of us are," amended she with a glare at the Bennet sisters, "almost as good as family. In fact, I cannot wait until the time comes when our families will share a closer connection."

Of those near enough to hear her words, Elizabeth looked skyward and shook her head at such blatant scheming, while Anne said nothing. If she was at all correct, she thought William too immersed in his study of Elizabeth to have heard her, which left only Georgiana.

"I apologize, Miss Bingley, but I do not understand your meaning. Perhaps I might persuade you to speak clearly?"

"Why," said Miss Bingley, "I refer to the ties which bind us together, ties which cannot be broken asunder by those persons who rely on subterfuge to impose upon families of consequence. In fact, I have often thought your turn of mind was similar to my brother's. I, for one, would be delighted to one day claim a closer relationship with you, dear Georgiana."

Georgiana's ability to stifle a laugh was admirable, in Anne's estimation. "Perhaps we are similar, Miss Bingley. But then again, you must remember the saying 'opposites attract.' It seems to me that your brother is happy where he is at present."

With a sniff of disdain, Miss Bingley looked to Lady Anne. "Have your guests settled in? No doubt they are awed by the surroundings, which are far finer than anything they have ever before experienced. How generous it is of you to sponsor them."

"They have settled in as if they were residents of this house; I thank you for your solicitous inquiry. And your words about the closer relationship between our families may bear fruit."

Miss Bingley preened until she noted where Anne's gaze rested. No one had to look at Mr. Bingley and Jane to determine the state of their feelings, but William was at that moment sharing a hesitant conversation with Elizabeth. When the full meaning of Anne's words became apparent, Miss Bingley turned a little green, excused herself, and went to sit beside her sister.

"That was almost cruel, Mother," said Georgiana, though the laughter in her voice superseded any reproof."

"You must own, the woman deserved it," replied Anne.

Then she turned back to her guests. Already she was anticipating the evening more than any event she had in some time.

CHAPTER VII

*F*or all Elizabeth had heard of the season in London, the beginnings of their stay with the Darcys were far tamer than Elizabeth had thought to expect. When asked, Lady Anne informed them that many of the families of high standing preferred to be fashionably late and many of the true spectacles were thus delayed.

That was not to say they spent all their time at home and never went out. There were several events for them to attend, including dinners, parties, a music recital or two, and even a poetry reading. Lady Anne confided to Elizabeth a week into their stay that the number of invitations they received far exceeded those they accepted.

"The Darcy family has ever been prominent, though perhaps not a large clan. Throughout the years, my son's ancestors amassed many connections to members of higher society, and while never peers themselves, there are few families who are not eager to curry favor with the Darcys."

"I had no idea your family was so prestigious, Lady Anne," said Elizabeth, a feeling of being overwhelmed settling over her.

Lady Anne smiled. "There is no reason you would have been aware. Our status is well known in society, but my son, as you have likely already apprehended, is not enamored of attention and attempts to avoid it whenever he can. It has, at times, given him the reputation of being above his company, but the reality is he has no patience for those who are eager to rise in society."

It was a brief conversation, but one which gave Elizabeth much on which to think. Though she still, in general, disapproved of Mr. Darcy's behavior while in Hertfordshire, for the first time, Elizabeth began to wonder if it was not understandable. Memories of her mother, eager to meet and capture wealthy gentlemen for her daughters coupled with those of the neighborhood's denizens whispering gossip about the two gentlemen returned, and Elizabeth wondered if Mr. Darcy put up with this kind of behavior whenever he was in society.

About ten days after their arrival in town, Lady Anne introduced the Bennet sisters to Mr. Darcy's closest titled relations—Lady Anne's immediate family. While it might be supposed would anticipate such a portentous introduction with a certain feeling of intimidation, it was just the opposite. Their acquaintance with Lady Anne had taught them the Fitzwilliams, if no one else, were people of little false superiority.

"So, these are the sisters of whom you spoke, Anne," said Lady Susan, when they had been introduced. "They are, indeed, as pretty as you had led me to believe. With your assistance, they will be the talk of the season."

Jane, as was her wont when anyone spoke of her in such flattering terms, blushed to the roots of her hair. Elizabeth was no less embarrassed by the obvious praise, but as she had always possessed more self-confidence than Jane, she weathered it better. Trying to ignore the discomfort which hovered about the back of her mind, she took stock of Lady Susan, noting her tall stature and stately air, though tempered with true good humor and an affectionate manner. Though she was likely ten years Mrs. Bennet's senior, if not more, she was a handsome woman, one who Elizabeth thought had been a beauty of some note in her youth.

"Come, Miss Bennet, Miss Elizabeth—let us sit for a time and become better acquainted, for I am eager to discover what has interested my sister so."

"Perhaps she has taken pity on us," replied Elizabeth, her tone more than a little bold. "The Bennets have been buried in Hertfordshire since before the flood—I know nothing remarkable about us."

Lady Susan laughed, far from being offended by Elizabeth's jest. "It seems to me you are an impertinent one, Miss Elizabeth."

"Only when meeting personages of great standing," said Elizabeth.

"I find that it is brought out by every attempt to intimidate me and serves to shore up my courage."

"Then you may put your impertinence away," said Lady Susan, still shaking her head and laughing. "Intimidating you is the furthest thing from my thoughts; I hope you do not find me at all frightening."

"For myself, no," replied Elizabeth, sneaking a look at Jane, who was watching the banter with interest and, perhaps, a little trepidation. "In your world perhaps it is commonplace, but where I was raised, it is not every day one meets the wife of an earl."

"Oh? Your words intimate you have met the wife of an earl before."

"You are incorrect, your ladyship. Until today, I have only ever made the acquaintance of the *daughter* of an earl."

Again, the ladies laughed at Elizabeth's sally. "Then, now that we have passed this formidable introduction, let us speak easily. And as for deference, Lady Susan will do—I have no desire to weave my way around 'your ladyship' every thirty seconds."

"Very well," said Elizabeth.

Their time with the countess was educational to the Bennet sisters, for in her they found a woman well aware of her position in society, but not full of that position. In many respects, she was much like Lady Anne, though she was a more open sort of character, whereas Lady Anne often tended toward a hint of the reserve so often displayed by Mr. Darcy. She was a skillful interrogator, able to winnow out their dearest secrets—or so it seemed—learning much about them both in the short time they sat together. Elizabeth decided she liked the countess very well, for she made herself easy to esteem by her interest and her manners, which were fine.

As the conversation began to wane, presaging their imminent departure, they were interrupted by the arrival of a young man, perhaps Mr. Darcy's age or a little older. He was not as handsome as the aforementioned gentleman, though not deficient, stood taller, broader of shoulders, and wearing the uniform of an officer. The way he looked at them suggested he had advance notice of their coming, and his interested glances informed Elizabeth he had a keen desire to know them.

"Mother, Aunt," greeted he, bussing their cheeks. Then he turned to Georgiana and said; "Well, Sprite, you are growing taller every time I see you!"

"Oh, Anthony," said Georgiana with a laugh. "I am eighteen now, you know. I do not know why you persist in referring to me with such nicknames."

"It is because, to me, you will ever be that eight-year-old girl who begged me to carry her on my back." The man winked and laughed along with his cousin, who shook her head and mock glared at him. Then he turned his attention to Jane and Elizabeth.

"Might I beg an introduction to your lovely guests?"

"By your words, I might have thought you surprised to see them here," said Lady Susan. "However, I remember informing you of our visitors today."

"Mother!" exclaimed the man, Anthony. "Do not inform them of my earlier knowledge! How shall I now convince one of them that I am overwhelmed by their beauty and hopelessly in love?"

Elizabeth laughed and cried: "I do not know if I should be flattered or fearful for my virtue."

"Concerned, most assuredly," said Georgiana *sotto voce*.

They all laughed again, though this time it was the man showing his cousin a mock glare. Lady Susan shook her head and addressed Elizabeth and Jane.

"Though I am not at all certain I should, I suppose there is nothing to be done. Anthony, these are Anne's guests, Miss Jane Bennet and Miss Elizabeth Bennet. Jane, Elizabeth, this scalawag is my son, Colonel Anthony Fitzwilliam. Usually, he is better behaved, but there are times like this when I wonder if he is not fit to sleep in the stables. Or perhaps the kennels."

Colonel Fitzwilliam laughed. "If you do not recall, Mother, Darcy and I attempted that when we were children."

"Perhaps we should have made it a permanent arrangement," said Lady Anne. "I do not think you could have turned out less well behaved."

"Enough, Aunt Anne! You are ruining my image to these lovely ladies!"

"I rather think you have already done that yourself," said Elizabeth.

"Corrupted already!" cried Colonel Fitzwilliam with a certain dramatic flair. "Another set of young ladies forewarned and forearmed against me. Whatever shall I do?"

Colonel Fitzwilliam's wink shattered any attempt to lament, firming Elizabeth's opinion of the gentleman as an incorrigible flirt. When he sat down to speak with them without the histrionics, Elizabeth learned he was an interesting man, albeit with a streak of teasing which rivaled her own. Entertaining, too, for everything he said was said with animation and verve, such that Elizabeth wondered if he had missed his calling in life.

"I must own to rarely being entertained so well," said Elizabeth when they rose to depart. "It may be best if you were to leave the regulars and join a theater troupe, sir, for you seem to have a gift!"

"But then who would protect you all from Bonny?" was Colonel Fitzwilliam's mischievous response. "No, Miss Elizabeth, I know my duty. Though I may have become world-famous in the theater, I must resign myself to the life of a fighting man. I must keep my family safe, after all."

"Then we shall depend on your diligence when Napoleon invades England, sir."

"If Napoleon invades England," replied Colonel Fitzwilliam, "I shall stand as your last line of defense, my lady."

"Oh, stop it, Anthony," said Lady Susan, glaring at her son with exasperation. "Can you never speak seriously about anything?"

"Not if I can help it."

Lady Susan shook her head and turned to Elizabeth and Jane. "Notwithstanding my son's manners, I was pleased to meet you, my dears. I do not know if Anne has informed you, but I hold a ball every year during the season. Anne and Georgiana are to attend, and I should like to extend the invitation to you as well."

"Thank you, Lady Susan," replied Jane for the sisters. "Elizabeth and I would be delighted to attend."

"Darcy!" boomed the sound of his cousin's voice. "Had I known that such beauties inhabited Hertfordshire, I would have resigned my commission and joined you at Bingley's estate!"

Darcy, ensconced in the comfort of his well-appointed study, looked up at his cousin in surprise, startled from recollections of one of the very women of which Fitzwilliam was speaking. Something must have shown in his countenance, for Fitzwilliam grinned and flopped into a chair on the other side of Darcy's desk.

"I am hard-pressed to remember meeting such a beauty as Miss Bennet, and Miss Elizabeth is quite the most interesting lady I have had the good fortune to encounter. It seems to me your mother has shown great discernment in inviting them to stay with you, for I cannot imagine they will not be a sensation in the coming season."

"You overestimate their charms, Fitzwilliam," said Darcy, still floundering after the unexpected interruption.

"Do I?" demanded his cousin. "If so, I should like to know in what manner. Only fifteen minutes in their company informed me they are well worth knowing. How can you say otherwise, when, it is said, you have been in their company for more than two months?"

"Oh, yes, very well worth knowing," said Darcy. "My mother has befriended two waifs with an improper family, little connection or wealth, and a mercenary mother who attempts to marry them off to any man with more than a tuppence in his pocket!"

"I have never heard you speak so, Darcy," said Fitzwilliam, his tone reproving. "Not even of Miss Bingley, whom you despise."

"I do not despise Miss Bingley," said Darcy with more shortness than he intended. "It is only that I do not wish to marry her."

"Then you must feel something for one of these ladies, for I suspect little more could induce you to forget yourself in such a manner as attempting to deny your attraction."

"You are dreaming," said Darcy. "As I said, I tolerate their presence, for my mother and sister have taken a fancy to them. Otherwise, I am in no danger."

The way Fitzwilliam regarded him, Darcy thought he did not believe Darcy's assertions. The wonder of wonders, Fitzwilliam did not press the matter, instead returning to his rebuke, which was no more palatable for Darcy's pique.

"Regardless, these ladies do not deserve your contempt, Darcy. As you have already stated, they are your mother's guests, and if for no other reason than that, you must curb your tongue lest you offend them."

"I have more control than that."

"Usually, I would agree with you. However, I have never seen you react like this to young ladies, regardless of their situation. I shall leave you to your disdain for them but advise you to take care to avoid saying something which cannot be unsaid."

Though Fitzwilliam claimed he would leave Darcy alone, he stayed in Darcy's study for some time, drinking his brandy and speaking of the Bennet sisters. Accustomed as he was to Fitzwilliam's ways and his composure restored, Darcy allowed him to wax eloquent, even agreeing with him on certain of his observations.

It was unfortunate, but Darcy's mood was not to improve to any great degree, considering the upcoming visit to the Bennet sisters' relations the very next day. As they sat in the carriage, Darcy beside his mother while the three younger ladies occupied the opposite seat, the excitement shown by the two sisters—shown more by the younger—was palpable. The carriage rattled from the Mayfair district through the streets of London, and soon they were making their way through narrower boulevards, though more heavily traveled. When they stopped, it was before a modest, yet comfortable and well-maintained home close to some business districts in the distance.

The Bennet sisters led the way up the stairs and into the house, where the housekeeper and a maid met the and then shown into a drawing-room where the relations awaited. There, waiting for them, were a man and a woman, the man showing a resemblance to Mrs. Bennet, perhaps ten years Darcy's senior, while the woman was five years younger, pretty, and slender of build. When they rose to greet the visitors, the Bennet sisters crowding close with fond greetings and embraces, the couple showed themselves to be both elegant of dress and possessed of fine manners.

"My lady," greeted Mrs. Gardiner when Miss Elizabeth introduced her again to Darcy's mother, "how lovely it is to see you again after all these years. I was never so surprised as when I heard you had invited my dear nieces to stay with you."

"And I am eager to renew our acquaintance, Mrs. Gardiner," said his mother with an unmistakable warmth. "I was also surprised to hear of the connection. But, please, let us dispense with the formalities."

"Of course," said Mrs. Gardiner. Then she turned to Darcy and Georgiana and greeted them, inviting them to sit. "Welcome to my home, Mr. Darcy, Miss Darcy."

"Again?" asked Darcy, puzzled. "I was not aware we were previously acquainted."

"It is not correct to suggest we were acquainted in any sense," said Mrs. Gardiner. "But I do remember seeing you in Lambton, for, as I recall, you came much as a young boy. As for your sister," Mrs. Gardiner turned to an interested Georgiana, "I remember her often in the company of your mother, and even held her once when she was a babe."

"Oh, I did not know that," said Georgiana.

"You were far too young," said Mrs. Gardiner. "But I remember it very well, for my youth in Lambton was among the happiest times of my life. I remember Derbyshire with great fondness and hope to return there someday."

Mrs. Gardiner turned and directed a smile at her husband, who was watching them all with interest and clear affection for his wife. "If my husband would hurry and build his business, we may even have the funds to purchase an estate someday, for living in the neighborhood would be one of my fondest dreams."

"All in good time, Madeline," said Mr. Gardiner with a laugh of good cheer. "She has long informed me of her desire to live again in

Derbyshire, but the matter is beyond my means at present. Perhaps in a few more years, it might be possible."

"I shall hold you to it, Edward."

The ladies all congregated together, their happy conversation and feminine voices rising over the room. It was apparent they were already getting on famously, a circumstance unsurprising to Darcy, given his mother's glowing comments about Mrs. Gardiner. As for the Bennet sisters, the easy and affectionate manner with which they interacted with their aunt suggested familiarity and esteem, and Darcy wondered if these people were the reason they were so different from the rest of their family.

"Well, Mr. Darcy," said Mr. Gardiner, pulling Darcy's attention back to his host. "It seems we are adrift in a sea of women and must rely on each other for sensible conversation."

Darcy arched an eyebrow at the man's humorous tone. "You do not consider Miss Elizabeth's conversation to be sensible?"

Mr. Gardiner laughed and shook his head. "No, Mr. Darcy, you have caught me out—as I am certain you are already aware, Lizzy is among the most sensible young ladies I have ever met, as is my dear Mrs. Gardiner. And yet, Lizzy's interests do not align with my own, though she has some startling observations to make about business, the war on the continent, and other matters which are usually a man's purview."

"Yes, I have noticed this about her." Darcy paused, regarding Mr. Gardiner with no little curiosity, and was induced to say: "If you will excuse me, sir, I am surprised, for you are nothing like your sister."

"'Sisters,' Mr. Darcy," said Mr. Gardiner, his amusement never dimming. "Trust me, you are not the first man to make that observation. For all Margaret is a good woman and Gertrude—Mrs. Phillips, my other sister—is loving, the Good Lord did not bless them with the highest sense."

"You are as unlike as siblings can be," said Darcy, unsure what to say and not wishing to cause offense.

"That we are. But they are good women, my sisters, though I will own they exasperate me at times."

From that awkward beginning, their conversation wove among several topics, and Darcy found himself enjoying Mr. Gardiner's company. Though not a gentleman, on that day when the man purchased his own estate, Darcy was certain he could fit in, his manners being more proper than some men he knew who sprang from stock ten generations deep in gentlemen.

When they left, after his mother extended an invitation to the Gardiners to join them at the theater in two days' time, Darcy was beset with the realization that his mother had been correct. Given his knowledge of Mrs. Bennet, he had made an assumption concerning their near relations and, in particular, Mrs. Bennet's brother. But much like Lady Catherine was nothing like her siblings, Mr. Gardiner was as different from Mrs. Bennet as night was to day. It was a lesson he had best remember.

"How fortunate it is for the Bennets and their relations that they have come to your mother's attention. Why, she has not only invited the eldest Bennet sisters to stay with you, but now she has taken a liking to their *tradesman* aunt and uncle and even invited them to society events. What singular behavior!"

Though Miss Bingley's words were not loud, the woman made no effort to modulate her tone either, making them clearly audible to Elizabeth who stood with Lady Anne and Georgiana at some short distance. A glance at Mr. Darcy showed the man as inscrutable as ever, but about his mouth was the tiniest hint of tightness, indicating he was not pleased with Miss Bingley for speaking so. Whether he might have agreed with her was not the issue, not that Elizabeth could determine from his demeanor if that was so — in so pubic a forum as this, he would not be pleased with the airing of his family's private business.

Covent Gardens' lobby was a busy place that evening for a showing of Elizabeth's favorite play, *A Midsummer Night's Dream*, and the presence of her dear aunt and uncle rendered the evening that much more agreeable. Given Miss Bingley's continued interest in Mr. Darcy, the Bingley party's absence was unthinkable, even if Mr. Bingley was not engaged in his usual habit of speaking with Jane to the exclusion of all others. The general hubbub meant that Miss Bingley's ill-bred attack *should* remain private. It was unfortunate for her someone other than Elizabeth had overheard her words, and *she* was not shy about speaking her opinion.

"Miss Bingley," said Lady Anne, turning and looking at the woman. "If I may have a moment of your time?"

It was a preening Miss Bingley who answered Lady Anne's summons, though how she could not see Mr. Darcy's mother was displeased with her was beyond Elizabeth's comprehension. As Lady Anne turned and addressed Miss Bingley where she stood, and though she had no intention of doing so, Elizabeth could hear the exchange as if they were speaking to her.

"I wish to inform you, Miss Bingley, that your supposition is completely incorrect. For, you see, Madeline Gardiner was known to me when she was a young girl—her father was the rector of Lambton, and I have many happy memories of her when she was a young girl."

"The daughter of a parson," said Miss Bingley, a nasty undertone in her voice. "Then she has stepped down in the world."

"She has married a good man, Miss Bingley, a man my nephew already esteems, one who is becoming known to my brother."

Elizabeth's gaze darted to where Uncle Gardiner stood speaking with the Earl of Matlock, and the way they spoke, animated hand gestures emphasizing some point, heartened Elizabeth, informing her that her beloved relations were people whom even the very highest of society could accept. To Elizabeth's sure knowledge, the earl had already expressed an interest in Mr. Gardiner's business, and both he and Mr. Darcy had promised to inform Mr. Gardiner if they heard of any estates for sale in Derbyshire.

"What you fail to understand," continued Lady Anne, "is that Mrs. Gardiner is the granddaughter of a gentleman—her uncle is still the proprietor of a large estate not far distant from Pemberley. As for Mr. Gardiner, his connections to the gentry are more distant but still exist nonetheless.

"I wonder," said Lady Anne, her voice harder, though Elizabeth dared not look in her direction, "do the Bingleys possess similar ancestry to the Gardiners, or even the Bennets, who have lived on their land for generations?"

"W-Well—" stammered Miss Bingley, only for Lady Anne to interrupt her again.

"Let us dispense with these ill-conceived attacks, Miss Bingley. In my opinion, a person's character is far more important than one's ancestry or connections, or even how much wealth one may boast. The Gardiners are excellent people—if you allowed yourself to know them, I am certain you would agree."

A figure moved in the corner of Elizabeth's eye, drawing her attention away from the ongoing reproach, and Elizabeth looked over to see Mr. Darcy regarding her. Though Elizabeth could not understand his thoughts, he gestured toward the doors and spoke.

"I believe you have been anticipating this evening, Miss Elizabeth. It seems to me you have stated your preference for Shakespeare's works—does *A Midsummer Night's Dream* meet with your approval?"

"It does, Mr. Darcy," said Elizabeth.

At that moment she realized that his intent was to distract her from what was happening between his mother and Miss Bingley, and Elizabeth was grateful, for though listening to Lady Anne defend her family was satisfying, eavesdropping was never to be praised.

"In fact," continued she, "it is among my favorites."

"Have you ever seen it performed before?"

"Once when I was much younger. During a visit to London, my uncle indulged me in an evening, knowing I favored it."

"Ah, then perhaps we should compare notes concerning this evening's performance and your previous viewing. I have also seen the play a time or two; adding my own observations to yours would be agreeable."

Feeling strangely flattered, Elizabeth accepted his proffered arm, as he gestured toward the entrance to the gallery. The rest of the party followed and split into two groups, Jane sitting with the Bingleys and Hursts in Mr. Darcy's box, while Elizabeth sat with Mr. Darcy, Lady Anne, Georgiana, the Fitzwilliams and the Gardiners in the Fitzwilliam box. It did not escape her attention that Miss Bingley shot her a look of pure poison, but as she was focused on Mr. Darcy, she ignored the other woman. For the first time, Elizabeth enjoyed the man's company.

CHAPTER VIII

$\mathcal{A}$s the events of the season continued, Elizabeth found it becoming more entertaining, the more she became accustomed to the activities, which differed greatly from what she experienced in Hertfordshire. Long accounted a social woman, Elizabeth enjoyed their forays into society, but it was the company of Lady Anne and Georgiana that Elizabeth appreciated most. Even Mr. Darcy showed himself to be more at ease and more affable. While Elizabeth could not yet call him agreeable, it was a marked improvement over his behavior in Hertfordshire.

Jane, of course, was content with the company of their hosts, but more so with that of Mr. Bingley, who, if he did not call daily, was in evidence almost every day, given their schedules were near identical. That Miss Bingley did not appreciate his ardent pursuit of Jane was without question, but as Mr. Bingley did not seem to be listening to her, Elizabeth put the matter from her mind.

One consequence of Elizabeth's stay in London was the inclusion in Georgiana's pianoforte lessons. "I should like it if you would attend my lessons with me," the girl had said soon after their arrival, indifference in her manner, though Elizabeth knew her request was anything but indifferent.

"If you believe the master will not mind, I would appreciate the opportunity to attend," was Elizabeth's reply.

Never having had access to a master, it pleased Elizabeth to discover that instruction from one who knew the correct techniques improved her playing. Georgiana showed exceptional skill, much more so than Elizabeth herself, but the improvement was welcome nonetheless. Should Mary be present, Elizabeth knew she would be eager to receive such an opportunity.

After they had been there for some weeks, an event occurred which had been long expected, by the Bennet sisters with interest, and the Darcys with a sense approaching exasperation or trepidation. With much fanfare, Lady Catherine de Bourgh and her daughter, Miss Anne de Bourgh, arrived in London for the season. The de Bourgh's owned a townhouse, from what Elizabeth understood, but as it was the practice for the de Bourgh ladies to stay with the earl and countess, that townhouse had been let out for some years. Within a day of their arrival, Lady Catherine and her daughter visited Darcy house.

A loud voice announced the visitors in advance of their arrival, and given what she had heard of the lady, Elizabeth deduced the identity of the visitor before the housekeeper led into the room. When she was, Elizabeth was treated to the sight of a woman dressed in a most expensive and ostentatious fashion, gliding in as if she was floating on a cloud. She was large, though slender, her features strong and not what Elizabeth might have considered beautiful, though she thought Lady Catherine would have been termed "handsome" in her youth.

By contrast, Miss de Bourgh, who followed her mother into the room, was a diminutive woman, with much more delicate features, which did not resemble her mother at all. She looked around with interest, her eyes falling on the Bennet sisters, curiosity written on her brow. There was nothing remarkable about her, though Elizabeth thought she was quite prettier than her mother was.

"Anne!" boomed the woman in greeting as soon as she had cleared the door. "How glad we are to see you. Though I cannot imagine why you would come to London so early in the season, it pleases me to be in your company at last. I trust you have been well."

"Very well, indeed, Catherine," replied Lady Anne. "And how are you, Anne?"

"I am well," was the younger woman's simple reply.

"Anne is always well," said Lady Catherine with a dismissive gesture. "The de Bourgh constitution is as strong as an ox, so we are never ill."

"I am happy to hear it. Now, if you please, I shall introduce my guests to you."

The lady's gimlet eyes found Elizabeth and Jane, leading Elizabeth to believe the woman had not even taken note of them. When Lady Anne performed the introductions and the curtseys had been offered — Lady Catherine only deigned to nod her head in response — the lady peered at them and addressed her sister.

"You have surprised me, Anne. I was not aware your guests were still present."

"I invited them to join us for the season, Catherine," was Lady Anne's reply. "As you are well aware, there are still several months before it ends."

"Yes, yes, I am. I merely express surprise they are *still* here. Should they not have returned to their home?"

"Again, Catherine," responded Lady Anne, a hint of laughter underlying her voice, "I invited them for the season. As there are several months left in the season, they remain with us."

Lady Catherine let out a loud huff and then focused her attention on the sisters. "Well, then, I suppose it must be so." The lady paused and began to speak as if the Bennet sisters were not even present. "Your guests seem to be genteel, pretty sort of girls. I have heard much of them from Mr. Collins, and it seems the praise, which was effusive, was not so unwarranted as I might have expected."

Given such a speech, Elizabeth was uncertain whether she should feel offense or laugh, but given her propensity toward laughter, she allowed her amusement free reign. In this she was assisted by the expressive look she received from Lady Anne and the giggle which Georgiana hid behind her hand. To know the lady's nearest relations were as amused by her manners was enough to allow Elizabeth to feel all the absurdity of the situation.

While the woman was many things, and Elizabeth could think of quite a few adjectives, as well as some invectives, to describe her, what Lady Catherine was not was foolish. This became clear over the next several moments in which she questioned the sisters with minute exactness, drawing from them the smallest details.

"Your sisters are *all* out?" demanded the woman with a raised eyebrow when Elizabeth owned the truth of it. "Are you not aware the convention is to wait to bring younger sisters into society until the elder are married?"

"We know of it, your ladyship," said Elizabeth, by now not taken aback by the lady's forceful ways. "With five sisters to bring into society, it cannot promote harmony for the younger sisters if they must wait because their elder siblings have either the lack of suitors or inclination to marry early."

"And you must own this is often done in country society," added Lady Anne. "Meryton is not London."

Lady Catherine grunted her agreement. "Perhaps it is so. But you must inform your mother most strenuously that she should not introduce her younger daughters in London until you and your sister have married."

As Elizabeth thought it unlikely her younger sisters would *ever* see the inside of a London sitting-room, she did not hesitate to give the lady her whole-hearted agreement. This was not all, however, for Lady Catherine was eager to dissect every detail of their lives, from the status of their relations to the extent of their education, to her mother's practices in managing the house. By the time the inquisition was over, Elizabeth wondered if those unfortunate souls in Spain had felt the same as she did now.

"Well, it appears you have not allowed unworthy persons to impose upon your better nature, Anne," said Lady Catherine, nodding with approval. "Given my parson's testimony, I had not thought it to be so, but one can never be too careful."

Then, as if the Bennet sisters were not even present, she turned her attention to Mr. Darcy, who had sat heretofore silent. "Darcy, I see you are looking as well as ever. I do not believe you have greeted your cousin."

"Anne and I exchanged our greetings while you were speaking with the Bennet sisters."

The way Mr. Darcy's eyes twinkled and from the slight pause in his words, Elizabeth was certain he had been tempted to insert "interrogating" in place of the words "speaking with." Lady Anne seemed to sense this too, for she bore a wide grin, as did Georgiana. Lady Catherine, however, noticed nothing, instead nodding with satisfaction.

"Does Anne not look well?" Before Mr. Darcy could reply, Lady Catherine continued: "Indeed, she does, for she exudes health and vitality, as I am sure you must see."

"I do," replied a noncommittal Mr. Darcy.

It seemed his lack of enthusiasm displeased Lady Catherine, though she hid it well—for a woman of her forthright nature, at least.

"Of course, she does. Perhaps this shall finally be the year, for she has anticipated our coming with unendurable excitement. And why should she not? It would be a great alliance, one which would be spoken of from one end of England to the other!"

"Please, Catherine," said Lady Anne. "Let us speak of something else, for it is not proper to speak of matters which are uncertain."

"There is little reason it should be uncertain," snapped Lady Catherine. "What can stand in the way of such a splendid outcome?"

"And yet it is undecided," replied Lady Anne. "Come, let us speak of matters in which all may take part."

With a huff, Lady Catherine turned the subject, though a return was never far distant. Though Elizabeth had heard not a whisper of such aspirations, it was clear Lady Catherine wished for Mr. Darcy as a son, and she continued to make comments designed to bring Mr. Darcy's attention back to her daughter whenever she could.

What was less certain were the wishes of the rest of her family. Miss de Bourgh was inscrutable, bearing her mother's officious attempts to pair her with Mr. Darcy with little comment. Lady Anne was, at times, openly exasperated, and her daughter, resigned, but Mr. Darcy was perhaps the greatest enigma. Though he spoke with his cousin more than once, Elizabeth could detect no regard for her which was out of the common way, though she supposed she may not understand him well enough to detect his esteem if it was present. The times when he grimaced in his own vexation suggested he did not wish to marry his cousin, but a man as independent as Mr. Darcy may be annoyed by his aunt's officiousness, regardless of his feelings.

At length, Lady Catherine seemed satisfied with how the visit had proceeded and rose to announce their need to depart. "We have several other friends we wish to visit today, so we shall depart now. I hope to see you all soon?"

Though Lady Catherine phrased it as a question, Elizabeth knew the lady had not meant it as such. Lady Anne, however, was not daunted in the slightest.

"Of course, we shall meet again soon. We shall attend events together as we usually do, and as Susan adores the Bennet sisters as much as I do, I anticipate being in a position to introduce them to even more of our acquaintances."

Lady Catherine's eyes found Elizabeth and Jane, apparently deep in thought, her manner searching as if she thought they may be a threat. "Yes, I suppose that must be true. Then we shall meet soon. For now, we must depart. Come, Anne."

With these final words, Lady Catherine and rose and ushered her daughter from the room, though Elizabeth noted her eyes were on Mr.

Darcy the entire time. As it happened, Mr. Bingley arrived as they were leaving, and while the lady clearly knew who he was, she responded to his greeting with a sniff before hurrying Miss de Bourgh away. Mr. Darcy greeted his friend and announced his intention to depart to see to some business, and Elizabeth and Georgiana took themselves to the music room, knowing Jane would not even notice them for some time after. Lady Anne called a maid into the room to act as a chaperone and then went to see to some tasks of her own.

"Well, what do you think of receiving your first taste of my aunt?" asked Georgiana after they had sat at the pianoforte for some moments playing together.

"I commend your mother's fortitude," said Elizabeth with a laugh. "Lady Catherine is far beyond what I expected, even after hearing your testimony, added to that of my cousin."

Georgiana made a face. "I assume you understood her wishes regarding my brother?"

"That, my dear Georgiana, was difficult to miss."

The two girls laughed together. "I suppose it was. Lady Catherine has wanted it for years and has never been subtle in informing us of her desires."

"And your cousin?" asked Elizabeth, curious about the young woman to whom she had been introduced but had exchanged no words.

"I am uncertain, as Anne has never vouchsafed her opinion to me. In the end, I believe she would accept William's proposal should he choose to make it, as to refuse would be to make her life immeasurably difficult."

"Yes, I suppose it would at that," murmured Elizabeth.

"Lady Catherine can do nothing to coerce William, for there is no contract for their marriage, though I understand she asked Father to sign one. But Papa declined, so there is nothing she can do legally."

"My husband did not sign a contract because I asked him not to."

The girls looked up to see Lady Anne framed in the doorway, watching them. The sense of amused exasperation with which she had greeted her sister's visit was entirely gone, and in its place was a sort of implacable intensity, such as Elizabeth had not seen from the genial woman.

"You asked Papa not to sign a contract?" asked Georgiana.

"I did," said Lady Anne. "However, I would caution you both to avoid repeating this where Catherine might overhear, for she does not know. In the interest of keeping the peace with my sister, I would prefer it remains that way."

There was no thought of saying anything to Lady Catherine, even if it had concerned her in any fashion. But Elizabeth could own to some curiosity as to why Lady Anne had declined, seeing the benefits of such a union, which were easy to divine. Lady Anne seemed to see Elizabeth's interest, for she explained her reasoning.

"Yes, Elizabeth, the union of my son with my sister's daughter *would* be a splendid match, in certain respects. It would not gain us any useful connections, as we are already closely connected, but I consider that the least matter of concern. The advantages of wealth and prestige *are* extensive, as the acquisition of Rosings would make my son one of the wealthiest men in England."

With his ten thousand a year, Elizabeth thought Mr. Darcy was already one of their number, not that she would say that. Lady Anne continued speaking, however, pushing Elizabeth's thoughts to the side.

"Of much more importance to me than wealth and prestige is my son's happiness. You see, I am convinced William requires something more in a marriage than dynastic advantages. In short, he requires a companion with whom he can forge a connection, one with whom he can share a deep and abiding affection."

"And he cannot find these with Miss de Bourgh?" asked Elizabeth, curious despite her urge to remain silent.

Lady Anne smiled. "My namesake is a good girl, Elizabeth, of whom I am very fond. But her interests do not coincide with William's to any degree, and she is a quiet girl, much like my son. A livelier, more outgoing sort of girl is what he requires."

"Do you have such a woman in mind?"

"There are a few on whom I have my eye," said Lady Anne. "The problem is, William has been wavering of late. I suspect he has even considered giving in to Catherine's demands."

"That would be unfortunate," said Georgiana. "I too like Anne very well, but I do not think she would be any happier in marriage with William than he would be with her."

Another piece of the puzzle slipped into place, though Elizabeth thought she was still missing several. Pushing such thoughts away, Elizabeth focused on her hosts.

"But why would he do so if he has no interest in her?"

"You must understand the world we inhabit, Elizabeth," said Lady Anne. "Though I have striven to raise my son to value other virtues than fortune and connections, many of our set marry for those reasons and no other. I do not believe William cares for greater wealth, and the adulation of the masses means nothing to him. However, he has not found a woman who interests him yet—if there is no woman to tempt him into marriage, why should he not accept Anne if Rosings is to be her dowry? If he did so, he would have a valuable estate to pass to his second son."

"Yes, I can see the lure," said Elizabeth.

"*You* would be the perfect woman for William."

Elizabeth turned her incredulous gaze on Georgiana, wondering if she had heard the girl correctly. Though Georgiana had turned a little rosy in embarrassment, she did not shy away from Elizabeth's gaze, meeting her without flinching.

"Though my daughter is correct," said Lady Anne, drawing Elizabeth's attention back to her, "there does not seem to be any interest in such a union, from either party."

"It is not my intention to pain you," said Elizabeth, choosing her words with care, "but I agree without reservation."

"Why?" asked Georgiana, her question more than a little improperly blunt. "My brother is the best of men—I should think *any* young lady would be privileged to receive his assurances."

"And I do not dispute your account," said Elizabeth, trying to remain diplomatic. "I do not deny that your brother is a good man, but I have seen another side of him during his sojourn in Hertfordshire, and it was not at all to his advantage."

"Do you speak of something in particular?" asked Lady Anne. When Elizabeth hesitated, thinking to demur, Lady Anne added: "If you do not wish, I will not require you to speak. It has often been a concern to me how William is perceived by others, for it is sometimes difficult for him to show himself in the best light."

"If he wishes to do so," said Elizabeth, a hint of her old annoyance with Mr. Darcy welling up within her breast, "he should avoid insulting young ladies in assembly rooms."

Having said this much, there was no way for Elizabeth to avoid revealing the entirety of the matter, and she did so, though not without reluctance. When she had shared all, mother and daughter exchanged a look and an almost identical rolling of their eyes. Despite the seriousness of the conversation, Elizabeth could not help but laugh.

"Though it pains me to say it, the picture you paint of my son does not surprise me. As I have said, William often struggles to show himself to advantage, and he is ill at ease with those he does not know. I have no knowledge of him openly insulting any other woman within her hearing, but I have often informed him he *would* someday if he did not guard his tongue."

"But he is not like that, Elizabeth," said Georgiana, the earnest nature of her reply endearing her to Elizabeth. "William is a very good man, though I will own my bias. There is no firmer friend than he, and once he gives his love to a woman, he would do it with his whole heart."

"Your defense of your brother is admirable," said Elizabeth. "However, I hope you do not expect to see me installed as your sister, for I do not see how it could ever happen."

"Of course, we did not bring you here to throw you in William's way," said Lady Anne. "I echo my daughter's words concerning your suitability for William, but I understand you might resent him at present."

"Indeed, I do not," said Elizabeth, surprising herself by meaning every word. "Since I have come to London, it is clear your son is much more than I ever gave him credit in Hertfordshire. Still, I cannot imagine him considering me a true prospective bride." Elizabeth gave them a wry smile. "And I would require him to atone for his behavior toward myself and my family. As I believe he has little liking for either, it is a hopeless business."

"My son might surprise you, Elizabeth," said Lady Anne. "But neither Georgiana nor I will attempt to influence you. We wish to have you here because we value your friendship—I hope you do not see our words as an attempt to persuade you."

"Not at all," replied Elizabeth with all the warmth she could muster. "Jane and I have enjoyed staying with you. We cannot be more grateful to you for your friendship. Though I know we must return to Hertfordshire at the end of the season, I believe we shall treasure this time together." Elizabeth paused and laughed. "Then again, since Jane seems well on the way to eliciting a proposal from Mr. Bingley, perhaps we shall not lose our friendship when we are required to depart."

"We will regardless," said Lady Anne. "Now that I have your friendship, I do not wish to give it up."

Elizabeth sensed the genuine regard in Lady Anne's words, and she felt as happy as she had ever been. Retaining this friendship was as important to her as it was to her hosts, and she meant to do it by whatever means she possessed.

"William, I would speak with you."

Her son looked up from some paper on his desk, and he smiled, putting it down and gesturing toward the dual chairs which sat before the fireplace. Anne, feeling annoyed with her son for his unthinking words which may have sabotaged what she thought would be an excellent match before it had a chance to succeed, sat next to him, but retained her upright posture. Her son would not be smiling for long.

"I should like to know, Fitzwilliam Darcy, what you were thinking when you insulted a young lady of whom I think highly." Her son frowned, and when he did not respond at once, Lady Anne added: "Do the words 'not handsome enough to tempt me' mean anything to you?"

William's frown grew deeper. "I seem to remember them, but I cannot place where I have heard them."

"*You* spoke them, Fitzwilliam," said Lady Anne, even more displeased than she had been only moments before. "You spoke them to a young lady you did not even know, a young woman as good as any I have ever met. And I think you must be blind, as she is as pretty a young lady as I have ever met."

All at once her son's eyes widened, and he gaped at her with confusion. "Miss Elizabeth overheard me speaking with Bingley?"

"I see your recollection has returned. Yes, she heard every word."

A haughtiness swept over her son's features, and he replied: "Perhaps it would be better if she had not eavesdropped, for then she could not have taken offense. My only purpose was to warn Bingley to stop importuning me to dance when I had no desire to do so."

"By Elizabeth's account," said Lady Anne, feeling very vexed with her son, "you spoke in a tone unmodulated, and she was sitting on a chair long before you came near. Should she have covered her ears with her hands to avoid overhearing you? Do you deny it?"

When her son did not, she knew he was aware there was no excuse. She nodded her head, pleased he had seen at least that much. "I would remind you, Fitzwilliam—this is not how your father and I raised you. I know you are not the proud and disagreeable man that some say you are, but sometimes you give the impression of it. Though your behavior in London has improved her opinion of you, there is still much work for you to do to rehabilitate it."

"And what if I do not concern myself with her opinion?" asked William in his continued defiance. "Though you have elevated her with your invitation, it is not as if she is of any consequence."

"*That* is most certainly *not* how your father and I raised you," snapped Lady Anne. She glared at her son, daring him to disagree, but he looked away. "A young lady is not worth less than you or I or Georgiana because she was not born with our privileges. You do not look down on Miss Bingley because of her origins—it is her behavior which draws your condemnation. Why is Elizabeth any different?"

It appeared her son was still without the ability to answer, confirming at least a part of Anne's suspicions. But now was not the time to press her point. The confidence she felt that Elizabeth would make an excellent daughter was as high as it had ever been, but she had given her word not to push, and Anne meant to keep that promise. But that did not mean she would not plant the seed in her son's mind.

"I think if you look within yourself, you will see that Elizabeth—and her sister—are not deserving of your disdain. In fact, Elizabeth is a wonderful girl, one who has fit in with our family and friends as if she has been among us all her life. And Jane is her equal, though she is not as lively as her sister."

"What of their family?" William's words carried a hint of petulance, but Lady Anne was not about to allow him to sulk.

"Their characters are undesirable, to be sure. But they may be amended. Regardless, our conversation was not about *them*, but about those Bennet sisters who are present.

"I believe, my son, you would see that Elizabeth is an estimable woman, one who is well worth knowing if you only allowed yourself to see past your impression of her family and the neighborhood in which she was reared. Put all notions of wealth, connection, and ancestry aside, and consider the woman herself. Do not judge her based on these things, for they are not the sum of her worth.

"You should also know," said Lady Anne, rising to her feet, "that Elizabeth does not have much respect for you, given your behavior in Hertfordshire. Your actions since her arrival in London have helped, but to earn her good opinion, there is still much to be done."

With those final words, Lady Anne departed, leaving her son to his thoughts. Maybe he would not allow himself to see Elizabeth's worth. Anne had done as much as she could—it was up to him to act on the facts she had presented to him.

CHAPTER IX

$\mathcal{E}$ verything was more difficult with Lady Catherine in residence, but Darcy had already known it would be. The lady had definite ideas about attending events during the season, and they did not coincide with opinions of the rest of the family. There were too many functions she thought it beneath her dignity, and her idea of an acceptable event was one given by those of the highest level of society, and even then, it could only be successful when Darcy was in constant attendance of her daughter, and if it was a ball, danced with Anne and no one else.

Furthermore, it was disturbing to Darcy that she attempted to exclude the Bennet sisters whenever possible. This was bad enough before she knew of the Gardiners, for she would insinuate they would do better to stay at home since there was no way they could live up to society. When the existence of the Bennets' family became known to her, the reaction was even worse.

"Then perhaps they should attend events at their relations' level of society," said she with a disdainful sniff. "If they did, they could pass themselves off with some degree of credit."

"Catherine, that is enough!" said Lady Anne, her tone brooking no opposition. "If you will insult my guests, I will ask you to leave. As I have said numerous times in the past, Jane and Elizabeth are *my* guests and attend events with *my* family. If you cannot abide their presence, you are welcome to assume a different schedule, for I will not exclude them."

Now, it may be supposed given the relative characters of the two sisters, that Lady Catherine might respond in kind, her more forceful disposition allowing her to dominate her more reticent sibling. But nothing could be further from the truth, and Darcy thought the reasons were twofold. First, his mother possessed a core of steel, and while she often allowed her elder sister to have her say without comment, when she felt she was in the right, she had no scruple in returning Lady Catherine's criticisms back on her. The second was because of Darcy himself—Lady Catherine did not wish to risk offending Darcy or his mother, so she often remained silent when Darcy knew she would much rather press her opinion. In this instance, she huffed with disdain and desisted.

However carefully Lady Catherine treated Darcy and his mother to avoid giving offense, she was not shy in putting Anne forward in every situation. Whether it was dancing at a ball, dinner, card parties, visits to exhibits, or any of the other entertainments in which they indulged, Lady Catherine was always there, directing him toward Anne.

"You will, of course, dance the first with Anne tonight."

"Does Anne not look beautiful tonight?"

"Lend Anne your arm, Darcy for she is fatigued."

"Anne has a wonderful voice, does she not? Hearing her read poetry is divine!"

By the end of a week, Darcy was at his wit's end. Though she said nothing regarding the Bennet sisters, Darcy soon realized that she considered them—or at least the younger, since Bingley was courting the elder assiduously—rivals for her desire for Darcy to wed Anne. Nothing Darcy said or did dissuaded her, and if anything, it only encouraged her.

The other matter was Miss Elizabeth. After the dressing down his mother administered, recollections of his time in Hertfordshire invaded Darcy's mind, and he could do nothing but conclude he had not behaved well. At the assembly when he had insulted Miss Elizabeth, he had not even realized until he next saw her that it was she he had insulted, and then he assumed she had not heard him. To learn that she *had* was mortifying in the extreme, such that though Darcy thought to apologize more than once, he found himself too embarrassed to approach her.

Two things were clear in Darcy's mind: the first was that he had always thought she differed from most other young ladies. The attraction he felt for her had led him to distance himself from her to avoid appearing to prefer her, as he did not wish to lead her to believe he might offer for her. That was a failure too, as, by his mother's testimony, she did not think much of him. The second was that his mother and his sister, the two dearest women in the world to him, esteemed the Bennet sisters greatly. If they did, it would behoove Darcy not to dismiss her. Thus, his resolution became to be more open with her, to see for himself how worthy she was. It was unfortunate this determination brought its own problems.

"It seems to me you have improved your playing since coming to London," said Darcy one day when he came upon Miss Elizabeth in the music room. Georgiana, who could usually be found there with her, was nowhere in evidence, allowing Darcy to take the opportunity to speak with Miss Elizabeth.

"Thank you, Mr. Darcy," said she. "I believe it has, though I must attribute it to the opportunity to sit with your sister in her lessons and my determination to practice more." She directed a searching look at him. "But I must inquire as to where you heard me play before, for I did not play at Netherfield, and I have no recollection of playing in your presence."

"It was at the party at Lucas Lodge not long after our arrival in the neighborhood," said Darcy. Leaving the door open, Darcy crossed the room and sat on the sofa, prompting her to take a chair nearby. "Though I would not consider myself a true connoisseur of music like my sister, it seems to me your playing was always exquisite — and now it has become even more so."

Miss Elizabeth laughed and fixed him with a playful look. "Now I must think you are intent upon flattering me, sir, for I know my playing pales compared to your sister's. I have always said I could play so much better if I took the time to practice, an opinion which I have proven by my recent efforts. Still, with your sister and your mother's examples, I cannot think you considered my playing to be anything special."

"There you are incorrect," replied Darcy, trying to inform her through his earnest reply that he was telling her nothing but the truth. "There are, perhaps, others who play with better technical proficiency than you, but you play with such a feel for the music that I think there are few who could disapprove."

After a moment of searching his eyes, Miss Elizabeth seemed to understand he spoke the truth, and she thanked him, though not without a little self-consciousness. Knowing it would not do to praise her to excess, lest she suspect him, Darcy decided to change the subject.

"The music you were just now playing—was it Mozart?"

"A sonatina by Clementi, actually," replied Miss Elizabeth. "Their styles are sometimes considered similar, though a true proficient like your sister would not have made such a mistake."

"I think we have covered the fact that I am *not* a proficient, Miss Elizabeth."

"Which is why I shall allow your lapse for the moment," replied she.

The silliness of the conversation induced them to laugh, and Darcy felt the cares of the world and his previous reflections melt away at the sound of her joy. Eager to continue the conversation between them, Darcy turned the subject to her preferences, asking:

"Do you find the works of Clementi pleasing, Miss Bennet?"

"Some, yes, though I would not call him a favorite." She smiled and added: "As I understand he considers England to be his home, I would find myself privileged to hear him play in person one day. But I appreciate the skills of many composers: Mozart and Beethoven, and Haydn and Scarlatti, to name a few. Your sister has convinced me of the wonders of Bach, though I had never heard of him before coming to London."

"Ah, yes," replied Darcy with a nod. "I have often heard my sister and my mother speak of Bach. Though I understand he was once considered to be a true master, his popularity has waned in recent years."

"Such that it is the true musicians who know of him," agreed Miss Elizabeth. "Many of his works I find beyond my level of skill, but I do appreciate his music for its genius."

They spent some time in the music room discussing their various likes and dislikes, with respect to composers, and musical forms and instruments. Darcy discovered Miss Elizabeth was knowledgeable, and that she loved the pianoforte, but appreciated many chamber styles as well. The opera was not to her taste, though she claimed to like certain works better than others, and she appreciated being in London, for it allowed her greater opportunity to hear music played with skill than she could experience in Hertfordshire. It was when the discussion was becoming interesting that they were interrupted by a most unwelcome source.

"Darcy!" boomed the voice of his aunt. "What are you doing in here alone with Miss Elizabeth?"

"Lady Catherine," said Darcy in greeting, rising to bow, noting Miss Elizabeth's curtsey at the same time. "Miss Elizabeth and I were discussing music, for I came upon her when she was playing the pianoforte."

The virago's gimlet eye fell upon Miss Elizabeth for some moments before his aunt sniffed and said: "If Miss Elizabeth attended to her practice more often, she might not play amiss. Unfortunately, she has not the taste that Anne possesses, which is not something that may be taught. Now, attend me, Darcy, for Anne expressed a desire to see you today."

Privately, Darcy doubted Anne had made any such declaration. More likely, she had made some comment and Lady Catherine had interpreted it—or expanded on its meaning—to convince herself her daughter was desperate to be in his company. Feeling resigned to their interesting tête-à-tête coming to an end, Darcy offered his aunt his arm and led her from the room. The thought made itself known, though it remained at the back of his mind, that the prospect of marrying Anne was losing its appeal. It always did when Darcy was in the company of his aunt.

"Miss Elizabeth Bennet!"

The voice, so close by when Elizabeth had not expected it, caused her to jump in surprise. Looking up, she noted Lady Catherine presence, as the woman stood over where she was speaking with Mr. Darcy, an expression of extreme displeasure etched upon her severe countenance.

"It seems to me you have forgotten your place, Miss Elizabeth, for it is clear to me you are attempting to distract my nephew from his duty."

"I am afraid I do not know—"

"Silence, and allow me to speak," interrupted Lady Catherine. "Since I found you alone with him in the music room three days ago, I have watched you, have seen the arts and allurements you deploy to attempt to capture my nephew. I will not have it, young lady. Darcy will never debase himself to offer for one such as you!"

"I have never attempted to distract Mr. Darcy from his duty, or from anything else," said Elizabeth, recognizing the tight note of anger in her own voice.

"If you will recall, I approached her, Aunt," said Mr. Darcy.

"Please do not berate my guest, Catherine," added Lady Anne, bringing her sister up short. "Elizabeth has not behaved improperly — and I will remind you again that nothing is decided, and I would thank you not to speak in a way which makes the engagement you wish for to appear a fait accompli."

Again, as had already happened several times, Elizabeth was treated to the sight of Lady Catherine swallowing her tongue. It was obvious the lady wished to snap a reply, but equally obvious she did not wish to offend her sister.

"Yes, well I know it will be decided soon enough." Her gaze swung back to Elizabeth. "Remember your place, Miss Elizabeth, and we shall not be at odds."

Then the lady stalked off, calling to her daughter to sit near Mr. Darcy and watching Elizabeth for as long as she was present. In truth, Elizabeth was becoming more than a little annoyed with the woman. Several days before, Mr. Darcy had begun to speak to her, his manner becoming less severe, his conversation more interesting. Elizabeth did not know what prompted this change and could only assume his growing comfort with her and Jane had allowed him to relax.

This change had not come without consequences, however, for whenever they were in company, Lady Catherine would watch them, her comments becoming more pointed the longer he persisted. That day had been the first time she had spoken in so severe a manner, but Elizabeth knew her reprimands would grow worse the longer the situation continued.

It was thus fortunate that Mr. Darcy recognized the problem and allowed a distance to spring up between them — or he did so when Lady Catherine was present. When she was not, his increased civility continued, and Elizabeth began to understand the gentleman more than she had ever thought possible.

Elizabeth was not the only one who drew Lady Catherine's ire. The lady would direct it at any young woman she deemed too close to Mr. Darcy — anyone with whom he shared even a few words. An amusing illustration of this occurred a few days after her first explicit words of warning to Elizabeth.

Though the Bennet sisters had now been in London for more than six weeks, there were still many to whom they had not been introduced, despite the fact that Elizabeth had by now met so many people, she could not possibly remember them all. Lady Susan and Lord Matlock had been a constant presence, though their schedules did not always coincide. On the day in question, Lady Susan planned for a large dinner party, and the residents of Darcy house were invited.

At dinner, Elizabeth and Jane were seated together, and neither was situated close to anyone of their party. Even so, Elizabeth found enjoyment in the evening, for there were always new people to meet and characters to study. After dinner, when the company retired to the house's sitting-room, Lady Catherine's irascible nature once again made itself known.

"Come, Miss Bennet," said Mr. Bingley, making his way to Jane as soon as the gentlemen rejoined the ladies. "Let us sit together and speak for a time."

Jane, as always, went willingly, her preference for Mr. Bingley's company as clear as ever. There were several other men who approached to strike up conversations with her, and while Mr. Bingley endured it, it was clear he was not happy with their interruptions. Elizabeth's amusement at the situation did not go unnoticed.

"It seems you are enjoying my friend's annoyance, Miss Elizabeth," said Mr. Darcy.

As she always did when Mr. Darcy approached her where Lady Catherine might see, she darted a look at the lady, noting some of the other matrons who were like her in character had distracted her. Thus assured a short conversation could proceed without her interference, Elizabeth turned to Mr. Darcy.

"I am not so much enjoying it, Mr. Darcy. But Jane is often the center of attention wherever she goes, and it is no surprise to me there are men in attendance who wish to speak with her."

Mr. Darcy peered at them for several moments, his manner grave, and Elizabeth wondered what he was thinking. For a time, Elizabeth thought he would not speak, but then he turned to her, as solemn as she had ever seen him.

"Though I would never accuse your sister of acting improperly, I wonder at her level of interest in my friend. Bingley's affections are obvious, but Miss Bennet does not seem to receive him with any more emotion than those other men who seek to interrupt them."

For a moment, Elizabeth was tempted to snap back at him, but she mastered her pique. "To one who does not know Jane well, I am not surprised her affections would be difficult to discern. I would tell you, however, to look closer, Mr. Darcy, for her character is, in many respects, similar to your own."

His countenance lightening a little, Mr. Darcy fixed her with a curious look. "That she is reticent is clear. Are you suggesting she holds my friend in esteem?"

"I will not presume to speak for my sister, Mr. Darcy," replied Elizabeth. "However, I would have you know that if she did not favor him, she would let him know, though, again, she would do so with tact and discretion. Should he misread her feelings, she would never accept an offer of marriage or even courtship if she felt she could not esteem him as a woman ought to esteem her husband."

The pause this time was much longer, as Mr. Darcy watched Jane and Mr. Bingley, his eyes sharp and inquisitive. When he turned back to her, Elizabeth could sense he was more at ease after hearing her assurances.

"I hope you will attribute my interest in the matter to a sincere desire to ensure my friend finds his happiness."

"As I hope you will credit my motives to be identical regarding my sister."

"Then we are agreed, Miss Elizabeth," replied Mr. Darcy.

At that moment Elizabeth noted Lady Catherine watching and could see Mr. Darcy had become aware of the same. Though they did not separate at once, by unspoken agreement they allowed a distance to grow in between them. It did not placate Lady Catherine to any great degree, for her suspicion remained unabated. At least she did not make a scene. Or she did not when *Elizabeth* spoke with Mr. Darcy.

At any such event when she was present, Miss Bingley did her best to garner Mr. Darcy's attention. This was fraught with danger, as Elizabeth had cause to know, even when a woman was not intending to tempt Mr. Darcy. That Miss Bingley most assuredly *was*, and yet Lady Catherine had not seen fit to reprimand her, Elizabeth attributed to the lady's surety that her nephew would never do something so crass as to offer for the daughter of a tradesman. It seemed Miss Bingley's actions were so overt that evening, however, that Lady Catherine could not ignore them. As Elizabeth was still situated nearby, she was close enough to hear Lady Catherine's reprimand.

"What a lovely evening this is, Mr. Darcy," exclaimed the woman, filling the space where Elizabeth had stood only a few moments before. "How lovely it is to make your aunt's acquaintance at last and to be invited to an intimate dinner at her house!"

If it was an intimate dinner, Elizabeth would liked to have known what a large one would be like—there were, by her count, over forty people in attendance! It was unfortunate for Miss Bingley, but her statement elicited little response from the gentleman, as was usual.

"It is not so intimate," said Mr. Darcy, echoing Elizabeth's thoughts.

"I am convinced it could not be termed so with more than half the present number, and most of those in the room replaced by extended family or intimate acquaintances."

Miss Bingley frowned at the way Mr. Darcy so easily rejected her claims of familiarity with his family, but it did not deter her. "Yes, well, I suppose there are some here who could not be called intimate." In the next moment, Elizabeth felt the heat of Miss Bingley's eyes on her back and knew the woman was glaring at her. "Our closeness *has* suffered to some extent, given those . . . undesirable elements who have latched onto your mother's train."

"Nothing could be further from the truth," replied Mr. Darcy. "My mother and sister have enjoyed our company, and I have not objected to their presence either."

The soft huff of exasperation which reached Elizabeth's ears attested to Miss Bingley's annoyance. "Well, be that as it may, our own intimacy seems to be increasing, and for that, I am well pleased." Miss Bingley paused as if expecting some response, and when none was forthcoming, she said: "Are you to attend the Davidson ball next week?"

"I would imagine we shall, given Davidson is a longstanding friend."

"Yes, well, I believe we shall attend too. Mr. Davidson and his wife are particular friends, you understand, for better or more elegant people cannot be found. Shall you anticipate it as much as I?"

"No more so than any other ball, Miss Bingley, which, as you know, is not my favorite pastime. Though I am not opposed to an evening in company with friends, I always find a ball to be tedious."

"Oh, I cannot disagree, Mr. Darcy!" exclaimed Miss Bingley. "As you know, I have often said conversation would be a more rational way to spend such an evening."

"Yes, I remember your opinion. I shall only observe, as your sister did on that occasion, that it may be more rational, but not nearly so much like a ball."

"I suppose not. However, I will observe, Mr. Darcy, that should you find the proper partner to pair for a dance, the evening would not seem so tedious."

It was all Elizabeth could do not to laugh out loud at the blatant suggestion that Mr. Darcy ask her for a dance—the first dance, no doubt—at a ball which was still a week distant. There was another who had moved nearby, and while she understood Miss Bingley's purpose as well as had Elizabeth, she was not so amused by it.

"For perhaps the first time in our acquaintance, I agree with you, Miss Bingley."

Elizabeth had moved to a position where she could just see the conversation out of the corner of her eye, and thus witnessed Miss Bingley's start of surprise at the lady's nearness. Lady Catherine, however, was not about to allow her to respond.

"And for the proper partner, it is obvious my daughter is the perfect option, for not only is she his cousin, she is . . ." Lady Catherine trailed off, and Elizabeth noted Mr. Darcy's stony visage, warning her to desist. Though with evident ill grace, Lady Catherine refrained, finishing her sentence by saying: "Yes, well, Darcy should choose someone who would complement him in *every* way, not only in lineage and wealth but in compatibility, shared admiration, not to mention the wishes of his family."

Again, Elizabeth held in her hilarity, as Mr. Darcy shook his head at his aunt's transparent suggestion—if suggestion it was and not a demand. Lady Catherine, however, was not finished with Miss Bingley.

"Let me warn you, Miss Bingley," said Lady Catherine, leaning in close to the lady, though her voice was no more a whisper than if she had put a trumpet to her mouth. "My nephew is not for you, so you had best cease your attempts to draw him in. Why you are wasting your time is beyond me, for you are no more suitable to be his bride than Miss Elizabeth. At least *she* possesses the ancestry to lay claim to the title of gentleman's daughter, something of which you have no claim. Do not seek to rise above your station, for it will go ill with you."

"I believe that will do, Lady Catherine," said Mr. Darcy, while Miss Bingley looked down in utter mortification.

Lady Catherine directed a critical gaze at Miss Bingley and nodded once. "Yes, you are correct."

Then she turned and walked away without another word or a second glance. Miss Bingley was far too embarrassed to say anything further, and she took herself away, appearing as if she wished to sink into the floor. A quick glance around the room informed Elizabeth that she was likely to escape infamy, for the confrontation appeared to have gone unnoticed.

For Mr. Darcy's part, he passed the rest of the evening in seeming annoyance, though Elizabeth caught his eye on more than one occasion. Those times, she smiled and shook her head, inducing him to respond with more wryness than she thought he felt. Lady Catherine was a meddling, persistent sort of woman, and Elizabeth had long determined the best way to deal with her was to allow the feeling of amusement at her antics. It was clear Mr. Darcy had not yet come to the same conclusion, but she hoped he would before long.

CHAPTER X

*M*argaret Bennet possessed the curious ability to take any situation, say something inappropriate and improper, embarrass her daughters, and make what should be a happy time into one anxious and mortifying. That she did not mean to cause such trouble was something Elizabeth understood. Mrs. Bennet could be a loving woman when she so chose. The worries of the entail, having five daughters of little dowry and few prospects often overwhelmed what little sense with which she was blessed, and her opinions concerning the best ways to attract husbands and her lack of understanding of proper behavior did not make matters any better.

If one observed the presence of the Bennet sisters in London, coupled with their mother's continued residence in Hertfordshire, the witness would be excused for assuming there was little she could do to discomfit said daughters. Sensible as they were of their mother's limitations, Elizabeth had little desire to endure her mother ruining the friendships forming between herself and those with whom she stayed in London. Unfortunately, a letter that arrived the day after the dinner threatened to do just that.

"It is from Mama," said Jane in a quiet voice when the post was delivered.

Mrs. Bennet was not a great letter writer, and what she did write was filled with nonsensical instructions and improper suggestions. Assuming it was more of the same, Elizabeth nodded and allowed the matter to rest for the moment to attend their hosts. Later, when they were at liberty to discuss the letter, she would discover what it contained.

Though Elizabeth was not in any condition to consider the matter rationally, she realized later that Lady Anne must have seen something in their faces, for she found them not long after, but once they had read through the letter. As the door opened and the lady stepped in, surveying them, Elizabeth fell silent, not wishing to debate her family's foibles in front of a woman whose opinion was becoming important to her.

"Is something wrong?" asked Lady Anne as she watched them both closely.

"We have just received a letter from our mother," said Elizabeth, attempting to portray it as nothing more than some correspondence.

Lady Anne directed a grave look at them both. "I have observed that your mother's letters often cause consternation. Furthermore, when I stepped into this room, it seemed like you were both eight years of age and caught in some mischief."

In any other circumstance, Elizabeth might have seen the humor in Lady Anne's comments. At present, however, with her mother's threats looming, there was little to be gained in laughing. Lady Anne closed the door behind her and approached them, her firm gaze never wavering, and when she sat nearby, she eyed them.

"If you do not wish to share your troubles with me, I shall not press the matter. However, I would have you both know that I am willing to help if it is something with which I may assist."

Elizabeth shared a look with Jane. Neither wished to portray their mother's character any worse than Lady Anne likely already knew. But as the letter primarily concerned Jane, Elizabeth allowed her sister to decide.

"Our mother has suggested she might come to town," said Jane in a quiet tone.

An elegant eyebrow rose, and Lady Anne said: "Though I would not presume to speak ill of your mother, it was obvious upon meeting her that she . . . struggles with proper behavior. Still, I would not have thought her capable of inviting herself to join you here."

Jane's eyes widened and she exclaimed: "Mama would never do that!"

Though Elizabeth suspected her mother might, in fact, do such a thing if it crossed her mind, she agreed with Jane in this instance. "If Mama came to town, she would stay with the Gardiners."

"Then why are you concerned?" asked Lady Anne.

"Because she no longer considers Mr. Bingley an appropriate suitor."

The words hung in the air between them, Lady Anne looking on with some gravity, while Jane attempted to look anywhere but at her host. For Elizabeth, the curiosity she felt was overwhelming her shame at this woman knowing of her mother's foibles.

"In what way?"

The question hung between them, but when neither sister responded, Lady Anne showed her insight. "Unless I am mistaken, is it because you are now staying with my family, and she considers your prospects as much higher than the son of a tradesman?"

Their expressions must have told her she guessed right, but Elizabeth would never have expected the slight smile which appeared on her face. For a moment she gazed at Lady Anne in shock.

"I offer my apologies for my mother's lack of tact, Lady Anne," said Elizabeth, uncertain what else to say.

"Do you suppose I have never seen similar behavior from any other woman of your mother's position in society?"

"Perhaps you have," replied Elizabeth. "But we are staying here because of your generosity. It would be poor repayment for your kindness if our mother were to insert herself into our midst and embarrass us all."

"I suppose it would be," said Lady Anne. "But I doubt it will come to that. Please, Jane, Elizabeth, tell me more about your mother."

Elizabeth sighed. "Mother was not born a gentlewoman, though, as you know, there are gentlefolk in her ancestry. This has left her with little understanding of how to behave in the manner those of her station should. As the entail has long been a concern, with no son to inherit, she has worried we will all lose our home when our father is gone, leaving us in a form of genteel poverty. Thus, she considers it best that we all marry, so we may be provided for."

"She is correct, you know," said Lady Anne, turning a pointed look on Elizabeth.

"Of course, she is," said Elizabeth, with a little more heat than she intended. "But I wish to have the right to choose my husband for myself and not be embarrassed by my mother's ways."

"That is understandable," replied Lady Anne.

Though aware they were spilling family secrets and embarrassing ones at that, Elizabeth felt they could trust Lady Anne. She listened as they spoke, injecting a comment or two where required, but there was little they did not share with her. When they fell silent, Lady Anne remained quiet herself.

"Your frustration is understandable," said she at length. "Though I would not seek to cast blame and I am certain you understand already, some of the responsibility belongs to your father. As your mother is not equipped to move in the society to which your father has raised her, it was his responsibility to educate her, and he has not."

Jane was uncomfortable with the criticism of her father, though Elizabeth knew Jane could not dispute it. For Elizabeth herself, it was a subject which had always given her consternation, though she could never escape the truth.

"But all is not lost." Lady Anne favored them with genuine affection and added: "It seems to me your mother must learn a little decorum. From what I saw at the ball, her manners are not beyond all redemption."

"Who will teach her?" asked Elizabeth, Jane nodding by her side. "My father will not, and she will not listen to a mere daughter."

"Oh, you never know when someone will become a mentor." Lady Anne's manner was mysterious. "I have seen her like many times, I assure you, so it is not uncommon."

"The lady directed a serious look at them, and then spoke again, saying: "I must assume your youngest sisters are another concern for you?"

"You have met them," was Elizabeth's simple reply. "Kitty and Lydia are nothing short of wild."

"That is unfair, Lizzy," said Jane, though the tone of her voice suggested her protest was more because of loyalty than conviction.

"I have only seen your sisters one evening in company," said Lady Anne, directing sympathy at Jane, "but from what I witnessed, I can say without reservation your sisters require much amendment before their behavior will be acceptable in society. They should not even be out in Meryton, given how they behave."

The tendency for Jane to defend the indefensible was on display, as she struggled to find a response. When it became apparent she could muster nothing, Lady Anne leaned forward and patted her hand.

"Do not concern yourself, Jane. Or you Lizzy," added she with a smile. "There are some years yet before your sisters reach maturity, and much may change in the interim. In the meantime, I suggest you write to your father, asking him to step in. Your uncle also seems to be aware of his sister's shortcomings — perhaps if he wrote to your mother informing her he will not host her at present, that would be enough to foil her plans."

"Thank you, Lady Anne," said Elizabeth. "I shall do just that."

And so Elizabeth wrote the letter and dispatched it, along with a note for her uncle, explaining the situation to him. Now there was nothing to do but hope it would be enough.

The sigh that escaped Anne's lips when the Bennet sisters left the room was as inexorable as the tide, though it was not directed at those two wonderful girls. To be nothing but honest, her annoyance was not even directed at Mrs. Bennet, for she knew the woman could not help her nature. It was not even Mr. Bennet who earned her pique, though matters would be much easier if he had not abrogated his responsibilities toward his wife and daughters.

There was no help for it, she supposed, for the situation was what it was. Though for a time Anne had wondered if her son would ever see the gem in front of him, she was now convinced he was coming around. If he decided Elizabeth was the woman he wanted, nothing would stand in his way.

Other than Elizabeth herself, thought Anne with a smile. The girl was perhaps the most independent Anne had ever met, which was interesting, considering she was not truly unfettered given the financial situation of her family. Elizabeth, however, would not accept William if she was not convinced of his ability to make her happy — or her own to make *him* happy. Her situation would not factor into her decision.

It was this, in part, which would make her such a wonderful wife for Anne's son. Many were the lady who attempted to capture William's attention, and all for his position in society and the wealth of the Darcy family. There were not five women in all England, Anne estimated, who would refuse William's offer of marriage on such grounds. And William needed such a woman for a wife, or he would be miserable.

The question was, what to do about the Bennets. Other than a tendency to laughter when he should be a mentor, Mr. Bennet was acceptable, and Anne did not think he would be much in society regardless. The behavior of the middle daughter, Mary, was also not a major problem, though there were issues which would need to be addressed. No, the real problems were the characters of the mother and the youngest two daughters.

Anne was convinced Mrs. Bennet's behavior could be amended with little difficulty, for she was so much in awe of them that Anne could bring her to heel without difficulty. If that did not work, an introduction to Susan, who would be eager to assist, would do the trick. The younger girls were a different matter altogether. Titles would not impress them, and their eyes would be fixed solely on the amusements of society.

That would be their undoing, and the undoing of the entire family. Society could be cruel when a woman's behavior did not measure up to what was expected; except when the offender possessed standing or fortune—then all could be ignored. Young, unknown ladies such as Misses Kitty and Lydia would have none of this protection and would quickly find themselves a laughingstock. This would, in turn, affect the Darcy family, and by extension the Fitzwilliams. That would not do.

Though Anne was not certain what to do yet, she knew something must be done to improve them, lest the Bennets embarrass them all. Should the marriage between William and Elizabeth come to fruition, Anne would need to take steps at that point. Perhaps school would be an option, or perhaps she could take a hand herself. Mr. Bennet would be no impediment, and if Anne succeeded in amending Mrs. Bennet's behavior, she would see the need to improve her daughters as well.

Another sigh escaped her lips and Anne rose, determined to think on the matter no more. This was all hypothetical unless William made an offer to Elizabeth. Until then, she would bide her time. But she would not hesitate to act if events played out the way she expected.

It was at another gathering of the extended Darcy family that Elizabeth found herself amused by Lady Catherine's antics. The woman was in fine form that evening, pushing her daughter and Mr. Darcy together at every opportunity, speaking incessantly of their upcoming union, and speaking of it as if it was a matter already decided. Mr. Darcy, it was clear to see, was becoming aggravated, for his responses to her words were becoming less patient and ever more clipped.

Miss de Bourgh's feelings on the matter, however, were opaque, for the woman did not speak much, and made no attempt to induce her mother to cease her machinations. Even the occasional pointed comment from the earl did nothing to stem Lady Catherine's incessant meddling. Thus, it was a relief when her sisters finally distracted her.

A moment of observing Miss de Bourgh convinced Elizabeth she would like to come to know the woman better to understand her. Thus, when Elizabeth was certain Lady Catherine was occupied and would not protest Elizabeth contaminating her dear daughter, Elizabeth rose and made her way to where Miss de Bourgh was sitting.

"Do you mind if I join you?" asked Elizabeth.

Miss de Bourgh appeared surprised to be so approached, but she did not object, motioning with her hand for Elizabeth to sit. True to what Elizabeth had observed of her character, however, she did not speak.

"How are you this evening, Miss de Bourgh?" asked Elizabeth. "Though my sister and I have been staying with your aunt, we have not taken the time to know each other, and I thought we should rectify that lack."

Miss de Bourgh's next act of sneaking a look at her mother—who was still distracted—informed Elizabeth of her companion's concern for what her mother would say. Then she looked back at Elizabeth and seemed mystified.

"Is there any point? You are not to stay with my aunt forever."

"The length of my stay does not determine the extent of my desire to form new acquaintances."

When Elizabeth smiled, Miss de Bourgh returned it, albeit in a tentative fashion, and Elizabeth wondered if she had ever had anyone she could call a friend. Though she might have thought Lady Catherine would allow her to associate with those of like status in the world, it was possible the woman was so focused on Mr. Darcy as a son-in-law that she had protected her daughter against acquaintances of any kind, and not just gentlemen seeking a wealthy wife.

Thus began a conversation which was slow and halting, but gradually became easier. Elizabeth had the distinct impression that her initial thoughts were correct, that Miss de Bourgh's social skills were not well developed, though she had been out in society for several years now, being Jane's age. But soon Elizabeth found her eager to make a connection, though perhaps not adept at going about it. Reticent though she was, Elizabeth thought she would make a good friend, if Lady Catherine should allow it.

After speaking together for some short amount of time, the subject turned to their presence in London during the season, and Elizabeth learned some things about Miss de Bourgh which did not shock her.

"Oh, we attend the season every year," said Miss de Bourgh. "Mama believes in keeping up appearances."

"Do you enjoy attending?" asked Elizabeth.

Miss de Bourgh's answer was a shrug, coupled with a softly

spoken: "London is more interesting than Rosings, I suppose, but many of the events I do not care for." Then she paused and spoke under her breath: "Not that Mama concerns herself with my preferences."

As Elizabeth was certain Miss de Bourgh had not intended her to overhear, she did not mention it, though it confirmed her suspicions. Instead, she changed the subject to preferences and was interested to discover that Miss de Bourgh loved art and music and possessed some talent in painting. What she did not enjoy as much were the social aspects of the season: balls, dinners, parties and the like. Then the subject turned again.

"Am I to congratulate you on your forthcoming engagement?"

Miss de Bourgh snuck a look at Mr. Darcy, who was speaking with Lord Matlock, and then at her mother—Lady Catherine had become aware of Elizabeth's conversation with her daughter but was still occupied with her sisters.

"Mama *does* wish for it, but I do not know what William means to do."

"Do you not wish to marry him?"

"I cannot say," said she with a shrug. "Though I do not have any real desire to marry William, I am not opposed to it either."

"If you will pardon my saying so, it seems to me that one should have an opinion on such an important subject as one's partner in marriage."

A slight smile appeared on Miss de Bourgh's face. "I will not say you are incorrect, but I will point out *you* are not the daughter of Lady Catherine de Bourgh. Since my earliest years, my mother has told me I will marry William, and as she is not a woman to hear any dissent, I keep my own counsel."

"Then if he proposes, you will accept?"

"I suppose I likely will," replied Miss de Bourgh. "But until he does, there is little point thinking of it, and to contradict my mother would make her angry. If William decides he wishes to marry elsewhere, Mama will rage and storm, but though *she* does not acknowledge it, she possesses little influence over her sister and less over William. Once the storm has passed, the matter will be at an end. Perhaps then I may find myself free to direct my affections where *I* wish."

Then Miss de Bourgh shook her head and added: "Then again, knowing Mama as I do, she will then search high and low for a man of high position in society, if only to prove to William that she is unaffected by his rejection."

"Anne, Miss Elizabeth, of what are you speaking? Tell me at once, for I must have my part in the conversation."

The way Lady Catherine was glaring at her suggested thoughts of contamination were now foremost in her mind. Miss de Bourgh, however, showed a quick wit for she replied before Elizabeth could.

"I was speaking to Miss Elizabeth of my painting, Mama."

"Oh, yes!" said Lady Catherine with unfeigned enthusiasm. Even so, Elizabeth was not certain she believed the lady's suspicion was extinguished. "Anne has the most exquisite taste coupled with such talent as is rarely seen. Some of her efforts are wondrous to behold.

"And she receives it all from me, for Sir Lewis was not a man of any artistic talent."

The grins Elizabeth could see out of the corners of her eyes informed her that most of Lady Catherine's words were nothing more than a boast. With such self-importance on display, Elizabeth could not keep from challenging the woman.

"I did not know you painted, Lady Catherine. If the situation presents itself, I should love to see some of your work."

"I do not paint, Miss Elizabeth," snapped Lady Catherine. "But had I ever learned, I should have been the talk of London, for I would have stopped at nothing to be the best.

"You would do well to take my example," said Lady Catherine. "If you practiced more, your performance on the pianoforte might be adequate. Nothing is achieved without practice."

"Thank you, Lady Catherine," said Elizabeth sincerely. "I believe you are correct."

As Miss Elizabeth toyed with his aunt, Fitzwilliam turned his attention back to his cousin, peering at her, curious as to what he had just seen. Unlike his aunt's initial lack of awareness concerning Miss Elizabeth and Anne's tête-à-tête, Fitzwilliam had seen the young woman approaching his cousin, interested to see what Anne's response would be.

Though he had only met her a few times, Fitzwilliam had already developed a healthy respect for Miss Elizabeth. She was a bright light, one at home in any situation, one able to pull a grin from the dourest of countenances. Among that number, Fitzwilliam counted his cousin Darcy, who often seemed as if he did not have any joy in his life, though Fitzwilliam knew his cousin was not at all unhappy. There remained much unresolved between Darcy and Miss Elizabeth, he suspected, and how it would end remained uncertain.

Those thoughts, however, were not Fitzwilliam's focus. Instead, it was the person of his cousin who drew most of his attention. If there was anyone who had experienced little joy in life, that person was Anne. Fitzwilliam did not think she was discontented, exactly, but her mother controlled so much of her daily life that Fitzwilliam did not think she had ever been in a position to live. The family tended to forget Anne or to consider her as nothing more than an extension of her mother, perhaps the same as a child who had not yet left the nursery.

But a strange thing had happened when Miss Elizabeth sat and spoke with Anne, and Fitzwilliam did not know if it was a function of her ability to charm anyone, or something more emerging from his shy cousin because of another paying her a little attention. Though she had started as reticent as usual, as they spoke, he saw Anne beginning to show a little more enthusiasm, a little cheer in what was a monotonous existence. And Fitzwilliam, for the first time in seeing her as a cousin, began to feel the appeal of a young woman who was not lacking in feminine attributes. It was intriguing, and he wished to know more.

Aunt Catherine was, as usual, intent on pushing Anne toward Darcy after interrupting the two younger women. Soon, however, she was again distracted, and given the opportunity, Fitzwilliam moved closer to his cousin, curious about her, aware he had not engaged her in conversation in quite some time.

"Anne," said he in greeting as he sat beside her. "I see you are as well as ever."

Far from the expected civility he expected in return, Anne gave him a level look, as if she did not know him. "I suppose I am," said she after a moment. "It does cross my mind to wonder why you would choose to approach me now."

"Should I not?" asked Fitzwilliam nonplused.

"It has been some time since you have."

"Yes, well . . ." stammered Fitzwilliam, painfully aware she was entirely correct. "At times I have not known how I would be received, and at others . . . Well, your mother."

While Fitzwilliam thought his last words were perhaps the stupidest he had ever spoken, Anne's response was a tinkle of laughter, which Fitzwilliam found intriguing, wishing to provoke that laughter more often.

"The Darcy conundrum," said she after a moment.

"Indeed," replied Fitzwilliam. "I do not know if you recall, but during a visit several years ago, when I sat beside you for some few moments, your mother took me to task after warning me against attempting to infringe upon Darcy's territory."

"She could not have said that!" exclaimed Anne, though with an undertone of laughter.

"Perhaps not in so many words," replied Fitzwilliam. "But that was the general message."

With a sigh, Anne looked over at her mother, shaking her head. "Oh, Mother, this obsession has ruled your life for so many years, it pains me, but there is little else for you to live for."

"Are you telling me you do not wish to marry Darcy?" For some reason, it seemed of utmost importance that Fitzwilliam learn the answer to this question.

Anne turned and regarded him. "This is the second time I have been asked that question tonight, and for the second time, I must say that I simply do not know. I have always assumed I would marry him if he decided he wished to have me for a wife, but I have never considered my own desires."

"Perhaps it is time you should."

For a long moment, Anne remained silent, watching him as if trying to understand him. Then, from her mouth issued three small words, words which seemed the most important in the world at that moment.

"Perhaps it is."

CHAPTER XI

The night of the Davidson ball soon arrived, and Darcy began to wonder if the women of his family were arrayed against him.

The intervening days had been characterized by a lull in society, a brief respite, but one welcome, nonetheless. In those days, those residents of his house spent most of their time at home relaxing, and when they did venture out, their activities were sedate and not taxing.

Though Darcy was not certain what had happened, the Bennet sisters had been ill at ease for some days before, but the arrival of a letter the day before the ball seemed to provide relief. Even Miss Elizabeth's laughter had seemed forced during those days. Darcy had no direct knowledge of what the letter contained — though it seemed to him his mother did — and while there were a few educated guesses he could make, he decided against thinking about it.

The ball and their preparations soon dominated the ladies' talk, such that Darcy often found himself at sixes and sevens amid a group of four females, excited for a coming amusement he did not find nearly so interesting. Fitzwilliam was much more in evidence those days, which provided some relief, though the ubiquitous presence of Lady Catherine and her daughter did not. Darcy and Fitzwilliam often employed tactics they used to avoid Lady Catherine when at Rosings, and though the lady did not seem to appreciate it, Darcy could bear her displeasure cheerfully.

On the night in question, the lingering questions which had persisted in Darcy's mind, grown larger as the ball approached, began to manifest in his mind, leading to growing suspicion. He might have ignored it and enjoyed the ball as much as he could, if not for the actions of his sister.

There was a tacit agreement between siblings since Georgiana's coming out that they open every ball together. Not only did it prevent Lady Catherine from insisting he open with Anne—much to the woman's chagrin—but Georgiana, who was in her first season, avoided showing similar favor to any of the young men on the hunt for a young lady of fortune. On that night, however, Georgiana seemed to have a different agenda.

"I can hardly believe Jane and Elizabeth have been with us for almost two months, William. Do you not agree they have provided life to our party this year?"

"Yes, I suppose you are correct," said Darcy. As Georgiana was speaking, Darcy was scanning the ballroom for Miss Elizabeth, though he could not see her. There had been some conversation between her and his mother, so it was possible there was some problem with her gown, or they had stopped to talk with some acquaintance or another.

"As I recall, you were not in favor of inviting them to London," continued Georgiana. "What do you say now, William? Was Mother's invitation not inspired?"

Darcy turned back to his sister. "What do you mean?"

Georgiana laughed. "I mean exactly what I have said. Their presence, especially Elizabeth's, has been a blessing in so many ways. I could not have wished for the support of better friends in my first season."

"I had not realized you had become so close to them," murmured Darcy, wondering at the significance of his sister's words.

"Then it appears you have paid little attention, Brother. In fact, I now count Elizabeth as one of my closest friends. Jane, too, though as she is much engaged with Mr. Bingley, I have not come to know her so well as Elizabeth."

As his sister continued to wax poetic on the subject of the Bennet sisters and how happy she was to have made their acquaintance, Darcy's eyes found Miss Bennet and Bingley where they stood together not far away in conversation. Though Darcy had watched them with the close attention the fox paid to the hare it was stalking, Darcy had seen nothing in the young lady's manners which indicated false feelings designed to capture a man of fortune. This had led Darcy to concede his suspicions of the lady had been unfounded. Given their intimacy, it was clear he had made the right choice to avoid aligning himself with Miss Bingley.

Miss Bingley was not happy about the situation, of course. While she paid every arrear of civility to Miss Bennet to her face, she disparaged the young woman as unsuitable whenever the opportunity presented itself. At first, Darcy was certain she had been attempting to induce him to support her, but afterward, it seemed to have become habit. Mrs. Hurst, by contrast, had accepted the inevitable and was now openly friendly with Miss Bennet. At present, Miss Bingley was watching her brother with some distaste, while she shot glances at Darcy, an invitation for him to approach her for the first dance. Darcy had little trouble rejecting the notion, for he had no interest in his friend's sister.

"Perhaps we should change our usual arrangements tonight."

The comment penetrated Darcy's thoughts, and he turned to Georgiana askance, only to follow her eyes to where Miss Elizabeth had appeared in the company of his mother. The attraction he had felt for her from the earliest moments of their acquaintance had increased tenfold by now, for she was divine in the pale-yellow ball gown his mother had purchased for her. Again, Darcy had not favored Lady Anne's decision to show them such favor as to purchase clothes for them, but he was forced to acknowledge the results were stunning.

"Do you not agree, William?"

"How do you mean?" asked Darcy with an absence of mind while he contemplated Miss Elizabeth's perfections.

"Why, that we dance with different partners to open the ball. I am certain there are many willing men who will open the ball with me, and if I am escorted by some other man, you would be free to dance with Elizabeth."

The suggestion prompted Darcy to turn to his sister, wondering what she meant by such a suggestion. "You wish to dance with someone else?"

"I might have thought *you* would wish to dance with someone else," said Georgiana, her chin jutting out in Miss Elizabeth's direction.

"You cannot avoid dancing the first, and if I do not dance with you, those dances may be taken by a man you would as soon not favor."

"Oh, do not concern yourself for me," said Georgiana. "Elizabeth has helped me gain so much confidence, I am certain I shall be well. There, it is decided—I give you leave to dance with her, for I am certain that is what you want. You have scarcely removed your eyes from her since she and Mother entered."

There was something cheerful about Georgiana's words, something that rang false. Oh, there was nothing amiss with the sincerity of her friendship or esteem for Miss Elizabeth, for Darcy could see both were genuine and true. But this suggestion that he dance with Miss Elizabeth, seemed to be calculated for some other purpose than what she was saying. Given his mother's assertions concerning Miss Elizabeth, Darcy suspected her of pushing the young woman as a suitable partner, and perhaps more. The old defensiveness rose in Darcy's breast, and he disabused his sister of any notion he would open the ball with Miss Elizabeth.

"There is no need for that," said he, his words more clipped than he had intended. "We shall open the ball together, as we always do, for I have no desire to alter our agreement."

Georgiana frowned. "What if I wish it?"

"Do you?" asked Darcy, directing a pointed look at his sister. "Is there some young man who has caught your eye?"

"Of course not," said Georgiana, a hint of annoyance making itself known. "To be honest, I thought *you* would."

"I have no desire to dance with another at present. Thus, we shall open together."

The way Georgiana looked at him, Darcy thought she was not quite willing to believe him, but Darcy did not care to further speak on the subject. Thus, when the music began, Darcy grasped his sister's hand and led her to the floor, leaving no opportunity for her to protest. Georgiana came willingly, for it seemed her words about having no one else she wished to dance with were nothing but the truth. That begged the question of what her purpose had been—it would take a fool to misunderstand—but Darcy did not wish to consider it, so exercised his well known stubbornness and turned his mind to other matters.

"Look, there is Jane dancing with Mr. Bingley."

Darcy allowed his gaze to wander to his friend, and he noted Miss Bennet's smile in response to something Bingley said. Though Darcy was still of the opinion that Miss Bennet smiled too much, there was now no choice other than to acknowledge Miss Bennet's affections for his friend were nothing less than genuine. When his sister voiced her opinion of their future felicity, Darcy grunted in agreement.

Then he saw it. Near to her sister, just to one side, Miss Elizabeth was also dancing the first, and with a man who Darcy counted as a friend. While Darcy might have thought nothing of Miss Elizabeth dancing with Tidwell, for he was a good man and a good friend, as Darcy caught sight of her, she laughed at something he said, her countenance bright and her eyes sparkling as they always did when her mirth was released.

A wave of jealousy swept through Darcy. The glare he directed at his friend might have frozen him into a block of ice. But Tidwell's focus was on Miss Elizabeth and he did not notice, which was likely for the best. For the rest of the dance, Darcy could not pull his eyes away from Miss Elizabeth. Georgiana continued to chatter about some matter or another, but Darcy heard nothing of it. When the dance concluded, Darcy considered marching to Miss Elizabeth and demanding a dance.

What held him back was the sight of Miss Elizabeth standing with her sister and Bingley and the thought of the fool he would make of himself if he took such an action. Discretion, however, while it might be the better part of valor, had its own price. For while Darcy was standing by the side of the dance floor fuming, wondering why he should feel so angry, a most unwelcome companion joined him.

"I see you are beginning to understand the truth, Mr. Darcy."

"You have my apologies, Miss Bingley, for I have no notion of what you speak."

"Why, the Bennet sisters."

Darcy darted a look at Miss Bingley, noting her customary sneer, the way she glared at the two women of whom she spoke. Knowing of her distaste for anyone she considered lower than herself in society — whether warranted or not — Darcy attempted to ignore her. Not that she received his message he did not wish to speak to her. Then again, she never did.

"It is unfortunate you did not support my efforts to separate my brother from Miss Bennet," said Miss Bingley, "for it makes it much more difficult now. It still may be accomplished, but if we do not act soon, it will all be for not."

A pause ensued, in which she waited for him to speak and agree with her. That Darcy did not reply seemed to cause her little grief, for she continued as if he agreed with every word she said.

"It is also unfortunate that your mother found herself so imposed upon for an invitation to London. That, I suppose, is the one event which led to Miss Bennet's continued proximity to my brother and the subsequent deepening of his infatuation. Of course, I would never presume to cast blame upon your mother."

"Miss Bingley," said Darcy, what little patience he had for this woman fraying to the point of breaking, "unless my recollection of the event is faulty, the Bennet sisters used no improper means to intrude upon my family party—my mother invited them of her own volition and without hesitation."

Miss Bingley sniffed with her usual disdain. "As I was not attending the conversation between them, I cannot say."

"*I* was," said Darcy, knowing she was dissembling. "And even if they made the attempt, do you not think my mother possesses the ability to reject such stratagems?"

"In this instance, I must suppose she did not," snapped Miss Bingley, her deference giving way to her frustration.

"Then you suppose incorrectly," said Darcy, his tone short. "Though I cannot say why, my mother invited them and, I suspect, went to Longbourn that day intending to do so. There was no *imposition* on the part of the Bennets. Furthermore, my mother *and* my sister hold the Bennet sisters in the highest of esteem and claim them as the most intimate of friends. I do not feel likewise—this I will own. But to speak of my mother in such a manner diminishes her. Please desist."

It was no less than obvious Miss Bingley would like nothing better than to continue to protest, but the woman swallowed her bile. "I offer my apologies, Mr. Darcy, for I had no intention of casting shade on your excellent mother or insinuating she is not capable of avoiding those undesirable elements of society."

Darcy ignored the insinuation of the Bennet sisters comprising those elements. Any hope that Miss Bingley would cease speaking was dashed when she shifted her line of attack.

"Be that as it may, I will not have Jane Bennet as a sister. We can separate them, but as I said before, I must have your support to succeed."

"And you shall not have it," was Darcy's short reply. Then he turned to her and said in a voice which stated his feelings without the possibility of misinterpretation: "There is nothing anyone could say which would induce me to interfere in your brother's affairs. He is his own man. Only a simpleton could fail to see how much affection has grown between them—yes, on Miss Bennet's side as well. You may do as you please, but I shall not attempt to persuade him, not when I believe it is doomed to failure."

With a short bow, Darcy moved away before she could hint at her desire to dance with him. The conversation had unsettled him, and Darcy cast about for a way to put Miss Bingley and her words behind him. Miss Elizabeth, it seemed, had gathered another partner to her for the next dance, and while Darcy tried to tell himself he did not care, he found it difficult to stop glaring at this man. In time, resentment began to build in his breast for the way this woman had captured his attention and refused to let it go.

Thus, when he was looking about, desperately seeking some means of distraction, he caught sight of another. And though it was foolhardy, he thought she just might suffice.

For the first time she could remember, Anne de Bourgh found herself enjoying a ball. There were many factors contributing to her evening, she supposed, one of which was that her mother, recognizing Darcy would dance the first with his sister, had not insisted she dance with him, though it was only a matter of time before she would. Another was Anne's steady stream of dance partners. Never one to take pleasure in a ball, Anne found that evening was an exception, and while not all of her partners were agreeable, watching Miss Elizabeth had allowed Anne a hint of insight as to how one may lose themselves in the demands of the moment.

The third reason was the behavior of her other cousin, Colonel Fitzwilliam. Though Fitzwilliam—Anthony, as she had usually called him—had always been a man difficult for her to understand, that evening he was no less than charming. The why of it she could not be certain, for Anthony had always been a man who, it seemed to Anne, enjoyed his diversions. This, coupled with a tendency toward a casual outlook toward life, rendered him the more exasperating cousin, one who could be great fun when he was not being utterly infuriating.

Tonight, however, Anthony charmed, rather than annoyed, speaking to her with clear fondness, something in his tone and manner which spoke to different intentions from his usual teasing. And Anne enjoyed herself more than she might have thought possible. Then she was interrupted, much to her surprise.

"Cousin," intoned Darcy as he stepped close. "Might I have this dance?"

Anne regarded him with astonishment. "You wish to dance with me?" Anne reflected on how pleased she was her voice was as steady as it was.

"Yes," was his short reply.

Given his tone of voice, Anne might have thought him discussing crop rotation with a neighbor rather than asking a young lady to dance. In the past, though Anne had suspected he was on the verge of giving into her mother's continuous demands, he had never danced with her, except under her mother's duress. That he had done so that evening was surprising, and Anne could not understand why. His tone did not suggest he *wished* to dance with her, neither did she think he wished to complete his duty to her before her mother could return and demand it of him.

Thus, when he led her to the dance floor—she had given him her assent, as to do otherwise would curtail her enjoyment of the evening—Anne attempted to discover his reason for approaching her.

"I must own to surprise, Cousin," said Anne after almost half the dance had passed without a single syllable spilling from his lips. "The last time you danced willingly with me is an occasion I cannot recollect."

"You are mistaken," was his short reply. "Have I not always danced with you when we have attended the same ball?"

"Yes, you have," replied Anne. "But always after my mother insisted, leaving you no choice. Yet tonight you have approached me with my mother absent from the room." Anne paused and fixed him with a smirk. "Do you not know that if she does not return until after the dance has ended, she will force us into another?"

"You are mistaken," replied Darcy, his tone and manner defensive.

"If I am, then I do not know how," Anne shot back, all mirth replaced with annoyance.

Darcy did not respond, but his feelings were a match for hers if the clenching of his jaw was any indication. By now certain there was some other reason for his sudden departure from his usual ways, Anne was determined to discover it. And the only way it would be possible, she knew, was to confront him with it.

"You and I both know this application is unlike you," said Anne. "I wish to know what you are about, Cousin."

"It is nothing."

"It is *not* nothing," growled Anne.

Though it took some doing, by the end of the dance, she had pulled from her cousin's unwilling lips his discussion with Miss Bingley. The bit about Miss Bingley's continual insistence on rising above her station Anne dismissed without another thought—it was nothing more than Darcy's usual annoyance with the woman. The business about Lady Anne inviting the Bennet sisters, however, revealed something more than Anne thought Darcy wished. It spoke to possibilities she had never considered. While Anne did not know precisely what to think at that moment, she pushed the thoughts to the side to concentrate on the infuriating man with whom she danced.

"I do not appreciate being used as an outlet for your annoyance with Miss Bingley, Cousin."

"Why do you suppose I am doing so?" was his sullen query.

"There is no other explanation, given your aversion to dancing with me under normal circumstances. I know you have never been eager to marry me on my mother's command, but I would remind you I am a woman with a woman's feelings."

"I have never thought you anything else," replied Darcy.

"Then I trust you will not ask for a dance again under such circumstances."

Darcy's grunt was enough confirmation.

"Then I expect you to weather mother's demand we dance if she has not witnessed us standing up together, for if you request another set, I shall refuse you, notwithstanding the effect it will have on the rest of my evening."

Though she thought Darcy wished to say something further, in the end, he only favored her with a curt nod. When the dance ended, Darcy escorted her to the side of the room, bowed, and walked away. It was fortunate he offered no other comment, for Anne did not know how she might have responded.

It did not miss Elizabeth's attention that Anne and Mr. Darcy had exchanged words on the dance floor that evening. However, it completely escaped Lady Catherine's attention, for while she had noticed them, disharmony was far from her mind.

"What a charming couple you make," said the lady as soon as she could reach her daughter. "I am certain this is a presage of greater events to follow, for Darcy cannot resist you. Of course, I knew how it would be, for you are so wonderfully matched in fortune, connections, and temperament, there was no other result possible!"

While the lady continued to speak in such a manner at great length, it was clear to Elizabeth's eyes that Anne, though she did not reply, was not of the same opinion. Anne's manner was serenity itself, eschewing any response to Lady Catherine's crowing. Given what she was seeing about her, Elizabeth thought the other dancers were well aware of the lady's wishes, and not at all as confident as she was to the outcome. It was not until later that Elizabeth learned her daughter, for one, was of a much different opinion.

"What fun this evening has been!" exclaimed Anne after two more sets had passed, in which she had danced both, and seemed to enjoy herself without reservation. "I cannot remember a night I have enjoyed so much."

Elizabeth cast a wary eye about the room, wondering what Anne's mother would see in her daughter's emphatic declaration, but Lady Catherine was on the other side of the room speaking with some acquaintance. Confident she would not make a scene at present, Elizabeth turned back to her friend.

"You usually dance at these events, do you not?"

"I do, Elizabeth," replied Anne. "But I find that I feel freer than I ever have before, and it has resulted in my enjoyment being increased."

"Oh?" asked Elizabeth. "And what has caused such an alteration?"

Anne turned and directed a pleased look at Elizabeth. "Because, I have decided once and for all that I will not marry my cousin, despite what mother might say. I should have resolved to decide my own future many years ago, for if I had, I know I would have been happier."

"Has some other man caught your eye?"

It was subtle, not more than a glance to another side of the room, but Elizabeth saw it nonetheless, though it was not clear to whom Anne had directed that glance. "No," said Anne, denying the evidence Elizabeth had already witnessed, "but I know for a fact that Darcy and I would not suit. My mother will bluster and demand, but should Darcy ever attempt to offer for me — and I am convinced he will not — he will receive my refusal."

The way Anne regarded her, Elizabeth wondered if she expected some reaction or another from Elizabeth, but at that moment the subject of their discussion approached and bowed to them both. Elizabeth curtseyed in return, but she noted that Anne's was rather careless.

"Might I ask for your next dance, Miss Elizabeth?"

After their last dance, Elizabeth wondered if it might be better to refuse him. But there was no good reason to do so, which prompted her to give her assent. Anne seemed amused, for she gave Elizabeth a smirk and excused herself. If Anne had thought to leave them so they could speak in privacy, however, she was mistaken, for the few moments in which Elizabeth stood with Mr. Darcy, he did not utter a word.

The dance seemed to Elizabeth to proceed as Anne's had. Why Mr. Darcy requested her hand was a mystery she could not fathom, for he did not seem to take any pleasure in her company, instead dancing in silence, looking for all the world like he little wished to be there. It was, in some ways, a disappointment for Elizabeth, for she had begun to think better of him than she had in Hertfordshire. Moreover, the dance was not at all like the one at the Netherfield ball, for then he had regarded her in earnest contemplation, not at all like the feel of annoyance which hovered about him now. The memory of that dance welled up within her, and Elizabeth felt a hint of mischievous amusement.

"Well, Mr. Darcy," said she, peering at him, feeling the corners of her mouth rise along with her amusement, "it seems we are doing no better now than we did the last time we danced together."

The gentleman fixed her with a frown. "To what do you refer?"

"Why, that we have become no better at conversing while dancing than we were then. I still maintain it is odd for two people to spend an entire half hour together and yet remain as silent as the grave."

Mr. Darcy's gaze bored into her, sending the corners of her mouth down in response. "Why should it be odd?" demanded he. "By my account, half of those around us have not spoken two words to each other."

Resisting the instinct to glance about, Elizabeth regarded him, uncertain whether she should take offense to his tone. "Perhaps some of them have not. But we are well acquainted by now, are we not? Surely we can find something of which to speak which will interest us both."

A snort was Mr. Darcy's response, followed by an acerbic: "Ah, yes—I remember your penchant for saying something which will be handed down to posterity with all the éclat of a proverb." Mr. Darcy's growl was even more unpleasant. "Perhaps, however, there are those who do not consider rattling away to be the mark of good manners."

Elizabeth gasped at the rudeness of his words. "So, you believe I am nothing but a vapid female, continually speaking of matters of which I know nothing for no other reason than the love of my own voice?"

"*You* said it, Miss Bennet—not I."

Fury churned in Elizabeth's stomach as she considered what this poor excuse for a gentleman had just said to her. "It seems, Mr. Darcy, that you have developed the habit of insulting me in a ballroom. While I might have thought you would know me well enough to know that I am not some mindless chit babbling about anything and everything, it seems I was mistaken. Then again, it does not seem to me you have ever taken the time to know me."

With an imperious glare, Elizabeth turned and stalked away from the gentleman in high dudgeon. The music had just come to a stop, which prevented Elizabeth from making a scene. However, not allowing him to escort her to the side of the floor was still bound to attract attention and cause whispers among those present. Elizabeth caught sight of Miss Bingley, watching her, glee flowing from her sardonic grin in waves. But Elizabeth ignored the woman, as she ignored everyone else who regarded her, looks ranging from curious to contemptuous.

Perhaps it was best not to attempt any further sketch of Mr. Darcy's character, for the man was ever-changing. At the very least, Elizabeth did not intend to ever allow him the opportunity to insult her in a ballroom again!

CHAPTER XII

৵৵৵৵

W hether there was something in her face or manners, or whether Lady Anne had noticed the nonexistent greeting Elizabeth had given her son the following morning, it was clear the lady knew something had happened. Elizabeth could not call Lady Anne forthright—that appellation more correctly belonged to her sister—but she was also not one to allow matters to fester. Thus, some time after breakfast the following morning, she found Elizabeth in the library, trying—and failing—to read. Upon spying her, Lady Anne closed the door behind her and approached, sitting near Elizabeth and fixing her with a look which spoke to her determination to obtain answers to her questions.

"Though I have often noted your forced cordial manners with my son," said the lady without preamble, "it has seemed to me you were warming to him. And yet, this morning your greetings were as cold as I have ever seen."

Elizabeth snorted with some disdain. "Was there a greeting in our interaction this morning?"

It was a rhetorical question, and one Lady Anne seemed to understand did not demand a response. "Exactly," said she, concentrating on her statement rather than Elizabeth's reply. "If I have learned one thing about you, Elizabeth, it is that you do not become spiteful on a whim. Did something happen between you and William last night?"

By now Elizabeth knew this woman would not take her son's side regardless of where the fault lay. However, it was not Elizabeth's wish to speak ill of her family even knowing that. Therefore, she attempted to obfuscate.

"Not every disagreement is one which should be dissected, Lady Anne."

"But there *was* a disagreement between you," said Lady Anne, fixing on that one word.

"There was," said Elizabeth with a sigh. "Despite that, I have little desire to speak of it, and less to enumerate your son's faults as I see them."

It was Lady Anne's turn to laugh. "You say that as if you think I am not aware of his faults." Lady Anne raised her hand and began ticking the points off on her fingers. "Fitzwilliam is taciturn, thinks entirely too well of himself, can be harsh when he puts his mind to it, and possesses a distressful habit of forcing his foot into his mouth. There, have I left anything out?"

Elizabeth could not help the laugh escaping her lips, though she did her best to stifle it. Then she directed a mock glare at the other woman. "I should not dare attempt to add to that prodigious list, Lady Anne. I will, however, say that he is also handsome, seems firm in his friendships, is very intelligent when one can slip past his defenses, and is a conscientious man, not only in his care of you and Georgiana but in the management of his duties. Would that I could say as much about my father!"

"There!" said Lady Anne with a grin. "Even given his insult— which is what I suspect happened last night—you are capable of seeing his good qualities. It is much more than many women would allow, and if they did, they would no doubt mention his position in society, connection to my brother's family, and great estate and wealth."

"Those are matters to consider," replied Elizabeth, "but I am not foolish enough to suppose happiness can be purchased."

"Which is one of the reasons I believe you are perfect for him." When Elizabeth frowned and opened her mouth, Lady Anne waved her off. "Yes, I know, Elizabeth. I have agreed not to push you in this matter, and I will keep my promise. More and more, however, my conviction of your suitability is turning to certainty. That you still can credit him with a measure of good regardless of his attempt to push you away only firms my opinion."

A thought which had been niggling at the back of Elizabeth's mind for some time worked its way to her conscious thought, and she asked: "And what of Anne?"

Lady Anne smiled and grasped Elizabeth's hand, squeezing it, showing her affection. "Not only are you perfect for him, but you are also perceptive. William would be required to work to keep up with you, should he ever succeed in winning your hand."

When Elizabeth glared at her hostess, Lady Anne chuckled and said: "Yes, Elizabeth, the thought of preventing William from marrying Anne is a part of my thinking."

"Do you think so little of your namesake?"

"No, Anne is a good girl," replied Lady Anne. "What she is not, however, is lively. Should a reticent man such as my son pair himself with a woman his equal in quietude, I doubt they would exchange more than two words a day. William *would* gain Rosings in the bargain, and his wealth and power would grow accordingly, but unlike my sister, I have always thought there is more to happiness in life than great wealth.

"I have always loved Anne, for in some ways she reminds me of myself. But I would wish more in marriage for my son *and* for my niece. Should William choose another, Anne would be free to search for a man who would suit her." Lady Anne's eyes twinkled. "In fact, I believe she has already found such a man, and it is not her cousin."

The amusement with which Lady Anne stated her belief suggested there was some joke inherent in her words, but Elizabeth was too busy considering her own situation to give it much heed. Lady Anne had already given her word not to interfere, reinforced with what she had said today. But good intentions were sometimes superseded by other considerations, especially, the desire to see a beloved son happy in life.

Before Elizabeth could voice this concern, however, the lady continued. "Georgiana and I have enjoyed your presence here, Elizabeth, along with that of your sister. I would have invited you to stay with us, even if I had not thought you the perfect woman for my son. However, I hope you understand I would have said nothing, made no attempt to push you together if I thought you did not suit."

"I understand and appreciate that," replied Elizabeth. The lady's words, her obvious affection for Mr. Darcy, spoke to the truth of this assertion.

"Now, will you not share with me what happened between you last night? Trust me—my constitution is hearty enough to withstand whatever misbehavior in which my son engaged."

While Elizabeth did not wish to speak, something about this woman's request, firm yet not intrusive, induced her to explain. By the time she had finished her recitation, Lady Anne was shaking her head in exasperation, though not at Elizabeth.

"It seems my son has a way of insulting you far beyond any behavior I might have expected of him. It is a wonder you have not yet informed him exactly what you think of him in language which cannot be misunderstood— it is equally shocking you still think of him as anything other than a highborn lout!"

The words set off a chain of thoughts in Elizabeth's mind, leading her to wonder at her feelings for the man who had now insulted her in two ballrooms. From the moment of his first slight, Mr. Darcy had impressed Elizabeth as a proud and disagreeable man, but something had always drawn her back to him. Whether it was their sparring or her wish to humble him she did not know, but she was not usually given to extending a second chance to someone who had impressed her as unworthy of her notice.

Mr. Darcy, however, had seemed to become something of a different man since her arrival in London, and Elizabeth had found herself responding to him in some manner beyond her ability to understand. Even this latest slight had not, beyond the initial flame of anger, caused her to dislike him any more than she already had. Any other man would have been beneath her notice after such poor manners. Then why was Mr. Darcy any different?

"Perhaps I should speak to my son," said Lady Anne, pulling Elizabeth's attention back to her.

"I wish you would not," said Elizabeth, not eager for Mr. Darcy to learn of her discussion with his mother.

Lady Anne peered at Elizabeth for a moment before she nodded slowly. "Yes, I can see why you would not wish it." She paused and grinned. "I promised I would not push you together, Elizabeth; I did not promise not to take my son to task when he is misbehaving."

When Elizabeth made to protest further, Lady Anne laughed and patted her hand. "Do not concern yourself, for I shall keep my own counsel. However, I would urge you, Elizabeth, to speak to him should the opportunity arise."

"Why would you have me do so?" asked Elizabeth, feeling more than a little uncomfortable.

"Because, my dear," said Lady Anne, rising to her feet, "no one should tolerate such boorishness, whether in my son or the Prince

Regent himself. Unless I am very much mistaken, you did not take him to task over his remarks at your first meeting, did you?"

Elizabeth shook her head.

"I understand why you would avoid the subject. But maybe you should have confronted him. If you had, it would have been clear to him you would not put up with it. William should not need that reminder to behave himself, but it seems he does."

With a smile, Lady Anne excused herself, leaving Elizabeth to consider what she had said. As she sat pondering the matter, a conviction came over her that Lady Anne was correct. Should the opportunity arise, Elizabeth was determined to ensure Mr. Darcy knew she would not allow him to treat her in such an infamous manner.

Being out of sorts was not a feeling Darcy relished. Sitting in his study, avoiding contact with anyone else in the house—Miss Elizabeth in particular—Darcy knew without any doubt that he had not behaved as he ought the previous evening. In his defense, the woman upset his equilibrium, left him twisting in the wind uncertain of what to do or how to act. That was not an excuse, to be certain—or, at least, it was not a *valid* excuse. Feeling unequal to being in her company—or, heaven forbid, apologizing—Darcy remained in his study with naught but his own ruminations for company.

That changed with his cousin's arrival.

"Good morning, Darcy," said Fitzwilliam as he stepped into the room and sat in one of the pair of chairs facing Darcy's desk. Fitzwilliam's lack of anything other than a distracted greeting and his pensive mien differed from his usual behavior when he would give a hearty greeting, help himself to a glass of Darcy's brandy, and rest his booted feet on the edge of Darcy's desk. For that matter, Fitzwilliam was not dressed in his regimentals that morning, which was odd, as Darcy had not thought his cousin was on leave from the regiment.

"To what do I owe the dubious pleasure of your presence?" asked Darcy, attempting to spark a hint of the man he knew through his jest.

Even then, Fitzwilliam gave him nothing more than a distracted grin. "Need I have a reason to visit my favorite cousin?"

"A reason, no. However, when you come into my room with much less than your usual joviality, I must own to confusion. I have rarely found you this introspective."

It seemed Fitzwilliam had not realized his demeanor was any different than usual, for he started in surprise. A moment later, however, a rueful grin came over his countenance.

"Have you not longed for this sort of behavior?"

Darcy could not help but laugh. "I suppose there has been a time or two when you have been an annoyance."

Rather than prompting the return to his usual insouciance, however, the brief banter faded away with Fitzwilliam assuming a more serious demeanor. "I suppose I have been distracted, Cousin, but I believe it is with a good reason."

"Oh, and what reason would that be?"

"What are your intentions regarding our cousin?" asked Fitzwilliam instead of answering.

Darcy was shocked. "Our cousin?" asked he, unable to fathom Fitzwilliam's question.

"Anne," clarified Fitzwilliam. "You know, the cousin our Aunt Catherine continually insists you marry?"

"Yes, I am acquainted with her," said Darcy, coming to his senses, but still curious as to Fitzwilliam's meaning. "What of her?"

"I thought my words were plain enough," replied Fitzwilliam. "In case, however, your wits have deserted you, let me elucidate: Anne, the daughter of your mother's sister, the woman your aunt has insisted you marry for almost as long as any of us can remember. For years, you have avoided speaking of the matter with Lady Catherine, never giving her encouragement, yet never denying your interest. The rest of the family has, of late, thought you were beginning to consider offering for Anne, though you are damnably difficult to read."

"You wish to know if I mean to offer for her," said Darcy, taking care to enunciate his words so he understood.

"I do," confirmed Fitzwilliam.

"Why?" asked Darcy.

"Does it matter?" rejoined Fitzwilliam.

"It does," averred Darcy. "As you have stated, I have not given Lady Catherine encouragement, nor have I warned her off, but at the same time, no one in the family has ever asked me concerning my intentions. There are only a few reasons you would bring this up now, and I would know which of my suppositions is true."

"Can you not just answer the question?" demanded Fitzwilliam, his annoyance rising.

"I might say the same, Cousin," said Darcy. "Why do you not inform me of the reason for your query?"

Fitzwilliam threw up his hands and leaned back in his chair, glaring at Darcy. "Very well," growled he after a moment. "As you have likely guessed, I am interested in paying court to Anne myself. However, if you are set on offering for her, I would never dream of stepping in where I am not wanted. Thus, I thought to ask you, to discover the truth once and for all."

"You wish to pay court to Anne?" asked Darcy, feeling the confusion well up within him.

"I do," snapped Fitzwilliam, his growl deepening. "Have you been so blinded by our aunt's ubiquitous soliloquies on the subject of your future that you have missed the fact that Anne has become a desirable young woman? Or have you decided that any woman will do as you lack interest in any of them?"

"Is that what you truly think of me?" asked Darcy, surprised and stung by the vehemence in his cousin's voice.

"I would if I did not know you better," said Fitzwilliam. "I *know* you are not heartless, Cousin, but at times you give the appearance of it."

Darcy was shocked anew, but his cousin's pointed glare was enough to inform him he could not sit back and refuse to give an answer. The problem was, he was not even certain of the answer himself. Though Darcy knew his mother's feelings on the subject of Lady Catherine's continued insistence he marry Anne, Darcy had never given much thought to it himself. The reason was simple, if not a flattering portrayal of his character: Darcy had looked on it with a certain level of fatalistic acceptance. It was not that his aunt's arguments moved him in any way, or the thought of her displeasure caused him to shrink. It was rather that his years in society had jaded him. Society teemed with young misses who saw him as nothing more than a pocketbook or a ticket to an easy life, and while there were many good and intelligent women among their number, many were insipid, could speak of nothing more than fashion or the latest gossip, and the behavior of many men, who married women they could not tolerate, solely for fortune or connections and then kept mistresses, repulsed him. Darcy found himself tired of such games and uncertain if he could find a woman who interested him. If there was no one with whom he felt he could connect on a deeper level, then did it matter whom he married? And if so, why not Anne? She was comely enough, and he had known her all of his life; there should be nothing standing in the way of their making a good life together. Rosings was a consideration, but not a large one, though the increase in wealth the estate would bring was, again, a factor.

As these thoughts ran through Darcy's mind, however, the sound of tinkling laughter replaced them, and a pair of bright, intelligent eyes looking back at him with amusement. Possibilities he had never allowed himself to consider clamored in his mind, refusing to be silent, forcing Darcy to ponder what he wanted. And what he wanted, he decided was not his cousin. No matter how much he respected and esteemed her, Darcy knew Anne was not the woman he wished to marry, no matter how much her dowry would enrich him. Had he not disdained such grasping for wealth all his adult life? Keeping Anne in suspense was unfair to her, as it was to allow Lady Catherine to forever hope for the union. Darcy now knew he wanted no part of it.

When Darcy was again at liberty to consider his cousin, it surprised him that Fitzwilliam had allowed him to contemplate the matter as long as he had, for Fitzwilliam was impatient for an answer. It was so unlike his cousin to be this tense, but Darcy could see Fitzwilliam waited with bated breath, desolation warring with hope. Darcy could not allow him to continue in this state — Fitzwilliam was his cousin and his dearest friend all in one. Fitzwilliam had always joked about how he needed to marry a woman with a substantial dowry; should he feel something for Anne, he would make a much better husband than Darcy.

"Given your manner of approaching me and your words concerning Anne," said Darcy, "can I suppose your wish to court Anne is based on something more than your oft-stated need to marry a woman with a handsome dowry?"

It seemed to Darcy that Fitzwilliam was on the verge of saying something caustic. But he maintained a hold on his temper, paused for a moment, considered the question, and then answered.

"I am not in love with Anne if that is what you are asking. In my defense, I have never considered her as a potential wife, given Lady Catherine's continued statements concerning which cousin she wishes Anne to marry. In the last weeks, however, I have begun to consider what I never have before, and I believe it is possible to achieve that level of regard for her."

"Then you should go to it, Cousin," said Darcy. "I have given the matter some thought of late, and I am convinced that Anne and I would not do well together. As I wish Anne every happiness, I have little compunction in stepping aside in your favor."

All at once the tension drained from the room. Fitzwilliam leaned back again in his chair, heaving a great sigh of relief, attempting his usual grin. It took no great insight to see it was forced.

"Given your behavior of late, I was uncertain of the response I would receive. I thank you, Cousin, not only for your assurances but also for seeing the truth of the matter."

"And what would that truth be?" asked Darcy.

"That you should not marry Anne," replied Fitzwilliam, his gaze pointed. "Most of the family have been skeptical for some time now, but none of us knew your opinion."

"I did not know my own opinion until you compelled me to think on it," confessed Darcy. "Now that I have, however, it is nothing less than obvious."

"As it should be."

A knock on the door interrupted the conversation, and when Darcy called permission, the butler opened the door, allowing Bingley to enter. It was clear his friend was in an ebullient mood, for he seemed like he was walking on a cloud, greeting them both with the cheer which had been Bingley's hallmark for as long as Darcy had known him.

"What brings you here, Bingley?" asked Fitzwilliam with a knowing grin. "I might have thought you would be in the sitting-room paying court to your lady."

"That would be my preference," agreed Bingley. "At present, however, she is unavailable, though I was informed she will receive me in half an hour. As I am forced to wait, I thought I would visit my good friend."

"You see, Darcy," said Fitzwilliam, gesturing to Bingley. "This could be you, should you only find a woman as suited to you as Bingley's is to him."

"It was my understanding that Darcy was to marry his cousin," said Bingley, throwing them both an interested look. "Has something changed?"

"Darcy, it seems, is blind to our Cousin Anne's charms," replied Fitzwilliam. "I have agreed to step into his place, for I will not be foolish and dismiss them."

Bingley laughed. "In fact, I agree with Darcy—I could never see him marrying your cousin. But I would not wish to be nearby when your aunt discovers this change of plans."

"I think we shall refrain from telling her for the moment," said Fitzwilliam.

"Given how she watches both her daughter and your cousin, I cannot imagine it will be a secret long."

"No," replied Fitzwilliam. "But perhaps she will become used to seeing us together. I shall provide many examples of my willingness to pay court to Cousin Anne, for she is an angel."

Bingley grinned at him. "I must think you daft, Fitzwilliam, for there is only one angel, and she is *mine*."

The two men began to debate the merits of their chosen ladies, their arms gesticulating to make their points, their claims growing wilder by the moment. Though their antics amused Darcy, there was somewhere he would rather be, and after a time of listening to their banter, he excused himself, not missing the looks exchanged by the other two. But Darcy said nothing, content to leave them to their amusement.

A quick query of the butler gave him the location of the woman he sought, and Darcy felt all the bemusement of learning she was in the library next to his study. Carefully, Darcy opened the door, looking in and noting her presence, sitting in a chair immersed in her book. For a moment, Darcy stood and watched her, noting her utter absorption in whatever she was reading, the way she nibbled on her lower lip, the light of intelligence in her eyes.

The danger of her noticing his scrutiny prompted him to move long before he might have wished, for he did not know how she would react to such knowledge. Miss Elizabeth looked up as he made to enter, the barest hint of a frown settling over her face as he stepped forward. The way she put down her book was deliberate, careful, as was the look she bestowed on him as he approached.

"Miss Elizabeth, I was wondering if I might have a word with you," said Darcy without preamble.

"Of course, Mr. Darcy," said she, the formality of her tone almost leading him to flinch. "How may I assist?"

"Assistance is not what I require," replied Darcy, favoring her with a faint smile. "Rather, I believe I owe you an apology for my behavior last night, and I wished to offer it without reservation."

Miss Elizabeth watched him for a moment, the hint of surprise playing about the narrowing of her eyes emphasizing to Darcy he had behaved poorly. Though he had already known it, the reminder was difficult.

"Thank you, Mr. Darcy," said Miss Elizabeth. "I appreciate your gesture."

"It is obvious to me that I have allowed my pique at matters completely unrelated to affect my behavior," said Darcy, knowing he was not being truthful, for Miss Elizabeth and his attempts to remain unaffected by her were at the root of his mood. "For that, I apologize and promise to amend my conduct, for you do not deserve my censure."

"Oh, so I am not a witless female speaking of matters of which I know nothing?" asked she, one eyebrow raised in an elegant arch. "Does this mean I am also worthy of being asked for a dance, or are you still concerned about my being slighted by other men?"

It was all Darcy could do to hold his countenance and avoid wincing. "You are right to ask me, Miss Elizabeth," said he. His mother had told him of her hearing those words but learning of it from her own lips made it strangely real. "I offer no excuses and apologize without reservation. I hope you will allow me to prove that I am not the man such behavior would paint me as being."

For a long moment, Miss Elizabeth seemed to consider this, and Darcy sat, dreading the manner her response would take. Years of being sought after by every matchmaking mama and their daughters had not prepared him for the possibility of rejection.

"I thank you for your apologies and accept them, Mr. Darcy. Let us begin anew."

Though Darcy still did not know what he wished from this woman, he felt as one saved from damnation. A bright smile lit his face, and he thanked her and began speaking of other subjects. In the back of his mind, he determined he would not allow himself to treat her in such an infamous manner again.

Chapter XIII

$\mathcal{M}$r. Darcy proved himself as good as his word. So much so that Elizabeth wondered why he had not shown himself to such advantage from the very beginning. The Mr. Darcy Elizabeth came to know during those days was perhaps not charming, as it was not a part of his character to charm a woman with the force of his personality, soft, yet deep voice, or even a flirtatious manner. But he was a lot more appealing than Elizabeth had ever given him credit for possessing when she had despised him in Hertfordshire.

As the days passed, they were not always together— Lady Catherine's behavior on seeing them so much as exchange a few words in passing rendered such continuous intercourse inadvisable. Elizabeth found, however, that the gentleman was much more open on the occasions he could be, more willing to sit and speak, and consequently, seemed much less judgmental than he had before.

Their conversations consisted of various subjects, for Elizabeth found no lack of suitable material for them to discuss. When Mr. Darcy gave his opinions, he gave them in a tone which suggested confidence but lacked arrogance. Furthermore, when she spoke, he was willing to listen, agree when her opinion aligned with his own, and argue his point with intelligence, but offered no condescension when they did not agree. This was not common to all men with whom Elizabeth had experience, as some were not hesitant to show they did not consider the opinion of a woman worth much. Not Mr. Darcy—when he thought she made a worthy point, he was quick to point it out, and her opinions, he allowed her, even when he disagreed.

What this new openness on the part of the gentleman might presage, Elizabeth could not say, for as ever, he was unreadable—often to a maddening degree. It may be nothing more than his realization he had misbehaved and was now attempting to correct his error.

Such thoughts, however, were put in doubt by the recollection of Elizabeth's discussions with Lady Anne and the lady's assertion of Elizabeth's compatibility with her son. Though Elizabeth would not have given the notion any credence only a few weeks earlier, now she began to wonder. Was Mr. Darcy considering his mother's assertions and paying attention to her with the aim of determining for himself if he wished to make an offer? The very idea of it almost set Elizabeth to laughing, but further thought told her she could not dismiss the notion entirely.

There was something in his manner which Elizabeth could not interpret, something which suggested feelings to which she was not privy. Mr. Darcy was not like Mr. Bingley, whose feelings were open to anyone who cared to look. The gentleman's admiration for Jane was open, shining from his words, his countenance, from everything he did while in—or out of—her company. Mr. Darcy, by contrast, did not show admiration openly. But when he looked at her, his intensity, which she had taken for disapproval, suggested a similar, if muted, admiration of his own.

In the end, Elizabeth decided there was little she could do but accept him for whatever he was and deal with the consequences later. Having always agreed with Jane that nothing but love would induce her into marriage, Elizabeth knew she could not accept a proposal from this man if he chose to offer for her. But as time wore on, she wondered if her opinion was not changing.

After a week of this, Elizabeth became privy to a conversation between Mr. Darcy and his mother, one which she did not mean to overhear. The library in the house, she had discovered, was next to Mr. Darcy's study, a configuration mirrored by his study in Pemberley, he had informed her. It was useful, for if he needed to consult with a book in his library, it was ready at hand, which did not require him to keep a large selection of books in the room itself. That morning, Elizabeth had come to the library, looking for something to read, when she heard words floating out through the adjoining door, which had not been closed completely.

"Yes, Mother," Mr. Darcy was saying. "I apologized to Miss Elizabeth, and I believe you can see the result."

"It seemed to me that was so," replied Lady Anne. "I have seen how you often seek her out, though I will commend you for your forbearance when in Catherine's company."

"It would not do to send her screaming back to Hertfordshire," replied Mr. Darcy, his tone rather dry.

Lady Anne's tinkling laughter spilled through the cracked door. "Surely you do not think Elizabeth so weak as to flee from the dragon."

"No, she is not. But it seems to me better to avoid it regardless."

"That it is."

A pause ensued, in which Elizabeth could well imagine Lady Anne considering her words. An awful feeling welled up in Elizabeth's breast, as she wondered what the lady might do to promote her as a bride for her son.

"I am happy you are on better terms, William. The lady is highly favored, in my estimation, as I am certain you well know."

"Is this where you now promote her to me as a suitable bride?" asked Mr. Darcy, the humor in his voice clear to where Elizabeth stood.

"No, William, I will not push you." Elizabeth could not help but breathe a sigh of relief. "Not only have I given Elizabeth my word I will not interfere, but I know of your contrary nature. You are apt to do the opposite of what I say, simply to prove you can."

"I do not think I am quite so obstinate, Mother."

It was at this point Elizabeth decided discretion was the better part of valor and retreated to the far side of the room, and from thence out the door. When she had reached the hall outside the library, she swiftly made her way toward the stairs in order to return to her room. There was nothing she wished less than for Mr. Darcy and his mother to learn she had overheard their conversation.

One consequence of Mr. Darcy's burgeoning friendship with Elizabeth was the deterioration of Miss Bingley's behavior. It seemed to Elizabeth that the woman's objections to her brother's courtship with Jane were growing weaker by the day. In time, she had all but ceased paying any heed to that situation, and for that Elizabeth had to give the woman credit. This capitulation, however, made things more difficult for Elizabeth, for Miss Bingley began to focus everything on Mr. Darcy.

"I can see what you mean about Miss Bingley," said Jane one evening.

That day had been particularly difficult for Elizabeth, as Miss Bingley had all but invited herself on an outing to Bond Street. While the woman was not so lost to propriety that she would disparage Elizabeth to all and sundry, that did not mean she did not insult with little demeaning comments designed to prick Elizabeth's confidence, nor did she cease to state her distaste for Elizabeth to Mr. Darcy.

"What, in particular?" asked Elizabeth, though she knew very well to what Jane referred

"Do not tease me, Lizzy," said Jane, understanding Elizabeth's ways as well as she did herself. "I know you sometimes think me naïve for looking for the best in others, but that does not mean I am blind. While I will own my appreciation that Miss Bingley has ceased her objections to *me*, I can see her continued attempts to attract Mr. Darcy's attention."

"Miss Bingley, it seems, has always wished to be mistress of Pemberley," replied Elizabeth with a sigh.

"And she sees you as a threat," replied Jane. "Even more so than Anne."

Elizabeth flashed Jane a wry grin. "Everyone but Lady Catherine can see a cooling of whatever existed between Anne and Mr. Darcy — I cannot think Miss Bingley has not seen it herself."

"But you must own his attentions to you have risen to fill the void."

"I cannot dispute that," replied Elizabeth, "but I still do not know what they signify."

Jane fixed Elizabeth with a look she might have expected to see from her mother. "Do you not?"

"Come now, Jane," replied Elizabeth, "*I* am accounted the observant one, and I cannot see anything in Mr. Darcy's manners which suggest admiration. His actions *imply* he admires me, but that is not enough to convince me when nothing in his demeanor confirms it."

It seemed Elizabeth had made a point Jane could not dispute, for she was silent for a moment, considering it. "I will grant you that Mr. Darcy's manners are not in any way similar to Mr. Bingley's." Jane paused, her cheeks pinking, as they often did when the gentleman was mentioned. "But there is something in him which I cannot find anything but pleasing, for his attentiveness to you is beyond what I might deem polite."

"I suppose you are correct," replied Elizabeth with a slow nod of her head. "But I will not consider him a suitor until such time as he makes his intentions known."

Once again Jane leveled a long look at Elizabeth. "Do you wish for his attentions?"

"At present, I hardly know," replied Elizabeth. "The gentleman *has* shown himself better than I might have imagined since we came to London, and even better in the past week. Is that enough to disarm my prior opinion of him? I cannot say."

"I would not have expected any other answer," said Jane, rising from the bed on which she sat. She bent over and kissed Elizabeth on the head and added: "But I urge you to keep an open mind to the possibility of the gentleman's admiration, Lizzy. Though I know you did not begin well with him, it is on my mind that Mr. Darcy is a more estimable gentleman than any of us gave him credit." Then Jane excused herself.

The conversation stayed with Elizabeth and, in part, provided the foundation for her behavior in the coming days. Even with Mr. Darcy's improved manners and her own ruminations on the subject, Elizabeth had never considered the possibility of his admiration likely. Jane's words, however, opened her eyes to the possibility, and even the likely interpretation of the situation. Elizabeth resolved to allow matters to develop and not to close her mind to anything.

The situation with Miss Bingley, however, continued to be vexing for Elizabeth, and unless she missed her guess, to Mr. Darcy as well. Lady Anne did not hide her disapproval for the woman's overt attempts to garner her son's attention, and Georgiana, it appeared, was no less annoyed. That they stayed silent was a relief to Elizabeth, for she did not doubt that Miss Bingley's private vitriol would grow in intensity and nastiness if she saw her chances slipping away. It was fortunate, therefore, the matter had come to a head only a few days earlier.

As spring was now in full flower, Elizabeth found herself drawn once more to the out of doors; the Darcy family lived close to Hyde Park, after all, and while it was not the wild paths of her father's estate, it more than sufficed during her sojourn in London. In this the family indulged her, one of whom almost always accompanied her on her walks, dispensing with the need for a footman to escort her. Of late, her companion was almost always Mr. Darcy.

"Perhaps we should walk together in Hyde Park," said Mr. Bingley on that day. The gentleman and his sister had arrived during visiting hours, Mr. Bingley to continue in his efforts to woo Jane, while the lady had her own wooing in mind.

"Oh, yes," said Miss Bingley, looking to Mr. Darcy with a clear hope he would invite her to walk. "It is such a lovely place, so excellently situated. The present hour is too early, of course, for anyone of any consequence will stroll the park at a later hour."

"That is a concern only if one wishes to be seen," said Elizabeth, tamping down on her amusement. "When I walk, I do so for the love of nature and for the exercise, not for some nebulous enjoyment of knowing someone will take note of me."

"Which is why you do not fit into this society," said Miss Bingley with an unpleasant sneer. "Country manners do not account for the need to socialize with one's equals in a higher setting. Then again, it is obvious to any making your acquaintance that you are not of their level, so I can see why you might wish to walk early and avoid the disgrace of being ignored."

Elizabeth, though she supposed she should be offended, was instead inclined to laughter, though she refrained with effort. As Miss Bingley knew Lady Anne did not appreciate her disparaging her guests, her comments were usually vaguer in nature, the more cutting ones delivered to Elizabeth's ears alone. For her to have been so open in her criticism showed her growing desperation.

"I do not care a jot for others' opinions," replied Elizabeth.

"As you should not," said Mr. Bingley, directing a glare at his sister.

"In my opinion," said Mr. Darcy, "this business of seeing and being seen by all and sundry shows nothing more than a narcissistic sort of pride and arrogance."

Those words silenced Miss Bingley far more effectively than anything Elizabeth or Mr. Bingley might have said. It did not stop Miss Bingley's fiery glare in Elizabeth's direction, but at least the woman did not attempt to denigrate her further.

In the end, the younger members of the company decided to walk out, including Jane and Mr. Bingley, Mr. Darcy, Georgiana, Miss Bingley, and Elizabeth. Lady Anne, though she peered at Miss Bingley with growing distaste—Miss Bingley affected ignorance—wished them a pleasant walk and announced her intention to speak with her housekeeper. A few moments later, the company had dressed in their outerwear and had left Darcy house to walk toward the park.

The initial composition of the party was exactly what Elizabeth might have expected. As there were two gentlemen and four ladies, each of the men escorted two women as they walked down the street toward the distant greenery. Jane was with Mr. Bingley, of course, and equally unsurprising, Miss Bingley had latched onto Mr. Darcy's arm with the strength of a hawk capturing its prey. Georgiana frowned at Miss Bingley and seemed to be working her way to some caustic comment. Elizabeth, eager to maintain the peace, smiled at her and accepted Mr. Bingley's other arm, allowing Georgiana to accept her brother's escort. Elizabeth did not miss the expression of cruel triumph with which Miss Bingley regarded her, but she also did not misunderstand Mr. Darcy's clear annoyance.

When they arrived in the park, they stayed that way for some time, though Elizabeth released Mr. Bingley's arm to enjoy the meandering path on her own. It was a lovely day, the sun warming them as they walked, accompanied by birds chirping and the murmur of the stream in the distance. It was almost as good as walking the paths of her father's estate.

After a time of this, however, Elizabeth noted Georgiana attracting Miss Bingley's attention to her, and raised her hand to her lips to stifle a laugh at the girl's blatant attempts to distract the woman away from her brother. Miss Bingley, seeming pleased and flattered, allowed Georgiana to lead her away, after which Mr. Darcy was not slow in approaching Elizabeth. Jane and Mr. Bingley had already walked on ahead.

"It seems to me you are in your natural state, Miss Elizabeth," said Mr. Darcy, his voice betraying some hint of emotion to Elizabeth, who was in the act of raising her face to the heat of the sun, her eyes closed in pleasure.

"Do you think me some wood nymph, Mr. Darcy?" asked Elizabeth, turning to smile at him.

"No, Miss Elizabeth," replied he. "Though it is clear you are at home in the woods and fields, with every hint of the allure those mythical women possess, I do not consider you anything less than human."

This was the first thing Mr. Darcy had ever said which seemed to reveal his admiration, and Elizabeth regarded him for a moment. "I am at home in the woods and fields," said Elizabeth at length. "As you are aware, I can rightly claim to be an excellent walker, for it is one of my favorite pastimes."

"Though I am almost afraid to ask, does Hyde Park suffice?"

Elizabeth laughed and waved a finger at him. "You accuse me of thinking ill of this wonderful bit of nature amid all this humanity? What utter contempt you must hold for me!"

"Never that, Miss Elizabeth."

"Then I shall inform you," said Elizabeth, still grinning, "that Hyde Park *is* wonderful, but it is not my home. At Longbourn I can walk for many miles in fields and woods, across streams and by ponds, and experience nothing but the wonder of nature. Hyde Park, though marvelous, is not the equal of the country."

"I am much fonder of the country myself," said Mr. Darcy. "Perhaps . . ."

The gentleman paused, seemed to consider the matter for a moment, and Elizabeth was certain there was an air of embarrassment about him.

"In the future," said he at length, "it is possible my mother might invite you to Pemberley. If she does, I dare say you will find much to appreciate, for there are enough paths on the estate to satisfy even your prodigious thirst for nature."

"Will you tell me about it?" asked Elizabeth, curious to learn what she could about his home.

They continued to walk, Mr. Darcy sharing his recollections Pemberley, his love for it shining through every word, every distant gaze, as if he was seeing it in his mind's eye. As he spoke, Elizabeth began to understand Mr. Darcy a little better, gaining a higher insight into his character. He was tied to his estate with bond greater than her father possessed for Longbourn, and knowing he was a conscientious master, Elizabeth gained a greater respect for this quiet gentleman.

Such circumstances could not last, unfortunately, as it was not long before Miss Bingley became aware of Elizabeth's present position walking by Mr. Darcy's side. As this was a condition which she could not allow to persist—and Miss Bingley's glare at Georgiana suggested she understood how the girl had distracted her—she hurried to join them. Though Elizabeth might have been content to allow the woman to have her way and laugh at her ridiculous behavior, it was the application of her designs which brought the ire of them all down on her.

"Mr. Darcy," exclaimed the woman, her voice nearly a screech, "shall you not walk with me toward the Serpentine?"

As she said this, Miss Bingley hurried forward and inserted herself between Elizabeth and Mr. Darcy. While Elizabeth had not been holding the gentleman's arm, she had been walking close, and as Miss Bingley was taller than Elizabeth, she stumbled when the larger woman's frame impacted with her own.

"Have a care, Miss Bingley," said Mr. Darcy, stepping around her, while avoiding her talons reaching for his arm, as he attempted to steady Elizabeth.

"Oh, you need not worry about Miss Elizabeth," mocked Miss Bingley. "I dare say she receives worse than the brush I gave her from the swine among which she walks when traipsing about her home."

"At least the swine know how to behave themselves," snapped Elizabeth, her endurance for this woman reaching its breaking point.

The malevolent glare with which Miss Bingley regarded her accompanied the woman's opening of her mouth, no doubt to deliver some stinging retort. Her intention, however, was interrupted by the gentleman.

"Miss Bingley," said he, his own stern glare more than equaling hers, "I believe the time has come to clear whatever misunderstanding you might have harbored, so you may cease your assaults on Miss Elizabeth's person and character."

Eyes wide, Miss Bingley said: "I cannot imagine what you mean. I have not assaulted Miss Elizabeth—if she believes it of me, it is because of her own lack of understanding concerning the behavior of those of our level of society."

Mr. Darcy quirked an eyebrow at her mention of *their* level of society, and the sudden flush of her face suggested she did not misunderstand his unstated rebuke. To castigate her for her continued attempts to claim a higher level than was warranted would have been far too obvious, and Elizabeth thought useless. Thus, Mr. Darcy ignored her assertion.

"I do not think Miss Elizabeth can misunderstand anything you have said or done, Miss Bingley, and shouldering her aside is not the action of a gentlewoman. That you do it because of your designs makes it even more contemptible."

"Designs?" echoed Miss Bingley, feigning lack of understanding.

Mr. Darcy only glared at her with impatience. "Come, Miss Bingley—no one who has spent any time in your company can misunderstand your desire to be mistress of Pemberley. Do not insult my intelligence by thinking me witless."

"I could never imagine such a thing," replied Miss Bingley. The woman showed him a coy smile, the sight of her batting her eyelashes almost causing Elizabeth to burst into laughter.

"Then you will also believe me when I say there was never any possibility I would offer for you."

Had it not been so very pathetic, Elizabeth might have laughed when the woman's jaw fell open. Apparently, Georgiana, who had followed Miss Bingley to them, had no such compunction, for her giggle served to snap Miss Bingley's lips back together. The glare she fixed on Georgiana was like nothing Elizabeth had ever seen before for one of the Darcy family.

"Can you not see the benefits of offering for me?" said Miss Bingley, turning a sweet smile back on Mr. Darcy. "What more could you want in a wife?"

"I will not discuss my requirements in a wife with you, Miss Bingley," replied Mr. Darcy. "Suffice it to say that you are my dear friend's sister, and that is all I have ever thought of you. There is nothing which will induce me to offer for you, so you are wasting your time."

"As I have told you more than once," came the voice of Mr. Bingley. He and Jane, having noticed the rest of the party had stopped, were striding toward them, the gentleman's eyes fixed on his sister. "Now that Darcy has told you himself, will you now believe me?"

Miss Bingley's countenance was ablaze with affront. "Then do you mean to make Miss Elizabeth your wife?" She snorted in utter disdain. "I must commend your confidence, sir, for it will take much work to make her in any way presentable for society."

"I will not trade words except to warn you." Mr. Darcy's look seemed to challenge her to continue, a challenge Miss Bingley declined. "I know not what you think, Miss Bingley, but Miss Elizabeth and I are not engaged, nor are we even courting.

"Your comments about her suitability for society, however, make me wonder if you have been blinded these past weeks. The Bennet sisters have been welcome wherever they go, and before you say it is because of my mother's support, you should know that it is much more than my mother's approval. Thus, in answer to your question, I do not consider her unsuitable at all, not that it is any of your concern."

For a moment, Miss Bingley watched him, her gaze suggesting an attempt to determine how serious he was. The answer must not have been to her liking, for her expression turned forbidding.

"Then I hope you find your happiness with your countrified wife, Mr. Darcy," snapped she.

Then she turned and her heel and stalked off in high dudgeon, leaving them all watching her as she departed. Mr. Bingley shook his head and fixed Darcy with an amused grin.

"I suppose I should at least follow her to ensure she does not come to harm." Then he glanced at Elizabeth and patted Mr. Darcy's arm. "Though my sister will not appreciate the irony, perhaps we shall be brothers after all."

With the departure of Mr. Bingley and Jane, who turned to follow his sister—albeit at a more leisurely pace—Georgiana flashed a grin and followed them. Elizabeth, having finally obtained Mr. Darcy's open declaration of interest—or at least that he considered her appropriate—remained where she was, watching the gentleman as his attention turned to her. They remained in this attitude for several long moments.

"Am I to understand that I am not only handsome enough to tempt but that I am apposite to be considered for the position Miss Bingley is so desperate to hold?"

"I should hope you will forgive me for those intemperate words, Miss Elizabeth," replied Mr. Darcy.

"Oh, I already have," said she, feeling mischievous and elated all at once. "That does not mean I will allow you to forget them."

For the first time in their acquaintance, Elizabeth was treated to the sight of Mr. Darcy laughing with abandon. There had been a time when she might have thought he was not capable of it. Recent events had disproved that supposition.

"Of course, I would not dream of it," replied he when his mirth subsided to chuckles. He then turned a more serious look on her. "If I *were* to consider you an appropriate prospective bride, would you consider *me* a potential husband?"

"Perhaps," replied Elizabeth, not stopping to think. "But I should warn you, Mr. Darcy, that Jane and I have always determined to marry for love. With my elder sister's excellent example, you can hardly suppose I would foreswear myself now."

"Then we understand each other," said Mr. Darcy.

The gentleman offered his arm, which Elizabeth took, and turned them back toward the house, following the rest of their party. Though Elizabeth had just given Mr. Darcy far more encouragement than she had ever thought she might, she could not help but feel content with her decision. Perhaps there was something more to Mr. Darcy than even she had thought these past weeks. If nothing else, she was certain she would enjoy learning if she was correct.

CHAPTER XIV

*H*ow they kept their growing affection for each other from her mother, Anne de Bourgh would never know. Then again, Anne did not know whether this was growing affection or more of Anthony's insouciance. That he appeared more earnest than she could ever remember him being was a good sign, but it did not answer all her questions.

Not that her mother did not notice when Anthony was often in Anne's company. In fact, she commented on the matter more than once. But Anne had known for some time her mother possessed a curious blindness, one which induced her to see what she wished to see, to interpret events according to her own desires. Though Anne knew a confrontation was looming, she did not wish to provoke it before it became necessary.

"You are much in evidence of late, Fitzwilliam," said Lady Catherine on one of these occasions. "Have you no duties to attend to at your barracks?"

"My duties are light at present," Anthony replied, not at all intimidated by Lady Catherine's manner. "What I have I attend to, you may be assured."

Lady Catherine eyed him for several moments, her gaze darting to

Anne. "And what of your recent interest in Anne?"

"Are we not living in the same house at present?" asked Anthony, neatly diverting her. "It seems serendipitous, does it not? It gives me an opportunity to come to know Anne better, and as she is a dear cousin, I am not hesitant to make good on the chance."

The reference to their situation living together in his father's house and his deliberate mention of Anne as a cousin seemed to do the trick, though it did not prevent Lady Catherine from issuing a veiled warning.

"I suppose you must be correct. As long as there is nothing more to it."

"We are cousins, Lady Catherine. Family is, after all, of utmost importance. Is it not?"

Finally satisfied, Lady Catherine allowed that it was and turned her attention to Lady Susan, who was watching them with evident amusement. Anne knew she was not as blind as Lady Catherine—whether Anthony had told her something of his intentions she did not know—and there was also a kind of hope about her which was becoming more pronounced the more Anne spoke with Anthony. Anne knew of her fears for her son, for he had been sent to war more than once. With the war with the French tyrant a constant threat, there was a chance he would be called into service again.

Which brought the other part of Anne's situation to mind and caused her to pause in consideration. The esteem she felt for her cousin, which was growing by the day, was tempered by the thought he might have *other* reasons for walking a path her *other* cousin did not wish to tread. If his behavior was due to a desire to retire from active service, should Anne allow it? She did not wish harm to come to her cousin, but Anne's confusion at present was such that she did not know what she felt for him, and the notion of relinquishing her newfound, though possibly illusory, freedom was not at all welcome.

As such, Anne decided it was a conversation she must have with him. The opportunity presented itself only a day or two after Anthony had put off her mother. As Lady Susan had Lady Catherine diverted by for the morning, Anne found herself at leisure, and as Anthony suggested a walk to Hyde Park, she agreed, thinking the privacy the walk would afford would be an ideal opportunity to learn what she wished to know.

As ever, the discussion was engaging—Anne had always known of his effortless ability to talk, sometimes without requiring a response. But as was usual of late, he spent much more time listening to her than was his wont. Anne used this to her advantage.

"It seems we have become much closer these past weeks, Cousin," said Anne.

"There were many things we each did not know about the other," said Anthony. "One would assume we each know the other well as we are cousins. Then again, your mother's obsession with Darcy has made it difficult."

"And yet, of late, we have ignored Mother's dictates," challenged Anne.

Anthony shrugged, a hint of his usual insouciance returning. "There does not seem to be any reason to refrain."

"Why? Has Mother's insistence on the subject changed?"

Turning to her, Anthony seemed to realize she was not of a mood to endure his nonchalance. "No, it has not. But I had not known what I was missing in not coming to know you before. This spring has taught me I should not care for Lady Catherine's displeasure."

That was an encouraging sign, Anne thought, though she still did not know how she should feel on the subject. "Then it is not your situation which prompts your attention to me."

Anthony appeared confused. "Situation?"

"Your oft-stated need to marry a woman who possesses wealth," said Anne, though she thought it should be obvious. "I must assume I am superior to any of *them* as I possess an estate as my dowry, rather than a sum of money."

Confusion turned to consideration and Anthony was silent for a moment. The moment soon passed, however, and he turned a look of some intensity on her. "I see Darcy's indifference has done you no favors."

This time it was Anne's turn to be confused. "I do not understand."

Sighing, Anthony spied a nearby bench and led her to it, seeing to her comfort before sitting himself. When they had situated themselves there, he paused for a long moment, looking about in seeming interest for their surroundings, though Anne was certain he was searching for the proper words.

"I can see how you might think that of me," said Anthony at length. When Anne attempted to speak, he held up his hand, clearly wishing to speak without interruption. Anne decided it was for the best. "I have, as you know, a sum of money set aside for me by my parents, and if I wished it, I could resign my commission now. But I have always thought it my duty to serve my country.

"I speak of my need to marry a woman of means in jest, though finding such a woman would be of immense assistance. For some time now, I have not searched much, as I have had my duty to occupy me. I often felt that any woman of means would do, never having had much of a romantic turn."

"And now?" prompted Anne.

Anthony turned to her, and he fixed her with a wide grin, and at that moment, Anne thought it possible to lose her heart to him. "Now I have discovered it is possible to aspire for something more than someone who can keep me in a style in which I wish to live. I now know it is possible to have that which many of our set have forgotten has much value—a union with a woman where we can both esteem the other and enjoy life. It has made me revisit what I want and revise my wishes accordingly."

For a moment Anne did not know how to respond. She wished to blush, gaze at him in wonder, declare her own similar desires, and ask him if he was as, indeed, in earnest, all at the same time. But something held her back, whether it was her own reticence, concern for her mother's reaction, or nothing more than the newness of it all, she did not know. For the moment, she knew she needed to consider the matter further.

"Then let us leave this subject for the present. For my part, I wish to assure you that I am not at all opposed to such a notion and am eager to see what may be."

Anthony favored her with a brilliant smile and stood, offering his arm to her. "Then shall we?"

Anne accepted and they continued their walk. And somehow, the day seemed brighter than it had been before.

It was a source of some amusement for Elizabeth that Lady Catherine focused on her as the impediment to her designs rather than looking to the other romance budding right under her very nose. Elizabeth was the interloper, the lowborn social climber intent upon diverting her future son-in-law's attention away from his duty. But Anne and Colonel Fitzwilliam were as focused on each other as any couple Elizabeth had ever seen, yet Lady Catherine ignored them.

Why this might be, Elizabeth could not say, though she had her suspicions. Among them was the notion that Lady Catherine could not imagine any way her daughter would not obey her and act as she desired. To the lady, Anne was the daughter who had always followed her every whim, whom she had dominated all her life, though Elizabeth knew the lady would not see it that way.

Elizabeth, however, had Anne's assurances she would not be prevailed upon to marry her cousin — or that she would not marry the cousin Lady Catherine had chosen for her! No matter how many times Colonel Fitzwilliam and Anne sat together under the lady's watchful gaze, no sign of suspicion ever showed in her manners, though at times Elizabeth thought the lady was exasperated with the colonel for taking up so much of her daughter's time.

"You must learn how to behave properly," the lady would say to Elizabeth, the moment she so much as glanced in Mr. Darcy's direction. Then she would turn to Mr. Darcy and add: "Sit beside Anne, Darcy, for she requires a partner at present."

That she made such statements, ignoring the presence of Colonel Fitzwilliam by her daughter's side, showed how blind she was. Elizabeth, though her annoyance would rise every time the woman attempted to castigate her, was at least amused by her antics. That Lady Anne was in much the same state, Elizabeth could easily see, but more than once she prevented Elizabeth from saying something caustic by interjecting herself and diverting Lady Catherine's attention.

This dynamic was displayed amply on one occasion, in particular, where the lady's harsh judgment of Elizabeth reached a new level. In that instance, Jane was absent, having been invited to the Hurst townhouse for the day by Mrs. Hurst.

"At least *one* of the sisters appears to have bowed to the inevitable," opined Elizabeth on learning of her sister's plans for the day.

Jane, as was her wont, responded with modesty and a hint of embarrassment. "I do not know that it is inevitable yet."

"Oh, I am quite sure it is," replied Elizabeth, amused at her sister's denial. "If Mr. Bingley does not propose within the next two weeks, I shall be very much surprised."

The hope Jane displayed endeared her all that much more to Elizabeth. Deciding against teasing her sister further, instead, Elizabeth assisted her in her preparations and accompanied her as she was leaving. Though Elizabeth knew she would lose the closeness she enjoyed with Jane — for a woman must cleave to her husband — Elizabeth was relieved Miss Bingley's efforts had been in vain.

Furthermore, thought Elizabeth as she watched the carriage transporting Jane disappear around a corner, Miss Bingley had not been in evidence much since the set down she had received during their walk at Hyde Park. Though Elizabeth had seen her at some events, Miss Bingley did not deign to talk to her or anyone of the Darcy party and had, instead, seemed to be attempting to curry favor to every man of consequence in London. Elizabeth could not say if she would find success in provoking a man to offer for her, but she seemed to have given up on her desire to wed Mr. Darcy.

Visitors to the house that morning after Jane left comprised some of Lady Anne's acquaintances, most of whom had already been introduced to Elizabeth previously. After some time of sitting and speaking, Lady Catherine arrived in all her grandeur with Anne in tow, along with Colonel Fitzwilliam. As was common in such circumstances, the pair sat near each other, though calculated to give Lady Catherine the impression they were not sitting *too* close. It seemed to work, for Lady Catherine noticed nothing. However, she did give Elizabeth a hard glare, as she always did, though Elizabeth was not situated anywhere near Mr. Darcy.

Then Lady Catherine glanced around, before fixing her gaze once again on Elizabeth. "I do not see Miss Bennet," said the lady, speaking to her sister, though she did not look away. "Has she returned to her aunt's house as she ought? If so, why is Miss Elizabeth still here?"

"Jane has been invited to spend the day with Mr. Bingley's sister," said Lady Anne in a tone of longsuffering. "As I have said before, I shall not surrender my guests' company until I must."

Lady Catherine sniffed with disdain. "At least she can keep the *other* social climber company today."

"It was his married sister who invited Jane," replied Lady Anne, her tone suggesting her sister leave the subject be. "If you are referring to Miss Bingley, she has not been at Darcy house much of late."

"Then my warnings seem to have done the trick," replied Lady Catherine. "If only all those who seek to interfere would have similar epiphanies."

Though it was clear Mr. Darcy, Lady Anne, and Georgiana — and even Anne — were annoyed with Lady Catherine's constant harping on the subject, the lady's words amused Elizabeth rather than offended her. After the weeks she had spent in the lady's time, Elizabeth was inured to her ways. If the lady knew her daughter had declared she would not marry Mr. Darcy, she would lose all interest in Elizabeth in favor of working on Anne. Then again, it would be, no doubt, Elizabeth's presence which caused such insubordination, so she would not escape condemnation.

"Catherine, I understand you have been assisting Susan in her preparations for the ball," said Lady Anne in a clear attempt to distract her sister. "How are they proceeding?"

"Oh, excellently, of course," replied Lady Catherine. "Though I find Susan's taste in these matters is sometimes bland, I have exquisite judgment and am able to guide her in the proper direction."

Lady Catherine continued to speak at length, her comments describing the preparations punctuated by frequent exclamations of how she had arranged this set of flowers or that candelabra. The self-congratulations were stifling, as evidenced by Lady Anne's expression of practiced patience. The rest of the room ignored the lady to carry on their own conversations, though Elizabeth was grateful her host had taken the lady's attention to herself.

"Tell me, Anne," said Georgiana, grinning at her cousin, "is Aunt Susan's taste truly as horrendous as Aunt Catherine claims?"

Though Colonel Fitzwilliam snorted, Anne returned Georgiana's grin and said: "For myself, I find that Aunt Susan's arrangements are lovely. Of course, Mother makes her suggestions and Aunt Susan humors her, but on no less than three occasions, I have seen matters returned to the way they were before Mother meddled. She cannot see it, for my mother cannot imagine anyone would think she could do better than accept her every command without question."

The group laughed, even Mr. Darcy, who was more often exasperated with his aunt than amused. This drew the two ladies' attention, Lady Anne's smile indicating understanding what they were discussing. Lady Catherine, however, scowled and shot them all a pointed look.

"Raucous laughter is for the lower classes. I should not wonder at your lack of restraint given the company you keep, but let your control not escape you again."

"On the contrary, Aunt Catherine," said Darcy, "Anne made a jest, and we all laughed quietly. There was nothing raucous about it."

Lady Catherine returned a sniff and turned her attention back to Lady Anne. Grins abounded between the rest of the company, but they altered their attention to other matters.

The visit continued in this vein for some time, Elizabeth enjoying her time with the rest of the company. In time she forgot all about Lady Catherine in favor of what was happening around her, and as such, did not note how the lady was behaving. When Mr. Darcy made some innocuous comment to her—Elizabeth could not even remember what it was moments after he made it—the lady once again made her presence known.

"Miss Elizabeth Bennet."

The tightness her voice informed Elizabeth the lady was not at all happy, and Elizabeth, not knowing what might have angered her, gave the lady her attention. "Yes, Lady Catherine?"

"I believe it is time you removed yourself from Darcy's presence and ceased to importune him with your attempts to distract him."

"I have no notion of what you speak," said Elizabeth. "Though you may think I have attempted it, I have made no attempt to distract, or even to bring his attention to me. Mr. Darcy is not even sitting beside me, for Georgiana is between us."

"It was I who spoke with Miss Elizabeth, Aunt," added Darcy. "I apologize if you dislike it, but good manners dictate I must speak with everyone who is part of the company."

Lady Catherine attempted to silence Mr. Darcy with a curt wave of her hand. "Since it seems to have escaped your notice—and that of my sister and everyone else—I shall remind you I am well acquainted with young ladies of Miss Elizabeth's ilk. She is eager to capture a wealthy man and has set you in her sights. Do not think your ambition will *ever* be gratified, young lady, for I shall never allow it!"

"That is enough, Aunt," said Mr. Darcy, rising to his feet. "Do not berate my mother's guest, especially when she has done nothing to earn your ire."

"It seems I must put her in her place, since you will not," rejoined Lady Catherine.

Mr. Darcy gave a sigh of exasperation. "Then perhaps it would be best to take myself from your presence."

"There is no need for that, Darcy. You should sit beside Anne, for she has not had your attention yet on this visit."

"Perhaps if you behaved better, I would stay." Lady Catherine's tight glare of anger informed them all of her growing pique. "Before I depart, let me only say this: nothing between Anne and me has been decided, and you should know it will likely not end in a manner you wish."

"I shall ensure it is," exclaimed Lady Catherine.

"It is interesting to hear you say it, for I should like to know how you intend to manage it," said Mr. Darcy. "I am my own man and not beholden to you—I need not propose to Anne if I do not desire it."

"Then you will marry a penniless girl of low status?"

"I have said nothing of the kind," replied Mr. Darcy. "But I should inform you that I—along with every other member of the family—am growing tired of your constant insistence on this matter. You will not browbeat me into doing what you wish, Aunt. Do not test me.

"You have my apologies, Anne," said Darcy, bowing to his cousin.

"It is not my intention to reject you or insinuate you are not fit to be my wife."

"No offense taken, Darcy," said Anne. "It has always been my understanding you may not make me an offer. I shall not be mortally offended should you choose not to."

Mr. Darcy bowed and looked to his cousin. "Shall we retire for a time to my study, Fitzwilliam?"

"Of course, Darcy," said Colonel Fitzwilliam. He rose and departed with the gentleman, though not before winking at Anne and grinning at Elizabeth.

Their departure, however, did not silence Lady Catherine. "This is all *your* fault!" growled the lady, gaining her feet and pointing one bony finger at Elizabeth. "If you would return to where you belong, Darcy would not be acting in so recalcitrant a manner."

"That is enough, Catherine!" said Lady Anne, rising along with her sister. "If you cannot refrain from berating my guest, I will ask you to leave."

"This Jezebel has bewitched you all!" cried Lady Catherine, spinning to confront her sister. "Send her back from whence she came, for I will not tolerate her presence any longer!"

"It is not for you to tolerate her," said Lady Anne, calmness marking her demeanor. "Elizabeth is *my* guest, as I have told you several times. If you will not behave with civility to her, then you are not welcome in my home."

"I never thought I would see the day when you would throw family over for those so unsuitable! What has happened to you, Anne?"

"Nothing has 'happened' to me. It is *you* who have grown unreasonable, who have allowed this fantasy of yours to consume your every thought."

"It is no fantasy!" screeched Lady Catherine, her voice most unladylike.

"Yes, it is," replied Lady Anne. Her countenance might have been chiseled from rock. "Let me tell you here and now, Catherine, that I do not favor this match you have so often insisted upon and will defend my son's right to choose his own wife. If he chooses Anne, then so be it. But I will not allow you to force him into it."

"We shall see about that!"

Lady Catherine spun on her heel and stalked from the room, her voice echoing behind; "Come, Anne!"

Anne rose and shook her head while glaring after her mother. Lady Anne approached and embraced her niece. "I apologize for this, my dear. I did not intend to fight this battle today."

"It was inevitable," replied Anne, showing a wan smile. "I am not offended. If William should propose—and I am convinced he will not," Anne paused and shot a grin at Elizabeth, "I shall reject him. For the moment, however, I shall refrain from informing my mother of that fact."

"That is for the best," said Lady Anne.

With that, the younger woman departed, leaving Elizabeth with Lady Anne and Georgiana. Before Elizabeth could even think of saying a word, Lady Anne turned to her and spoke:

"Do not even think to offer a word of apology, Elizabeth. No one other than Catherine is at fault for our argument."

"Thank you, Lady Anne," said Elizabeth, mustering a wan smile. "Since I did nothing to provoke her displeasure—other than my very presence—I had not thought to offer an apology. I will note that Lady Catherine is correct to a certain extent—it is my presence which provokes her displeasure."

"That is *her* problem," was Lady Anne's short reply. "Whether she considers you at fault is not at issue; Catherine has no right to berate guests in my house."

"This confrontation was inevitable, Elizabeth," said Georgiana. "Now we may be free of Catherine's presence for a time."

"My brother can control her if need be," added Lady Anne. "If it causes a schism in the family, it will be on her head."

"If you do not mind," said Elizabeth, "these events and talk of breaks in families have left me fatigued. I believe I shall return to my room."

"Come, Elizabeth," said Georgiana, looping their arms together, "I shall accompany you thither. I believe I would benefit from a rest as well."

With a few more words intended to comfort, Lady Anne allowed them to depart. Elizabeth did not wish to think on the matter anymore—she wished for nothing more than to lie down and lose herself in sleep for a time. This was unlikely, she knew, for her mind would work the matter over until she grew frustrated. But perhaps Georgiana's presence would distract her.

CHAPTER XV

To the relief of the Darcy family, they did not see Lady Catherine for the next few days. As they were days leading up to the Fitzwilliam ball, each of them knew they would be required to endure her that night, but the distance allowed them to shore up their defenses for her next offensive.

No one was more relieved than Elizabeth. Though she had thought her courage had been sufficient to ignore the lady's disapproval, Elizabeth realized in those days free of her presence that she had become tense and irritable. When the threat of Lady Catherine's constant criticism was removed, she returned to her usual optimistic demeanor, a relief in more ways than one.

Dear Jane, not being present for the event, was not aware of exactly what had happened, though being an intelligent woman, she could well guess. "Lady Catherine has, indeed, behaved badly, Elizabeth," said she when Elizabeth related the confrontation to her. "But I suppose we must excuse her, for she is seeing the dream of her daughter being married to Mr. Darcy die before her very eyes."

Trust Jane to excuse the inexcusable; Elizabeth was not about to argue with her sister. "I suppose we must do so, though I cannot be easy with her continued censure."

Jane smiled, grasping Elizabeth's hand and squeezing it with affection. "I cannot imagine it is affecting you as much as you suggest, Lizzy. If it is, I must wonder where my indomitable sister is, the sister who allows nothing to intimidate her."

"She is still here, Jane," said Elizabeth, giving her sister an affectionate embrace. "There are times, however, when even *she* finds Lady Catherine too much to endure."

The disadvantage of the lady's absence was her inability to be in Anne de Bourgh's company. Elizabeth did not expect her new friend would come to Darcy house, not with Lady Catherine's current anger with its residents—if Anne extended any measure of friendship to Elizabeth, her mother would become exceedingly angry, making matters difficult for Anne. Elizabeth was uncertain how the situation might be improved, for having come to know Anne, she was not willing to give up her acquaintance. Now, however, was not the time to push Lady Catherine any further.

On the other hand, the state of affairs between Mr. Darcy and Elizabeth continued to improve, unsurprising given the absence of the major limiting factor against their greater understanding. While Elizabeth had come no closer to clarity regarding her own feelings for the gentleman, at least she was able to see him with eyes unclouded by misunderstanding. With his declaration during their walk in the park, she now knew he was interested in her, though she could not predict how the matter would end. As a result, she looked on him with the eyes of a woman welcoming a suitor and was surprised to discover that notion was not as onerous as it might have seemed only a few months before.

"I believe I have had enough of balls and parties for a lifetime," said Georgiana one day when they were all together in the sitting-room.

"It is interesting to hear you say that," said Elizabeth, laughter in her tone. "As a member of society, you can expect to experience this every year during the season."

"Do not remind me," was Georgiana's sour reply. Elizabeth thought her manner was more than a little melodramatic, as did Lady Anne, who watched her daughter, fondness evident in her slight smile and steady gaze. "I know not how those who take delight in the season do it every year, for it is exhausting."

"And yet, your aunt's ball is approaching," said Lady Anne.

"I have no wish to offend Aunt Susan," replied Georgiana. "But I hope for the next few days we may avoid similar events, for I have tired of them."

Lady Anne glanced around the room, saying: "Yes, it seems to me we would all welcome a respite. Perhaps we may stay at home and refuse all invitations leading up to Susan's ball."

"There is also a new exhibit at the Royal Academy of the Arts," said Mr. Darcy. "Perhaps an outing to a museum would be welcome after the recent drudgery of parties and the like."

They all laughed at Mr. Darcy's choice of words. "Only you would call parties 'drudgery,' William," said his mother with a fond shake of her head.

"It was not I who complained of our recent activities," was his mild reply. "Though I will own I agree with Georgiana's assessment."

"Then shall we?" asked Lady Anne, looking at the rest of those present. "We may go tomorrow if you all wish it. Other than that one outing, we may stay at home."

The company all agreed, and thus their plans were made. The following day, they assembled to go thither, and they soon made their way to the Darcy carriage for the short journey to Piccadilly. It was unfathomable that an outing of this nature could be contemplated without Mr. Bingley's presence, and Elizabeth knew Jane had informed him of their plans during his visit to the house the previous day. Mr. Bingley waiting for them when they arrived was not a surprise—what was unexpected was the presence of Mr. and Mrs. Hurst, Miss Bingley, and another man to whom Elizabeth had not been introduced.

The gentleman was soon introduced to them—his name was Mr. Powell, though his connection to the Bingley party was not vouchsafed to Elizabeth. When he stepped up and offered his arm to Miss Bingley, she thought it possible that he may be an intimate of the woman's, possibly even a suitor, though she had heard nothing of the matter and the scene in the park had been too recent for a formal connection to have formed. As Mr. Darcy offered his arm to Elizabeth at the same time, while offering his other to his mother—Georgiana found herself escorted by Mr. Bingley—Elizabeth put the matter out of her thoughts.

As a party, they walked through the academy, looking at this painting or debating that sculpture. The building was large, far larger than they could see in the space of a day. After the activities of recent days, however, it was a welcome break, a breath of fresh air to people who had begun to find ballrooms and dining rooms of town stifling. Of course, not all of them felt that way.

"Oh, you find the pace of the season not to your taste, do you?" asked Miss Bingley in that superior tone of hers when she overheard

Elizabeth make some comment about the welcome distraction of the day. The way the woman glanced at Mr. Darcy and sneered suggested she knew something he did not. "Well," continued she, her tone condescending, "I suppose there is something to be said for training and lineage to prepare one for such activities. Perhaps a return to the country would be advisable, for the 'hectic' nature of the season, as you call it, will not trouble you there."

"I did not say I cannot cope with the pace of the season," said Elizabeth, her amusement, she thought, easily seen despite her best efforts to suppress it. "I only observed that a break from the busyness of the season is welcome occasionally."

"And I agree," said Mr. Darcy, interjecting when Miss Bingley would have responded, no doubt with some other veiled criticism. "I am not fond of most of the events we attend, so a respite is most welcome."

Even Mr. Darcy's words in support did not seem to prevent Miss Bingley's response, but the tug on her hand by the gentleman escorting her did the trick. Elizabeth noted his quiet words to her as they walked away, and she wondered if he was annoyed by her nastiness, though she could not determine that as they were facing away. A glance at Mr. Darcy showed him considering the same subject, for he glanced at her and grinned.

"It appears Miss Bingley is not completely cured of her desire to be mistress of Pemberley," said he, maintaining a straight face.

"Or perhaps she is," replied Elizabeth. "It may be nothing more than jealousy and a desire to prevent *me* from obtaining that which she was not so fortunate as to secure."

Mr. Darcy regarded her, a hint of a smile playing about his mouth. "If that is so, she may wish to take care. Envy can be a harsh taskmistress, and if she does not control it, her new beau may take offense."

"Oh, so he is a suitor?" asked Elizabeth.

"I do not think it correct to refer to him in such terms," replied Mr. Darcy. "Bingley mentioned he has called on her a few times, but I believe his interest is not yet sufficient to call him a suitor."

"Then I wish Miss Bingley well," replied Elizabeth, her manner mischievous. "For if he *is* a suitor, then she will have no choice but to give up her interest in you. Her words suggest she has not, even now, given up some measure of hope you will 'come to your senses.'"

Mr. Darcy chuckled and shook his head. "If she still does hope, she does so in vain. There is no more chance of my marrying her than of my dancing in the streets in naught but my waistcoat."

"That is an interesting picture," replied Elizabeth. "I think it will keep me amused for some time."

After an enjoyable time at the exhibit, the party made their way back to Mr. Darcy's house, parting with the Bingleys when leaving the academy. That Miss Bingley looked on her with added contempt, Elizabeth noticed, but she did not pay any attention to the supercilious woman. They traveled back to the house in silence, for they were all tired from their exertions, and when they arrived, they went their separate ways. Though Jane and Georgiana both returned to their rooms to rest, Elizabeth found herself less fatigued and took herself to the library to read. It was there that Lady Anne found her.

"Elizabeth," said the lady as she stepped into the room and approached. "It seems your years of walking have served you in good stead. Why, I thought Georgiana would fall asleep in the carriage, and yet you have chosen to forego rest in favor of the written word."

"Perhaps they have," said Elizabeth with a smile.

"I was also interested to witness your behavior with my son." Lady Anne paused and added: "Though I recognized a change before today, it was more marked than I have ever seen. Do you wish to share the reason for this change of heart?"

Surprised, Elizabeth gaped at the lady. "I do not think our behavior has been *that* different."

The soft smile with which the lady regarded her seemed to suggest to Elizabeth she was being daft. "While I am certain *you* did not notice, it was evident to everyone else present. Why do you think Miss Bingley forgot herself enough to speak openly in the presence of a man she hopes will be her suitor?"

When Elizabeth still did not comprehend, Lady Anne shook her head. "Is not inattentiveness to all about you the very essence of love? I myself spoke to you on one occasion and you did not even notice me speaking, and I know there was at least one other instance of the same. If Georgiana did not wish so much for you as her sister, I think she might be quite offended.

"Add to this how you never strayed from William's side," said Lady Anne, chuckling at Elizabeth's dawning realization, "and the way conversation flowed with effortless ease, and one might be forgiven for assuming there was already a courtship if he did not know."

The more the lady spoke, the more Elizabeth became embarrassed, which led to further amusement and, consequently, even greater blushing. When Lady Anne fell silent, Elizabeth could not muster a response, for every interaction, every word spoken between herself and Mr. Darcy she recalled, analyzed, and the fact of her inattention to anyone else became obvious to Elizabeth.

"I had not realized I was being so unmindful," managed Elizabeth at length.

"That is obvious, Elizabeth," replied Lady Anne. "I quite despaired of you after my son's last incident with you. But it seems you have mended that rift so well it might not have existed at all."

"He apologized," replied Elizabeth. "He promised to do better in the future, and so far, he is making good on his promise."

"That is good to know," said Lady Anne. "As I told you, William is not the man who offended you twice—I can only attribute it to his unacknowledged interest in you, and his misguided attempts to fight his attraction.

"Though I am sorely tempted to speak further on the matter, I shall restrain myself." Lady Anne then grinned and continued: "But I cannot refrain from informing you that should my son propose, I shall as a daughter. I have already informed you of Georgiana's desire for you as a sister."

Lady Anne stood and touched Elizabeth's cheek. "Do not concern yourself that I shall interfere. I doubt my interference is required now."

With those words, the lady departed, leaving Elizabeth alone with her thoughts. All thought of reading vanished, for her mind had focused on other matters.

At times, Elizabeth thought her thoughts were too chaotic for her to make any sense. They were a jumbled mess of feelings and impressions, of Mr. Darcy, herself, their recent interaction, not to mention the others in the house who appeared united in wishing to see a happy conclusion. Elizabeth even considered Mr. Bingley's courtship with Jane, noting their actions with respect to each other, wondering if what she was gaining with Mr. Darcy was in any way similar. Then she realized that it could not be the same, for she and Mr. Darcy were by no means like Jane and Mr. Bingley. No, she would have to forge her own path, just like countless others had before her.

It was fortunate the ladies had the Fitzwilliam ball to anticipate, for Elizabeth was soon able to shed some of her introspection in favor of the upcoming event. Georgiana was more excited than she usually was for an event of this nature, and even Lady Anne, who appeared unflappable, harbored much more enthusiasm than Elizabeth had seen before.

"You will both have more fun at the ball than I," said Georgiana one morning two days before the event. "For you have your beaux, who will be more than attentive." Georgiana turned and winked at Elizabeth. "I shall even give up my first sets with my brother should he so choose—I cannot imagine he would prefer to dance them with his much younger sister than with the woman he fancies."

"Oh, I am certain you will have beaux of your own," replied Elizabeth, teasing her friend in return. "Shall you require the gentlemen to vie for your hand for the first sets?"

Georgiana laughed. "That is an amusing picture, Elizabeth, and perhaps I shall attempt it. But at present, I am content to witness the romances taking place about me. I have no hurry to become attached to anyone."

"That is wise of you, Georgiana," said Elizabeth. "It is a lesson I wish our younger sisters would learn."

"If you delay long enough," said Jane with a sly look at Elizabeth, "perhaps Lizzy will have something to say about whom you marry."

Elizabeth glared at her sister in mock affront, but the other two girls could hardly contain their glee as they bantered back and forth. After a time of this, Elizabeth declared her intention of walking out, ensuring she informed them of her wish of escaping their teasing. The accusation only spurred them on.

"It is not often I am able to discompose you with teasing, Lizzy," said Jane. "It is usually the other way around."

"And I wish it to return to that dynamic," replied Elizabeth.

Kissing her sister, she rose and departed, seeking her outerwear and a footman to accompany her. But the walk she desired was to be denied by the coming of a most unpleasant visitor.

"Miss Elizabeth Bennet," the sound of Lady Catherine's voice interrupted her reverie as she began to descend the stairs. "How fortunate I have come upon you, for I must have words with you."

In Elizabeth's opinion, it was anything but fortunate, but she refrained from making that observation, knowing that Lady Catherine already had reason, in her own mind, to despise her. The lady noted nothing of these thoughts, for she drew breath and began to make her case, the contents of which Elizabeth knew before the lady ever uttered them.

"You can be at no loss to understand the reason for my wishing to speak with you in private," said the lady. "Indeed, I am certain you must have been expecting me to return to make my sentiments known to you."

"Yes, it was my expectation," said Elizabeth, impatient to depart. "That does not imply that I welcome it."

Lady Catherine's eyes bored into Elizabeth and the lady snapped: "It makes little difference to me what you wish. I have come to inform you of my displeasure, and you shall not move me from my purpose. If you were sensible of your own good, you would not act in such a way as to make my reproofs inevitable.

"Now, I shall not canvass matters which I have previously made known to you—by now you should know my sentiments. I will only say this: from this day forward, I require you to cease distracting my nephew. He is destined to marry my daughter, and I shall see that he will. No lowborn temptress will keep him from his duty—if you persist you will be censured and despised by all, for I shall see it done.

"In fact, it would be best for all if you returned to your home and let my family be, for your insistence upon imposing on my sister is most reprehensible. Regardless, I require you to stay away from my nephew, do you hear me?"

"I have heard you many times, Lady Catherine," said Elizabeth, her patience almost exhausted. "I will note that it will be difficult to stay away from him, considering our residence in the same house at present."

"Did I not inform you that you must return to your home?" retorted Lady Catherine.

"You did," replied Elizabeth. "But as I am here at Lady Anne's invitation and stay because of her wish for my presence, I hope you will forgive me if I count her wishes as superior to your own."

Lady Catherine's eyes blazed in outrage. "I am unaccustomed to such language, Miss Elizabeth. Do you not know who I am?"

"I know exactly who you are," rejoined Elizabeth. "That is what makes your behavior so reprehensible—I might have thought someone of your exalted station would conduct herself better than this."

"I will not be judged by one such as you!" cried Lady Catherine. "No, we shall not speak further, for speaking with you is as efficacious as speaking to a child. You will promise me that you will stay away from my nephew and that you will not even speak to him at the ball my sister is holding two days from now."

"If you think I will make such an outrageous promise, you are out of your senses," said Elizabeth. "I shall do nothing of the kind."

The lady stared at her for several moments, and Elizabeth thought she would continue to make her case. But she seemed to come to the correct conclusion, though Elizabeth knew she would not be silent for long.

"So, you refuse to oblige me?"

"I thought that was clear, Lady Catherine."

"Very well, I shall know how to act. Do not think your ambitions will ever be realized, for I will not allow it!"

Then the lady spun on her heel and made her way back down to the carriage, which Elizabeth noted had been waiting on the drive. At once Elizabeth realized she and the lady had aired their disagreement before the world, though she could see no one in the vicinity. As the lady's carriage pulled away, Elizabeth hoped their argument had escaped the notice of the gossips.

The intended walk forgotten and now unpalatable, Elizabeth returned into the house where the housekeeper looked at her askance. It was fortunate the woman did not speak, for Elizabeth was uncertain how she would respond. She divested herself of her spenser and bonnet and made her way back into the house, occupying her time by slowly walking the corridors of the house deep in thought. That was how Mr. Darcy found her.

"Miss Elizabeth," said he in greeting, his manner more formal than it had been in recent days. "I have been searching for you, for I wish to ask you a particular question. Will you do me the honor of opening the ball with me in two days' time?"

It was all Elizabeth could do not to burst out laughing, for she thought no man wished for a woman to laugh at him when applying for her hand for a dance. Something must have eked its way past her control, however, for he frowned.

"I hope my application was not amusing," said he, proving her supposition.

"No, it was not," replied Elizabeth, allowing free reign to her mirth. "But when you consider the conversation I had not fifteen minutes ago, it *is* ironic in the highest sense."

"Conversation?" asked Mr. Darcy with little eloquence.

"Lady Catherine," replied Elizabeth, feeling lighter than she had since the lady departed. The mention of the woman darkened Mr. Darcy's countenance, but Elizabeth shook her head. "I was departing for a walk and happened to meet her as she was coming to confront me. Among other things, she informed me I was not to even talk to you at the ball. Then again, given our previous dances, it is possible I could accept your application and still abide by her strictures!"

It was clear Mr. Darcy could not see the amusement in Elizabeth's account. "What did she say?"

Elizabeth gave him a brief explanation of her conversation with the lady, and by the end, she could see he was not at all happy, likely considering going to his uncle's house to berate her once and for all. While the lady would deserve every speck of her nephew's displeasure, Elizabeth did not think it would resolve anything. Thus, she proceeded to talk him out of it.

"I shall be happy to dance the first with you, Mr. Darcy. I hope we shall put our past missteps behind us and speak at length of many interesting topics. The opportunity to see Lady Catherine's countenance as she watches us when she explicitly warned me against you, will be more than worth the price she will exact later."

The quirk of his lips informed Elizabeth Mr. Darcy had seen the humor in her jest, though it was clear he was still annoyed with his aunt. To seal her quest to prevent his immediate departure, Elizabeth stepped forward and laid a hand on his arm.

"I am certain running off to confront Lady Catherine, though it might be satisfying, will resolve nothing, Mr. Darcy. Though I know she is your aunt, at present, she is being ridiculous. Is it not better to laugh than take offense?"

"You are unique among women, Miss Elizabeth," said Mr. Darcy, his anger relinquished. "I know of no other woman who would not take great offense at my aunt's insults."

Elizabeth shrugged. "There is little reason to do so and much more reason to laugh. As you know, I dearly love to laugh."

"Then I will count on you to induce me to laughter at the ball, for I suspect my aunt will provoke other emotions."

"I accept your challenge, Mr. Darcy."

"Thank you, Miss Elizabeth."

When Mr. Darcy said her name now, it was like a caress. Her walk, the confrontation with Lady Catherine, even her thoughts as she had paced the house she now forgot. There were many more interesting things on which she could think, and Mr. Darcy was foremost among them.

CHAPTER XVI

A day before the ball a letter arrived which astonished both Jane and Elizabeth. Though letters from home were plentiful, they usually contained little more than the gossip of the neighborhood. Their mother included words of "wisdom" on how they may go about catching gentlemen, her annoyance plain at being forbidden to join them in London, while Mr. Bennet, when he took the time to write a few lines, spoke of missing them and desiring their return. There was little enough from their younger sisters, and when they did write, Mary wrote of her studies of the Bible and Fordyce and her concerns for the wildness of her younger sisters, while Kitty and Lydia spoke of their exploits with the officers and their devastation that the regiment was to decamp to their summer quarters in Brighton.

That morning, however, the letter was different, for though it was from Lydia, the words she wrote were not gossip, but known fact. The subject of it returned Elizabeth's mind to Hertfordshire and the acquaintances—or one acquaintance in particular—she had left behind.

"I hope you do not have unwelcome news in your letter," said Lady Anne, pulling Jane and Elizabeth both from their shock.

Elizabeth glanced up and noted the way the lady watched them, her interest containing a hint of concern. When Elizabeth looked at her sister, Jane shrugged and motioned toward the letter. Since the matter was one which had already been decided, it was not gossip. Thus, Elizabeth decided to speak.

"It is from our youngest sister, Lydia," said Elizabeth, her caution inducing her to speak slowly. "Though her letters are often matters of little interest to anyone not of Meryton, she writes of a serious event which took place last week and concerns one with whom you are all acquainted."

At Lady Anne's confused look, Elizabeth clarified: "It is about Mr. Wickham."

"Mr. Wickham?" demanded the lady, her gaze finding her son at the other end of the table. "How are you acquainted with *that* gentleman?"

The manner in which Mr. Wickham had spoken of Lady Anne and Georgiana had soured her opinion of the gentleman many weeks ago, and as such, Elizabeth did not question why the lady seemed to hold him in as much contempt as her son. A glance down the table revealed that Mr. Darcy had laid down his cutlery and was now watching them intently.

"Mr. Wickham joined the local regiment of officers last year, Lady Anne," replied Elizabeth.

"I do not remember seeing him there, and I know would have recalled it. Did he not attend the ball?"

"He claimed business prevented his attendance," replied Elizabeth. "As he said some unflattering things about you and Georgiana, I learned to question everything he said. To my shame, I had accepted much of his tales before that, though my dear Jane had the foresight to caution me against giving too much credence to his assertions."

"Mr. Wickham did not make his claims to me, Lizzy," said Jane, attempting to show Elizabeth's mistake in a better light.

"It is kind of you to say it, Jane," replied Elizabeth, putting a hand on her sister's, "but I was completely at fault."

Lady Anne's eyes found her son. "Were you aware of Mr. Wickham's presence in the neighborhood?"

"I was," was Mr. Darcy's short reply.

"And you did not warn the Bennets or any of Mr. Bingley's other neighbors? What were you thinking?"

"It seems, I was not thinking at all," replied Mr. Darcy, making no attempt to defend himself. "Miss Elizabeth, will you not share what your sister writes of Mr. Wickham?"

Though Lady Anne's annoyance suggested the matter was not closed, she turned back to Elizabeth and waited for her to speak.

"It seems Mr. Wickham was paying court to a Miss Mary King who lives in the neighborhood. As I recollect, his interest started at Christmas."

"If you recall, Lizzy," interrupted Jane, "she had just inherited a fortune of ten thousand pounds."

The unladylike snort given by Lady Anne spoke to her derision. "Oh, yes, Mr. Wickham's ever-present lust for riches. I have little doubt ten thousand pounds would slip through his fingers in little time, and he would leave his wife destitute and alone."

Elizabeth nodded—the pieces were all there, and Mr. Wickham had shown his true colors. More than once, if Elizabeth were to be honest with herself, though she did not wish to think on the matter at the moment.

"There was a general expectation of an engagement in the neighborhood. But it seems Miss King's uncle became suspicious of Mr. Wickham and engaged a man to investigate him. Much of what Lydia writes on the subject is garbled and difficult to make out, but Mr. Wickham was found to be in debt with many reputable tradesmen in the town and had dallied with some of their daughters.

"Miss King's uncle took the matter to Mr. Wickham's commanding officer, who then had Mr. Wickham arrested. Mary King was then sent to Liverpool to the home of another relation and Mr. Wickham was court-martialled, stripped of his commission, and transported to prison."

"Then it is little less than he deserves," said Lady Anne. The way she glared across the table at her son suggested she dared him to argue.

"You will get no disagreement from me, Mother," said Mr. Darcy. "It has been many years since I thought only the worst of Wickham."

Lady Anne gave her son a curt nod. "Mr. Wickham was always a bad apple, though it was difficult for my husband to see it. Robert saw Mr. Wickham's genial manners and his ability to charm at will."

"Some of the blame must fall on my shoulders, Mother," said Mr. Darcy. "I should have taken the matter of Mr. Wickham's character to my father, but I did not. If I had, perhaps he might have turned out better than he did."

The opinion Lady Anne espoused of the suggestion was once again on display with her retort: "I doubt it would have made any difference, William. You know Wickham played on my husband's kindness and affected an innocence unbelievable in a child of five. If you had gone to your father, Wickham would have denied all and taken greater care to hide his debaucheries."

"If you will pardon me," said Elizabeth, feeling a little frustrated, but not at all certain she should ask, "but you have not yet said anything of Mr. Wickham's particular sins. Though I know it is an impertinence, and your words on the subject have given me some suspicions, might I ask you to be more explicit?"

Though Mr. Darcy's gaze was stern when he turned it on her, it soon softened. "It is not an impertinence, Miss Elizabeth, though you must understand that some of my account of him is not suitable for the ears of young gentlewomen."

The significant look he directed at Georgiana was not missed by any of them, nor by Georgiana herself. While she huffed, Elizabeth knew his concern, though primarily for her, was directed at them all.

"I have no need to know of the more lurid details, Mr. Darcy," said Elizabeth. "Only what you can say in polite society."

Mr. Darcy nodded, relieved. "Then you shall know what I can impart."

The gentleman paused for a moment, introspective, idly fiddling with his fork before he continued speaking. "I suppose Wickham must have informed you he was reared at Pemberley and that we were friends as children. Given your comments during our dance at Netherfield, might I also assume he informed you of *his* version of the events surrounding my father's will and the living at Kympton?"

"He did not mention the name," said Elizabeth. "But, yes, that is correct."

Shaking his head, Mr. Darcy said: "What makes Wickham's lies so insidious is his ability to mix them with enough of the truth that they appear to be completely plausible. Wickham *did* grow to adulthood at Pemberley, and as there were few other boys my age on the estate, it is only natural we were firm friends. That was when we were young, for as we grew into young men, I found that Wickham changed from the happy boy I knew into one who cared for nothing but his own gratification. I cannot say when this change occurred, for it happened too gradually, but by the time we were at Eton together, I began to disassociate myself with him."

"There is one point on which you are incorrect, William," said Lady Anne. "Those tendencies were always a part of Wickham's character. For my part, I suspect his mother, for the woman was a spendthrift, and taught her son to envy what he did not and could never have. Many were the times when I observed him looking on Pemberley with covetous eyes, and I remember, in particular, a time when you were perhaps thirteen when your father purchased a new horse for you. His jealousy was difficult to miss."

Darcy nodded, not replying to his mother's assertions. This was clearly a subject which they had discussed at some length.

"Regardless, by the time we were young men at Cambridge," continued Mr. Darcy, "my opinion of him was very poor. Though I will not speak plainly of his vices, you may be certain they included gambling, leaving debts wherever he went, not to mention exploits with the ladies of which I cannot speak. Both in Cambridge and Lambton, I discharged his debts to protect the Darcy name. I still have the receipts if you wish to verify my account."

"That is not necessary, Mr. Darcy," said Jane a heartbeat before Elizabeth could say the same. "Your word is enough for both of us."

Mr. Darcy nodded as Elizabeth softly voiced her agreement. "Of the living at Kympton, it is essential to understand that my father's wish was *not* a bequest—it was, rather, an instruction for me to assist Wickham in his future profession. The living was mentioned as a suitable means for Wickham to support himself, but the bequest consisted of a thousand pounds.

"A further condition upon any young man receiving a living is, of course, the man's willingness to attend a seminary and obtain his ordination." When the Bennet sisters nodded, Mr. Darcy continued. "Some time after my father's funeral, Wickham came to me to discuss the living. As my opinion of him by this time was very ill, I was relieved when he betrayed no interest in the living or the life of a parson. Instead, since he was not to benefit from the living, he proposed a more immediate pecuniary advantage. I agreed."

"You were not required to do so," said Lady Anne, her tone firm. "There was nothing in my husband's will which required you to so much as lift a finger beyond giving him the thousand pounds Robert left to him."

"I understand that, Mother," said Mr. Darcy, his agreeable manner again suggesting they had discussed this before. "But the spirit of my father's will meant I would not be fulfilling *his* desires if I gave Wickham his money and showed him to the borders of Pemberley. After some negotiating, in which Wickham asked for far more than was reasonable, we settled at an amount of three thousand pounds in exchange for his resigning all claim to the living. We signed a contract solemnizing this agreement."

"Three thousand pounds?" gasped Jane.

"In addition to the one thousand he received," added Elizabeth, "he could have supported himself on that money for many years if used with prudence. As he arrived in Meryton with little, I must assume he did not use that money well."

"Prudence has never been a part of George Wickham's character," replied Mr. Darcy. "Though I did not see Wickham for some time after, I received reports of his behavior from time to time. It was no shock to learn the money did not last long, for now being free to live a life of idleness and dissipation, Wickham threw himself into that lifestyle with little thought for the consequences. I hope, considering these facts, you will not blame me for refusing his entreaties when the incumbent retired from the living."

"Mr. Wickham came to ask you for the living after he resigned it?" demanded Elizabeth. Jane was no less incredulous.

"There are few audacities beyond Wickham's ability to rationalize," said Mr. Darcy. "His abuse of me when I refused him was in direct proportion to the difficulty of his situation, and he no doubt abused me to all and sundry. The last time *I* saw him until meeting him on the street in Meryton was when he left Pemberley after his application, this time under guard and with the instruction ringing in his ears that he would be turned over to the magistrate and his outstanding debts called in if he dared to return."

Though Jane did not appear to catch the emphasis of Mr. Darcy's words, Elizabeth recognized it and guessing his reference turned to Georgiana, who nodded in response to Elizabeth's questioning gaze.

"Yes, Elizabeth, you are correct." Georgiana paused as Mr. Darcy sat back, content to leave this part of the account to his sister. "When I was young, Mr. Wickham used to play with me, and as I grew older, he plied me with the force of his charm, telling me how beautiful I was growing and what an accomplished woman I would be. After my father passed, Mr. Wickham approached me while at Pemberley discussing the living, again trying to charm me. Though I did not know why then, I know now.

"This past summer, Mother and I were in Ramsgate enjoying a month vacation. You will not be surprised to learn that Mr. Wickham met me there, seemingly by chance, and continued his campaign to charm me, even going so far as to tell me he loved me and wished to elope."

Lady Anne huffed with disdain. "All that boy has ever loved is himself and whatever money he can extort from others."

"By that time, William had already told me of Mr. Wickham's

character, so I was on my guard. But I will own that had I been only a little younger, I might have fallen prey to Mr. Wickham's pretty words."

"And yet I, a woman two years your senior, was drawn in as if I were a child." Elizabeth shook her head, disgusted with herself. "I, who should know better, who have always accounted myself as being an excellent judge of character."

"Do not blame yourself, Miss Elizabeth," came the soothing voice of Mr. Darcy. "Wickham can be very convincing, and I gave you no reason to esteem my character."

Elizabeth was not ready to release her self-condemnation, but Georgiana took up her tale again.

"Mr. Wickham has supreme confidence in his own charms. I played upon his vanity and gave him to believe I was taken in by his charm, inviting him to come to the house that evening to meet me and my mother."

"And when he arrived, Thompson, one of our burliest footmen, met him at the door," said Lady Anne with a laugh.

"Wickham has reason to fear Thompson, for the man has never liked him," said Mr. Darcy, taking up the tale. "Thompson told Wickham in no uncertain terms that he was not welcome and that I had been called to Ramsgate, warning him of what would happen if he returned."

"It surprised us when the housekeeper brought word that Mr. Wickham was demanding to see Georgiana," said Lady Anne. "I would never have thought Mr. Wickham would show such courage in the face of an angry Mr. Thompson."

"I still believe it was desperation," said Mr. Darcy.

Lady Anne inclined her head and said: "That may very well explain it. Regardless, Georgiana and I went to confront him. Though his looks were nigh murderous, he was forced to abandon his scheme when Georgiana told him in no uncertain terms she knew everything of his character and would not elope with him."

"You have my apologies for believing him so implicitly," said Elizabeth. "Jane was much more perspicacious than I."

Jane reached out and grasped Elizabeth's hand in support, but Lady Anne said: "Were you not changed in your attitude toward Mr. Wickham when you came?"

Though Elizabeth had hoped they would not require her to explain further, she could do nothing but respond: "It was his words concerning you and Georgiana. He told me you were both proud and disagreeable, and as I had made your acquaintance—and had my aunt's testimony to back up my own observations—I knew his words were calculated, rather than an honest opinion."

"Do not concern yourself with offending me, Miss Elizabeth," said Mr. Darcy, seeing through to the heart of Elizabeth's hesitance. "Though it is clear you believed Wickham's tales of *me* and not of my mother and sister, it was my own fault."

"It also appears you are past that," said Lady Anne. "Thus, I suggest you do not allow such thoughts to plague you any further." The lady then turned to her son. "Will you do anything concerning Mr. Wickham's current situation?"

Mr. Darcy leaned back in his chair, considering the matter. "At present, I believe I shall do nothing, though I am certain I shall receive a letter from him asking for my intervention."

A sniff was Lady Anne's response. "No doubt he will be confident he can persuade you."

The nod with which Mr. Darcy replied showed his agreement. "It may be best to use his debts in Meryton, coupled with the receipts I hold from Cambridge and Lambton, to see to his removal from England altogether. If I give him enough money to go to the Americas, I may be able to convince him it would be best to seek his fortune there.

"Then again," said Mr. Darcy with a shake of his head, "it is possible he may succeed in returning. Thus, persuading the courts to sentence him to transportation to Botany Bay may be for the best."

"We shall have my brother's support if it comes to that," said Lady Anne.

"I know, Mother. But I hardly believe it should be required."

Lady Anne nodded. "Well, Mr. Wickham is neutralized for the moment, so we need not worry for him." Her gaze then found Elizabeth. "I hope this has not been too distressing for you, my dear."

"No," replied Elizabeth. "I had already determined Mr. Wickham was untrustworthy. I am only ashamed he preyed on me with so little effort when I first met him."

"Let us speak of it no more, Lizzy," said Georgiana. "Mr. Wickham is not worth a jot of your sorrow."

Deciding Georgiana was correct, Elizabeth gave her assent and turned the subject. For the rest of the meal, the company discussed their plans for the day and the ball on the morrow, the subject of Mr. Wickham now consigned to the dustbin of unlamented history. They stayed this way until the end of the meal, the company seeming more in harmony than Elizabeth had ever seen, even since her opinion of

Mr. Darcy had begun to improve.

As they were beginning to consider rising from the breakfast table, the sound of swift footsteps reached them through the door and before anyone could rise, Anne burst through, followed by the housekeeper. She was in a state Elizabeth had never seen, her countenance flushed and worried, her eyes almost wild. She caught sight of Mr. Darcy, who had risen halfway from his chair.

"William, you must stop my mother!" exclaimed Anne before anyone could speak.

"What has she done now?" asked Mr. Darcy.

"It is not what she has done, it is what she is planning to do."

The party waited for Anne to continue, when she appeared to wilt a little, which prompted Lady Anne to rise from her chair and escort Anne to it, calling for a restorative tea. "There, there, Anne, you are overwrought. Sit for a time and regain your strength."

Though Anne allowed her aunt to lead her to the table, she did not remain silent. "My errand cannot wait, for there is no time." As she was seated, she looked across the table at William, who was watching her with no little concern. "Mama has written to the Times, asking them to publish a notice of our engagement."

"What?" demanded Darcy, standing ramrod straight where he had been in the process of sitting again. "Is she mad?"

"She claims that since you will not oblige her, she will force your hand."

The vein working in Mr. Darcy's forehead spoke to his fury, but he controlled his anger, saying in a tight voice: "Anne, though I have spoken of this matter with others, and I suspect you have too, we have never spoken to each other. Do you wish to marry me?"

"No, I do not," came Anne's reply without a hint of a pause.

Elizabeth, who had been holding her breath unaccountably, let it out, though slowly, so she would not make a fool of herself.

"Then we agree," replied Mr. Darcy. "Mother, if you will excuse me, I shall go to the offices of the Times at once. If they dare to print anything which does not come from my hand, I shall file suit against them to the full extent of the law."

"Then you had best be about it, William," said Lady Anne. "They will be eager to print anything about us and not at all inclined to wait."

Mr. Darcy did not respond — instead, he bowed and strode from the room. In the aftermath of his going, Lady Anne turned to her namesake and addressed her.

"Did you walk here from your uncle's house?"

"It is not far," replied Anne, "and Mother would interfere if I called for the carriage."

"She will be furious you thwarted her schemes."

The grin which Anne returned was reminiscent of her more open cousin. "Why should she suspect me? I am the dutiful daughter who has always obeyed, even after I should have given her a piece of my mind. If I return to the house before I am missed, she will not suspect me, as she is engaged in celebrating her own cunning at present."

Lady Anne laughed. "Then perhaps Georgiana and I shall return you to my brother's house. Then you may credibly claim you were visiting with us and remove any suspicion she might harbor."

"Thank you, Aunt," replied Anne.

The servants delivered the tea, and Anne was served a cup while the two Darcy ladies left the room to prepare for their outing. Jane left to return to her room, and Elizabeth remained behind, curious as to her friend's actions that morning.

"It appears Colonel Fitzwilliam has made a greater impression on you than I had known," said Elizabeth, shooting her friend a grin. "You informed me you do not wish to marry Mr. Darcy, but thus far you have said nothing of the colonel."

"At present, I do not think there is anything to say," replied Anne.

"But you believe there soon will be," pressed Elizabeth.

Anne shook her head and smiled. "Yes, Elizabeth, I do esteem Anthony very much."

"And I have eyes enough to see he returns the sentiment." Elizabeth rose and embraced Anne, feeling this was a friendship she could easily retain for the rest of her life. "Then I shall wish you the best, my friend. I think you will be very happy."

"If I can convince my mother to accept it."

With a laugh, Elizabeth rejoined: "Rosings Park has a dower house, does it not?"

"It does, indeed, Elizabeth," replied Anne. "But I am not certain it is far enough from the main house to protect us from her displeasure. If it was in Scotland, the distance might be enough."

Again, Elizabeth released her mirth. "Then I suppose you will simply be required to meet your trials with fortitude. With such a man as Colonel Fitzwilliam by your side, I know you are equal to the task."

CHAPTER XVII

*B*efore that night at the ball, Elizabeth could not be certain of the outcome of Mr. Darcy's visit to the offices of The Times the previous morning. Or perhaps it was more correct to say she knew the outcome of the visit but was not aware of Lady Catherine's reaction to it.

"They agreed not to print it," Mr. Darcy had said when he returned from his errand. "Though they did not say it outright, I suspect my arriving before Lady Catherine's note influenced their decision. As the editor informed me, Lady Catherine's word, as a member of the family, could be deemed sufficient for them to claim including it in tomorrow morning's edition was warranted."

"Surely not," Lady Anne had replied with a frown. "Everyone who has been in society these past five years knows that Catherine has often pushed the match without regard for the claims of anyone else in the family."

"And that is the problem," said Mr. Darcy. "It has been rumored for so many years that it could be said to bridge rumor into certainty. That coupled with Lady Catherine's status as mother of the prospective bride might have been enough to protect them from a lawsuit.

"Regardless, I arrived in time and informed them of the truth of the matter, and they will not print it."

"Will rumors not begin because of Lady Catherine's attempt to force your hand as a result?" asked Elizabeth.

The look Mr. Darcy gave her was tender and firm all at once. "If they do, those rumors will redound onto Lady Catherine's own head. I will not appreciate being drawn into such gossip, but as it will affect her more than me, I shall not repine it."

It seemed, however, that The Times was more circumspect than this, however, for no word of the supposed engagement, nor Mr. Darcy's efforts to prevent its publication, were contained in the newspaper. Those at Darcy house were careful to examine the paper from one end to the other, ensuring there were to be no consequences of Lady Catherine's ill-judged attempts to force Mr. Darcy's hand. Whether any gossip had spread by word of mouth, they could not say, as they did not go out that day. In the end, they dropped the subject in favor of such topics as the amusement that night and their preparations to attend.

When Elizabeth arrived with the rest of the party that evening, she could not see Lady Catherine in attendance, but then again, Anne was not in evidence either. The earl and countess welcomed them, and though nothing was said in Elizabeth's hearing, their manner seemed to suggest knowledge of the situation. Anne had returned to the house the previous day, and Elizabeth supposed she must have informed them, if for no other reason than to ensure their opinion was aligned with her own.

For some time, they stood at the edge of the dance floor speaking and drinking punch, Mr. Bingley joining them a short time after they arrived. Though others attending the event drifted in and out, a few words here and a request for a dance there, they said nothing on the subject of Lady Catherine's efforts.

"It seems the editor I spoke to must have suppressed any hint of gossip," observed Mr. Darcy after some time of this.

"Of course, he would," replied his mother. "Though perhaps they could argue Lady Catherine had the authority to send an announcement to them, they must know that gossip would be less readily defended."

Given what Elizabeth had heard of the gossip sheets, she was uncertain this was the case. As no one was looking at her, pointing, or whispering behind their hands, she was content. When the music for the first sets began to float over the assembled, she was at ease and eager to accept Mr. Darcy's hand as he led her to the dance floor.

"What shall we speak of this time, Miss Elizabeth?" asked Mr. Darcy almost as soon as they began to dance. "I seem to recall from our previous attempts at dancing that you consider conversation essential to the art."

Elizabeth could not help but laugh. "And you mean to ensure there is a conversation between us to stave off misunderstanding?"

"Well, I *did* prove I was rather inept at it in the past, if you recall," said Darcy, his self-deprecation on display. "It would seem best to ensure we start this dance better than we have in the past."

"Then I am at your disposal, Mr. Darcy. I am happy to speak about anything you like."

Mr. Darcy's eyebrow rose in response to Elizabeth's words. "Am I to now understand you even consider books to be an appropriate ballroom conversation topic?"

Delighted with his teasing reply, Elizabeth said: "I shall tell you a secret, Mr. Darcy. If the conversation partner is intelligent, there are few subjects which would be inappropriate."

"Then I shall do my best to hold up my end of the bargain."

Thus, the first part of their dance was characterized by lively conversation, interesting topics, and intelligent exchange of ideas. Elizabeth found she had rarely been so entertained in a ballroom. As they continued to speak, Elizabeth reflected it would have been so much easier if Mr. Darcy had shown this side of his character to her when he came to Hertfordshire the previous month.

Then a sight caught Elizabeth's attention which pushed away all her heady feelings of deepening love. Her sudden grimace did not miss her partner's attention.

"May I take it Lady Catherine has made an appearance?"

The steps of the dance separated them at that moment, and as Elizabeth watched Mr. Darcy as he moved, she was aware of the exact moment when he saw his aunt. In that instant he turned from the congenial gentleman he had been throughout the evening into the cold and silent Mr. Darcy she had known in Hertfordshire. For her part, Lady Catherine seemed to recognize this and understand its reason, for her already forbidding frown became positively violent.

"I suppose it was destined to happen," was Mr. Darcy's short statement when they were close together again.

"Of course, it was," said Elizabeth, giving the gentleman an impish smile. "It was inevitable from the moment I accepted your request for this dance if it had not already been so before."

A brief smile appeared on his countenance. "Stay close when the dance ends, Miss Elizabeth," instructed he. "Though I well know of your ability to defend yourself against the likes of Lady Catherine, I believe it is best we face her together."

Elizabeth squeezed his hand, indicating her acceptance, and was gratified when he returned the gesture. The rest of the set saw little conversation between them, their enjoyment muted by the sure knowledge of the coming quarrel Lady Catherine would certainly provoke. Elizabeth knew she could withstand any slings or arrows the lady could cast in her direction, and even more, with the presence of this man by her side. In time, she began to feel more confident, even as the remaining minutes of the dance ticked away.

When the music faded, Mr. Darcy turned to Elizabeth and offered his arm, which she accepted without hesitation. He then turned her toward the side of the floor a little away from where Lady Catherine stood fuming and close to where his mother waited. This did not prevent the lady from making her sentiments known, but it put them among friends who would help in blunting her displeasure.

"Miss Elizabeth Bennet!" growled Lady Catherine as they reached their destination.

Before she could utter another syllable, Lord Matlock was there, stepping between Lady Catherine and Mr. Darcy. He looked at each of them in turn, his gaze quelling, before he said: "Let us take this to another location, shall we?"

Lady Catherine, it seemed, was not of a mind to delay for even a moment, but even she was forced to yield when her brother scowled. "Do you wish our disagreements to become fodder for the gossips?"

A huff escaped the woman's mouth, though she did nothing more than stalk off toward the room's exit. Lord Matlock watched her go for a moment, his annoyance clear for them all to see. Then he caught his wife's eye from across the room and nodded before turning back to Darcy and Elizabeth.

"I shall join my sister, for I believe she has gone to the library. Though I do not suppose this shall be completely hidden from the eyes of society, we should, at least, make the attempt. I shall try to calm her; follow us to the library once a few moments have passed."

Mr. Darcy gave his assent, and the earl turned and strode from the room. When he left, the remaining three looked at each other, Lady Anne giving Elizabeth and Mr. Darcy a penetrating look.

"Well, if you meant to announce your attachment to my sister, you could not have done it in a more effective manner. It is also one which will enrage her. I do not suppose a hint of her ire will remain unexpressed."

"And yet, when I asked Miss Elizabeth to dance, I did so with no thought of or interest in Aunt Catherine's opinion."

"You know she will not see it that way," said Lady Anne with a sigh. When Mr. Darcy opened his mouth to respond, she waved him off. "There is no question of your ability to act as you see fit, William— I might have preferred to have handled this in another fashion, rather than rubbing Catherine's face in it and prodding the wild beast."

Then Lady Anne laughed and added: "Then again, perhaps it is best to lance the boil and have done with it."

"I cannot say you are incorrect, Mother," replied Mr. Darcy.

"Then let us be about it. The longer we stay here, the more attention we attract, given Catherine's exit only a moment ago."

Though Elizabeth had not realized it, a quick glance around the room told her Lady Anne was correct. The eyes of many were fixed upon them, and though none of the whispers reached her ears, Elizabeth knew what was on their tongues. Lady Anne directed a look at Georgiana which suggested she should remain where she was and led Elizabeth and Mr. Darcy from the room. The sound of raised voices as they approached the library spoke to Lady Catherine's extreme displeasure. Then they were caught in the midst of the storm.

"There she is!" exclaimed the lady as soon as they entered the room. Lord Matlock, who had been speaking with her, attempting to calm her, was ignored as Lady Catherine rounded on the newcomers and approached, singling Elizabeth out with a finger jutted out in accusation. "Miss Elizabeth, you will pack your trunks and return to your home at once. You should have returned long ago!"

"Once again I shall remind you that Elizabeth is staying in *my* home, Catherine," said Lady Anne, stepping forward to confront her sister. "There is nothing you can say to induce me to relinquish Elizabeth's company before I wish to give it up."

"She has taken you in!" screeched Lady Catherine. "She and her grasping sister! Why can you not see this?"

"Lady Catherine," said Elizabeth, now becoming angry, "you may attack me as much as you like I and I do not concern myself with your opinion. But you will not speak so much as a syllable about my sister, who is the sweetest woman I have ever known."

"I will speak about whom I please when I please," snarled Lady Catherine. "For your sister, I care nothing, for if she chooses to marry my nephew's *tradesman* friend, it is nothing to me. As for yourself, I will thank you not to speak in such a fashion to *me*. I am so far above you by all measures of society as to prevent any comparison."

"And yet you shriek and storm and rant like a common fishwife," said Elizabeth evenly. "I apologize, Lady Catherine, but I was not aware that members of fine society behave in such a manner, otherwise I should have returned your insults in kind."

While Elizabeth could never have imagined provoking the woman to such a degree, it shocked her when Lady Catherine raised her hand to strike. The blow never fell, however, for Mr. Darcy moved in front of her to protect her, and moving even more quickly, Lady Anne put herself before her sister her scowl fearsome to behold.

"You will not even consider striking my guest, Catherine! Have you lost your mind?"

"When she behaves in a manner which demands it, I will not hesitate to deliver retribution. And it will be well-deserved!"

"Yes, she has lost her mind," came the voice of the earl, who, Elizabeth could tell, was incensed. Lady Catherine whirled on him, but he stepped forward, his countenance implacable, warning her she had best hold her tongue. "There will be no physical assaults perpetrated here, Catherine—remember this, or I will send you back to Rosings and bar you from my home."

"Perhaps it would be best if you turned your ire on this . . . this . . . Jezebel our sister has allowed into our company! Do you not censure her for the way she speaks to me?"

"Not when you deserve it," replied Lord Matlock.

"What is it about this young woman which has you all forgetting from whence you sprang?" cried Lady Catherine. "Do you mean to allow this farce to persist, Hugh? How can you justify such pollution of our family line as to admit so unsuitable a woman into our midst?"

"I only propose to allow Darcy the power of his own choice," said Lord Matlock, motioning for Mr. Darcy to remain silent. That Mr. Darcy did so was a surprise to Elizabeth, for the tense feeling of his arm under her hand suggested he was on the verge of an outburst. "If you think I possess the power to work on my nephew, I wonder at your audacity. Darcy is his own man and may direct his affairs without any reference to our feelings, whether displeased or no."

"My father would never have stood for such blatant disregard for his position," spat Lady Catherine.

"But my father is no longer the earl," replied Lord Matlock. "*I* am, and I am the head of this family. You would do well to remember that."

"How can I recall it when you insist on abrogating your responsibilities?"

"Have you heard nothing my uncle has said?" demanded Mr. Darcy, his temper frayed to the point of no longer holding his silence. "I am perfectly ready to do as I please, Lady Catherine, and I do not need your approval, nor do I need his lordship's, much though I respect him."

"As I have tried to inform you," added Lord Matlock.

"Furthermore," said Darcy, continuing over Lady Catherine's protests, "you should look about you and see that your objection to Miss Elizabeth is not echoed by anyone else in the family."

"Nor should it be," added Lady Anne, her shortness informing them all how angry she was. "Elizabeth is in every respect suitable to be among us, and a far better match for William than your own daughter, I dare say."

"Now I must think you mad," growled Lady Catherine. "To suggest she is better than Anne is utter lunacy!"

"Mother, do you not listen to anything anyone else has to say?"

As one, the four turned to the door to see Anne framed in it, accompanied by Colonel Fitzwilliam. How long she had been there Elizabeth could not say, but she sensed a determination about Anne the likes of which Elizabeth had not seen before in their short acquaintance.

"Aunt Anne said nothing about Elizabeth being better than I am," said Anne, advancing into the room. "She only said that she was a better match for William than I am. And in that she is correct."

"You have now infected my daughter with these ridiculous notions," cried Lady Catherine. "I cannot imagine where you have come by such thoughts, Anne, but I would remind you that you are both descended from the same great noble line on your mothers' sides, and equally ancient, though untitled lines on your fathers'. A match between you would be one of the greatest matches in our time, creating a dynasty which would be the envy of all. Why, Darcy could aspire to a title himself, further increasing our family's power. What can Miss Elizabeth offer that is greater?"

"You are the only one who craves such worldly adulation, Lady Catherine," said Mr. Darcy. "Do you not know that I care nothing for a title? I shall not give up the woman I love for such material concerns when I may aspire to something far greater." Mr. Darcy's glance found Anne and he added: "And I can only think Anne agrees with me regarding her own future."

"I do," said Anne without waiting for her mother to respond. "The issue, Mother, is your selfishness and insistence on enforcing your will on us all. Let me tell you here and now that you shall not work me by any means you possess to act against my inclination. Elizabeth and William will form a magnificent couple, and I can do nothing other than wish them every happiness.

"For myself, I have come to esteem Anthony, and it is *he* whom I will have as a husband, and not William."

It was Elizabeth's estimation that Lady Catherine had never had words directed at her, nor had Anne ever stood up to her mother with such force and determination. For a moment, Elizabeth thought apoplexy might strike the woman, so red of face and furious did she become. The moment passed much too quickly, for the lady soon found her voice.

"No, you shall not! I utterly forbid you to marry Fitzwilliam! What is he but a poor soldier, one who has spoken incessantly of his need for a wealthy wife?"

"He is the son of an earl, Catherine," retorted Lord Matlock, clearly at the end of his patience. "In fact, from the perspective of prudence alone, he is a much better match for Anne than Darcy is."

"I do not wish to marry Anne for such reasons, Father," said Colonel Fitzwilliam, never taking his eyes from the enraged form of his aunt. "I wish it based on nothing more than inclination."

"Oh, yes, it is inclination very well," cried Lady Catherine. "I know you have coveted your cousin's wealth all these years, Fitzwilliam. Do not think I have been blinded by your continued visits to Rosings with Darcy to see if you can displace him."

"Whatever your opinion, it matters little to me," said Anne.

"I am your mother," snapped Lady Catherine. "You will obey me."

"You *are* my mother, but I am of age," rejoined Anne. "I am my father's heir. My inheritance is not subject to your sufferance, nor am I beholden to obey your every whim.

"Furthermore, should you persist in this irrational objection, I will banish you to the dower house when I am married, for I will not have you bringing disharmony into my home."

"And I will support Anne," said Colonel Fitzwilliam. "Do not think I will be moved by your tantrums, Lady Catherine. You should know me better than to suppose this show of temper will have any effect on me."

For a moment, Lady Catherine said nothing. Her eyes flicked from Colonel Fitzwilliam to Anne, from thence to Darcy and then to

Elizabeth herself. When she made eye contact with Elizabeth, her lids narrowed, and her anger boiled over.

"Very well!" snapped she. "If you are fixed on this course of action, it seems there is nothing I can do to prevent it. I hope you all realize what a mistake this is. When you feel the full weight of your decisions today, as I have no doubt *this woman* will prove herself wholly inadequate to the level she aspires, then you will crawl to me, begging for my forgiveness. I shall not listen."

With those words and one final glare at Elizabeth, she marched from the room. As the door slammed behind her, Elizabeth thought it unlikely anyone would see her for the rest of the evening. The thought passed her mind that no one would repine her absence.

CHAPTER XVIII

"Well, it seems that particular problem has been resolved," jested Fitzwilliam almost the moment the door impacted the jamb behind Lady Catherine.

It was a well-practiced move for the family members present to roll their collective eyes at Fitzwilliam's irreverence, though Darcy noted that Miss Elizabeth laughed. The waggling of his eyebrows did nothing to return the atmosphere to the seriousness of the situation.

"Really, Anthony, can you not be serious for once?" asked the earl.

"Oh, aye, it *is* a serious business," replied Fitzwilliam, his grin belying his words. "I do not know about Darcy, but I am relieved Aunt Catherine's dissent has been removed from the equation."

The earl guffawed and exclaimed: "Yes, I suppose that must be a reason for celebration!" He then paused and glanced between Fitzwilliam and Anne. "While I will own to some knowledge of the interest between you, I had not known of your determination to marry. Is this not a little sudden?"

Anthony and Anne shared a look and turned back to Lord Matlock, Anne winding her arm through Anthony's. "Though it is still early, and we are far from an announcement, I believe both Anne and I know how it will end."

"I agree," added Anne. "As for the situation with Mother, I cannot repine what has occurred tonight. Since I have determined not to marry William, I have known this argument was inevitable."

"It is for the best, I think," replied Darcy, "for we shall both be happier with our chosen companions."

The stiffening of Miss Elizabeth's hand on his arm informed Darcy he may have been a little precipitous in stating his feelings before them all, but he supposed it was best she now understood his intentions. As the earl spoke, she remained silent, for now was not the time to discuss the matter.

"Then, I suppose the next step is to resign your commission. Your mother will be happy about that."

"Yes, she will, though that might be a little hasty. Nothing has been decided yet, after all."

"Anthony," said Anne, fixing him with a look, "I believe you may safely resign, for I have no wish for the war office to call you to the continent and claim your duty requires it of you."

With a brief glance at his future bride, Anthony turned back to his father. "It seems you have the right of it, Father. I shall notify my general tomorrow and begin the process of finding someone to purchase my commission."

The earl nodded and turned to Elizabeth and Mr. Darcy. "I will own I had no notion your own situation had progressed to such a degree."

"It has not," Miss Elizabeth was quick to say.

Darcy frowned a little when he looked down at her, but he sensed she was not averse to him as she might have been before and understood his comment had likely caught her more than a little by surprise. His uncle and mother shared in a moment of laughter at his expense, and when Miss Elizabeth noted him looking at her, she favored him with an impish smile. A weight seemed to fall from Darcy's heart at the sight.

"Well, perhaps it would be best to leave you alone for a moment," said Lord Matlock, "though we should take care we leave the door ajar. It would not do for rumors to spawn from your absence — or for them to gain any more foothold."

"If you wish a few moments together," said his mother, "I shall wait at the end of the hall and ensure no one intrudes upon you."

"Please, Mother, if you would not mind," said Darcy.

His mother must have given her agreement, for she nodded, rested a hand on Darcy's arm and grasped Miss Elizabeth's hand, and then led her family from the room. Darcy's eyes never left the woman who stood by his side. At the moment, she was regarding him in much the same way as he was watching her, openly, frankly, and with a hint of a curve in her eyebrow, as if daring him to speak. Darcy decided it was best to wait for her.

"Do you mean to say nothing, Mr. Darcy?" asked Miss Elizabeth. "Love was not a word I had heard you speak before you announced it to the room."

For a moment, Darcy wondered as to her meaning. "Would *you*, Miss Elizabeth, marry without affection?"

"No," was her prompt reply. "However, I did not just announce to my uncle and my mother that I was in love with you."

"Ah," said Darcy, fixing her with a grin, "but if you recall, I did not specifically declare love for *you*. I merely said I would not give up the woman I love for my aunt's demands."

"Then are you hiding some other woman in here?" asked Miss Elizabeth, casting a lazy glance about the room. "Perhaps under the sofa or—"

"Minx!" exclaimed Darcy, cutting her off. "Then I shall own to it. Yes, I have found you worthy of love. In fact, I have found it nigh impossible to remove you from my heart and mind, you have taken up such permanent residence there. While I should find it difficult to let you go now, I will not proceed unless you can assure me of a return of my sentiment. Do you think you can find it within yourself to return my affection?"

For a long moment, Miss Elizabeth regarded him, and had her lips not been turned up slightly, he might be worried for her response. It was, he supposed, something of a large alteration for her, for his heart had been engaged much longer than hers. In the end, he with her response did not disappoint.

"At present, I must own that it is all so new, Mr. Darcy," said she. "But I believe you may proceed, for I have great hope of a favorable outcome."

"Thank you, Miss Elizabeth," said Darcy with great feeling, knowing what a boon she had given him. "Then I shall seal our agreement."

Giving her no chance to respond, Darcy leaned down and captured her lips with his own, surprised and gratified when her arms snaked about his neck. Pulling her to him, Darcy was careful to keep his kisses light and playful, rather than releasing the passion which had built up in his breast and threatened to provoke him to actions highly improper.

It seemed Miss Elizabeth had no lack of passion herself, for though she was obviously inexperienced in the act, she more than made up for it in enthusiasm. When he pulled a little away from her and gazed into her beautiful dark brown eyes, he found them bright and peering back, lightly misted with the passion of their recent actions. Then her lips turned up in a slight smile, and she disengaged her arms.

"Had there been anyone present, I might have thought you eager to compromise me into accepting your suit, sir."

"No, indeed," replied Darcy. "But I would have you know, Miss Elizabeth—I mean to make you my wife. I will do everything in my power to ensure you believe me worth the risk of accepting."

In place of a response, Miss Elizabeth rose on the tips of her toes and placed a kiss again on his lips. "I begin to think your chances of success are good, Mr. Darcy. Continue in this charming manner, and perhaps they will rise again."

The sound of a cleared throat from beyond the door alerted Darcy to the continued presence of his mother and the fact they had been in that room alone for some time. It seemed Miss Elizabeth saw it too, for she inspected herself, ensuring there was nothing out of place, before turning to Darcy.

"Is my hair mussed?"

"It looks as beautiful as it did when we entered the room," said Darcy as she turned her head this way and that. "There is nothing out of place that I can see."

"Then you should escort me back to the ballroom, for I think we have been absent long enough."

With a bow, Darcy offered his arm for her to take and gestured toward the door, leading her thither. His mother had situated herself at the end of the hallway, though she turned as soon as they emerged, and approached them, looking to Elizabeth for signs of damage to her appearance.

"It seems your conversation did not have quite the destructive effect on your coiffeur I had feared," said she, regarding them with a grin she could not hide. "Then again, I know my proper and upright son would never trespass upon a lady's good reputation. Would you?"

"Of course not, Mother," replied Darcy, keeping a straight face. "Miss Elizabeth is entirely safe with me."

"And are you safe with Elizabeth?" asked his mother with laughing eyes.

"Perhaps not as safe as he was a short time earlier," replied Miss Elizabeth with her own brand of humor. "But I shall endeavor to keep myself under good regulation."

"Excellent," said Lady Anne. "Then we should return to the ballroom."

If there was one thing Darcy despised, it was being the focus of the gossip of others. On this occasion, however, he looked upon the whispers which were winging about the room before they entered — and rose noticeably when they returned — with a certain fatalistic acceptance. In deciding to marry a young woman who was an unknown in society, Darcy knew he was inviting the speculation. It was fortunate he would have such great sources of happiness attendant upon his situation, being married to a woman as wonderful as Miss Elizabeth, that he thought himself equal to withstanding any gossip, at least if they could avoid gossip which was mean-spirited or suggestive.

The mean-spirited sort Darcy knew would be Miss Elizabeth's cross to bear, for no one would say anything of the sort to *him*. There were enough men in society whose manners were not the best that Darcy knew he would be required to fend off suggestive comments not limited to the supposed *passion* of country girls. In this, Darcy was proven correct within minutes of returning to the room. Of course, not all the comments were of a bad sort. Some of his friends, in fact, were complimentary.

"I had thought you were wavering toward your cousin," said Hardwick, a good friend of Darcy's from his university days. "Not that Miss de Bourgh would have been a poor choice, as she is pretty enough and possesses a handsome dowry. But this sudden alteration is surprising, Darcy."

Darcy shrugged, keeping his eyes on Miss Elizabeth, who was moving about the dance floor with another man who was a slight acquaintance of Darcy's. "Yes, Anne is a good catch for any man, but I do not need her wealth, and managing another estate of such magnitude so far from Pemberley would be difficult."

"That is true." Hardwick laughed and slapped his back. "Though some will question your sanity for throwing aside a young woman of such advantages for a woman who, by all accounts, has little to her name, I cannot help but commend you. From what I have seen of Miss Elizabeth, she is a jewel of the first order."

'That she is, Hardwick," replied Darcy. "I feel fortunate I have recognized her worth is above the price of any dowry."

"And country girls are infamous for their passionate natures," interrupted Dowd, another of their acquaintances. Unlike Hardwick, however, Dowd was prone to being in his cups from time to time and speaking when he ought to remain silent, for all Darcy counted him a friend. "You shall experience it firsthand," exclaimed Dowd, throwing an arm around Darcy's shoulders, proving he was already a little top-heavy. "Leave us all envying you, eh?"

"Have a care, Dowd," said Darcy, divesting himself of his friend's arm. "Miss Elizabeth is a lady. You should not speak of her in such tones."

"I did not mean to cast aspersions on her character, Darcy," said Dowd, staggering as he stepped away. "A damn fine woman. Damn fine woman, indeed."

Hardwick shared a look with Darcy as their friend walked away. "It is a little early for him to be in his cups."

"Perhaps his mother has been difficult again. I have heard she is demanding he marry this year, and you know he is much more interested in the benefits of remaining single."

"Aye, that is true," laughed Hardwick. "Perhaps I should also begin to reflect on the benefits of marriage, my friend, and I might if you informed me if Miss Elizabeth has any other sisters than the angel Bingley cannot keep his eyes from."

"Three more," replied Darcy in an offhand tone, his eyes once again finding Miss Elizabeth.

"Then you must introduce me, my friend," said Hardwick, his jovial tone not hiding his seriousness in the slightest. "If they are in any way as pretty as your lady, I should be very happy to make their acquaintance."

The thought of the younger Bennet sisters brought a smirk to Darcy's face, which he noted his friend did not see, fixed as his attention was on the pair of Bennet sisters who were dancing close to each other. Though Darcy did not see any way those girls would be introduced to wider society anytime soon, the picture his mind painted was amusing.

"If there is an opportunity, I shall introduce you, my friend."

"Excellent!" said Hardwick. "I shall hold you to it."

Hardwick then turned away to seek a new partner for the dance while Darcy returned to his contemplation of Miss Elizabeth's perfections. Perhaps he should attempt to be sociable, but watching the young woman was far more satisfying.

Though Darcy was not aware of it, Elizabeth was soon to be the subject of those spiteful young ladies who were seeing the master of

Pemberley slip through their fingers. The chief among these was a pair to whom Elizabeth had not been introduced — they had not requested the introduction — but whom she had seen on several occasions. It took no great turn of thought to assume much would be said on her coming accord with Mr. Darcy, and as Elizabeth was expecting it, it was not a surprise when it came.

"It shall be great fun when we are sisters!" exclaimed Georgiana when she was in Elizabeth's company again. "I have always wanted one, you know."

"Let us not put the cart before the horse, Georgiana," replied Elizabeth, maintaining her calm. "I am not engaged to your brother yet, neither do I believe I am ready to accept a proposal."

"No, but I believe you are moving in that direction," said Anne, her tone teasing. "Else Mother would not have been so incensed."

"Mr. Darcy *has* watched you closely, and his ardor has grown apace," added Jane. "His looks are not possible to misinterpret."

"Perhaps they are not," said Elizabeth, a hint of embarrassment falling over her when she remembered their interlude in the library. "But I would not give the gossips material to fuel their whispers."

"Then you should not have stayed in the library so long after we all quit it," said Anne, casting a knowing glance at Elizabeth. "I suppose we should all be grateful your hair escaped serious damage and that your dress was not similarly affected, else it would have been plain for all to see."

Elizabeth swatted at Anne's arm, and she dodged it, her merriment ringing out over them all. The other two girls crowded in and offered their congratulations, though in a manner designed to tease.

"It *will* be so wonderful to all be related," said Anne when these teasing observations had been offered. "Though in my case it will be a little more distant, I shall count on your society in the coming years."

"I believe we may promise that, Anne," said Elizabeth, squeezing her friend's hand. "Regardless of what happens in the future, I hope to retain all your friendships."

Her sister and friends chorused their agreement. It was when this small group began to disperse, Georgiana looking for her mother while Jane's attention was caught again by Mr. Bingley, that the nastier elements of society struck.

"I will own I am not certain what Lady Anne was thinking," said a cold, affected voice near to where Elizabeth stood.

A glance to the side revealed the haughty person of Lady Eugenie Clark, with Miss Yates by her side. While the lady appeared as she had the first occasion Elizabeth had seen them—which had been unchanged in each subsequent instance—Miss Yates was altered. Gone was the insipid disinterest, the reliance on her aunt's ability to speak for her, and instead her expression showed cold fury.

"This is what we must expect, I suppose," said the girl, in an affected tone, yet one lacking any strength of character. "When one invites the lower classes to mingle with them, one cannot be surprised when they attempt to usurp the position held by their rightful betters."

Elizabeth declined to speak to them, instead turning her attention back to the dance. It appeared Lady Eugenie was not about to allow herself to be so summarily dismissed.

"Do you have nothing to say for yourself?" asked the woman, her voice shrill and displeased.

"I apologize, Madam," said Elizabeth, "but we have not been introduced."

"Do not feign misunderstanding," snapped Lady Eugenie. "I am well aware Lady Anne has informed you of my identity."

"Perhaps she has," replied Elizabeth, "but that does not change the fact that we are not acquainted. Perhaps you should apply to Lady Anne if you wish to speak with me, for I am not in the habit of giving consequence to those ladies who will not even show the good manners of requesting an introduction."

"I have no need to know you!" spat Lady Eugenie, while at the same time Miss Yates gasped and exclaimed: "Such insolence!"

Lady Eugenie shot her niece a quelling look which cowed the girl, though her baleful glare never waned. Her niece silenced, Lady Eugenie's malevolence once again found Elizabeth.

"Perhaps you do not know who I am, or it may be your witlessness has led you to misunderstand what it means to be in company with those who are your betters."

"Or perhaps you have confronted me with the purpose of trying to intimidate me," replied Elizabeth. "I know exactly who you are and what power you hold—should I be blamed for refusing to allow you to intimidate me? It would be best if you simply leave me be, for I am a guest in this house, which is, I am certain you must remember, the home of an earl."

At that moment behind Lady Eugenie, Elizabeth could see Lady Anne approaching with Lady Susan and had no illusions about how they would see this jumped up woman attempting to browbeat her. Lady Eugenie, however, did not take the warning she imparted.

"I shall see you ruined if you persist in speaking to me in such a manner!"

"As always," said Lady Susan when she had come close enough to overhear, "your opinion of your own power far exceeds the reality."

Startled by the sudden words, both of Elizabeth's tormentors jumped and whirled to see the sisters looking on them with no hint of friendliness in their countenances. Had Lady Eugenie been as haughty and confident as she attempted to appear, the sudden pallor would not have fallen over her, pale skin akin to the color of a sheet. The woman continued to sneer, but it was clear to all present it was nothing but bluster.

"No one will be ruined, Lady Eugenie," continued Lady Susan while the baroness was engaged in trying to recall her wits. "If, however, you mean to persist in accosting my guests, perhaps we shall see what stories those of society will invent when your ejection from my home is known to society."

For a moment the ladies stood and stared at each other, the baroness attempting to discover the resolve of the other two women. After a moment of this, Lady Eugenie seemed to come to the correct conclusion, for she turned to address her niece.

"Come, Clara," said the woman, "let us depart. It is clear there is nothing for us here."

"But Aunt," the whining voice of the younger woman floated back to them, "*she* is not good enough to marry Mr. Darcy. He was to be mine!"

The two women moved far enough away that they could be heard no longer, leaving Elizabeth to laugh, in which Lady Anne and Lady Susan joined with a will. For a moment, none of them could say anything for their hilarity.

"Perhaps we should allow her to have a go at William," said Lady Susan. "It would be amusing if nothing else."

Lady Anne huffed, her amusement forgotten in the face of affront. "To think *that woman* was filling her insipid niece with the notion of marrying my son! William would never even look at the likes of her.'

Though it was clear she agreed, Lady Susan shook her head in disgust and turned to Elizabeth. "I hope those two harpies were not distressing you, Miss Elizabeth."

"Not at all," replied Elizabeth. "I knew their insults would be ineffectual."

"That is a good word to describe them," said Lady Anne. The woman smiled and put a hand on Elizabeth's back. "It is unfortunate, but I doubt they will be the last. Should you have any trouble with any other ladies tonight, or any other night, be certain to come to Susan or me. We shall set them to rights."

"Do you not know?" asked Elizabeth, affecting a haughtiness similar to Lady Eugenie's. "My courage rises at any attempt to intimidate me and shall not be taken away by the likes of those two colorless women."

The ladies again laughed. "That is well, for I believe you will require that fortitude in the coming days."

Well did Elizabeth know it. Though many had been welcoming of the Bennet sisters, there were many more she could not trust to behave with the same degree of kindness. But Elizabeth would not concern herself. She knew the extent of her mettle.

As the strains of the supper set floated over the company, Lady Anne was given all the satisfaction of watching her son dance with the young lady she was certain he would marry. It had been difficult, for William had made it so, and at times Elizabeth was not any better. But it had all worked out. Catherine's ruffled feathers would take some time to smooth, but in the end, Anne was certain she would understand the benefits of Anthony for her daughter and accept that which she could not change.

"What a good night this has become!" said Georgiana from her side. "After Elizabeth informed us of William's actions in Hertfordshire, I had not thought to see this happy ending!"

"And yet, Elizabeth is forgiving, and not so unaffected by him as she might have liked to assert," replied Anne.

The pair passed close by to where they were standing, and Anne grinned at Elizabeth as she glided past. Elizabeth's cheeks pinked a little, though it was clear she was enjoying herself and happy. Perhaps the young woman could not state with a certainty she loved William, but Anne knew the feeling was there, simmering under the surface.

"Anne and Anthony appear happy too," observed Georgiana, drawing Anne's attention to the other couple further down the line.

"Our efforts were for her benefit as well," said Anne. "Though I do not think either would have been *unhappy*, I foresee a future in which she, too, obtains her heart's desire."

"Then we did well," replied Georgiana. Then she turned a mock glare on her mother. "However, I would beg you not to obtain a taste for matchmaking, Mother. I believe I can find my own partner well enough without assistance."

Anne laughed and drew Georgiana close. "As long as you find a man with whom you are well suited and can be happy, you may be assured of my support, dearest. If you choose awry, then you can expect my interference."

Though Georgiana glowered a little at that, Anne's grin did not dim a jot, and soon her daughter was laughing along with her. They turned to their watching of the couples, only a few words passing between them as they watched.

Georgiana was correct. Anne decided; they had well done. Who would ever have thought they would find the perfect woman for William in the wilds of Hertfordshire, far from the center of society? And yet they had, and Anne could only be grateful for it. There was work to do in the future, but for now, she allowed herself to bask in the success of seeing to her son's happiness. And she knew he would be very happy, indeed.

EPILOGUE

$\mathscr{P}$emberley was everything her new family had told her it was. The peaks in the distance, the long valley in which it stood, offering a myriad of paths for Elizabeth to explore, the proximity to the quaint market town of Lambton—all these factors were highly in favor of a place which had become Elizabeth's favorite place on earth. And in it, she found a home, a loving husband, a mother who supported and helped her, and a sister who was as dear to her as the sisters of her birth.

Georgiana was no longer at Pemberley, having met and married a young man of considerable fortune the previous season. Though it had been difficult to see her leave for her new home, Elizabeth knew she was happy, and took comfort in that knowledge. William had found it even harder to endure, for what man thinks any man is good enough for his baby sister? With Elizabeth and his mother standing united in their support of Georgiana, he had given way—not that there had been any question of his capitulation—but Elizabeth had seen his pensive mood on more than one occasion during his sister's courtship.

"Elizabeth!" exclaimed a voice as she entered the house from the back gardens.

With a smile, she handed her bonnet and pelisse to a waiting maid and looked up to see her husband striding toward her. The pensiveness she had noted during Georgiana's courtship was long gone, and in its place was vexation. Elizabeth could not blame him, for exasperation often seemed her constant companion these days.

"Yes, William?" asked Elizabeth, reaching out to accept his hand, allowing him to draw her close. "Has Cassandra escaped from the nursery again?"

A snort was William's response. "Cassandra is with her governess at present, though I do not doubt she is testing her as we speak. If I had known what sort of children we would produce, I might have thought twice before offering for you."

It was a well-worn jest, and Elizabeth laughed along with her husband. "Yes, perhaps you should have considered the matter more carefully. If you had asked my mother, she would have informed you of what kind of a child I was."

"Do you think she would have?" asked William. "Surely she would have avoided any subject which would have put her daughters in anything but the best possible light."

"Ah, but my mother thought it was charming. Or, at least she thought so in hindsight, for I can well remember infuriating her as a child."

William offered his arm, and they turned and moved further into the house. "Alas, I doubt it would have changed anything, for I was much too in love with you to consider any impediments."

A smile was Elizabeth's response and she looked up at her husband with devotion. Though most of society would not credit it, the man was loving in private, though he kept his mask on in public where others could see. Elizabeth could not imagine feeling more cherished if she had married the most demonstrative man in the world. They had their share of arguments, but they had promised early in their relationship never to say anything to hurt the other, and to ask for clarification instead of wallowing in misunderstanding. Thus far it had worked for them, as their marriage was as loving now, three years after their wedding, as it had been when they said their vows.

"At present, Cassandra is perfectly behaved," said Darcy. He showed her a grin and added: "I suspect, however, she will not be for long, for that look of mischief is alive in her eyes. No, at present I am vexed with your youngest sister."

Elizabeth sighed and they shared a commiserating glance. It had been a surprise when Lady Anne had proposed to take her family in hand and teach them proper manners soon after Elizabeth and Darcy had returned from their wedding trip. Elizabeth had not been eager to hand them off to her, for it was not her responsibility to see to the Bennet family. But the lady had won them over with good sense arguments and eagerness to be of use.

"As you know," said she when Elizabeth protested, "your family is part of who you are, Elizabeth. As it stands at present, your younger sisters can never be seen in society, and if some of those who wish for mischief seek them out, tales of their behavior could spread throughout London quickly. It is not my purpose to cast shade on them, but it would be best if they were in society, showing all and sundry you have nothing to hide."

When Elizabeth looked on her with skepticism, Lady Anne had laughed and patted her shoulder. "Do not concern yourself, Elizabeth. I do not think it will be as difficult as you believe. If they give me difficulty, I can count on Susan's help, for she and Hugh will not wish your family to be a detriment, if they cannot be a credit."

So, Lady Anne had, one by one, taken her family into her protection and taught them how to behave. To Elizabeth's great surprise, Mrs. Bennet's reformation had been easily accomplished, for her mother was so in awe of Lady Anne that she did as she was asked without question. That was not to say that Mrs. Bennet had changed to the extent that she was an informed and rational woman— she remained flighty, though her nerves were a thing of the past. But she now knew to hold her tongue in company, for Lady Anne had explained to her at some length how her words could be perceived.

"You have taken away my source of amusement, Lizzy," her father had commented on one occasion. "Your mother is now so well behaved that there is little at which to laugh."

Such words had struck Elizabeth as rather improper, and she replied, saying: "Would you prefer the return of the woman who embarrasses you at every turn?"

"Mrs. Bennet rarely embarrassed me," was her father's irreverent reply. "I had rather grown inured to her ways."

"All jesting aside," Mr. Bennet hastened to say when he saw Elizabeth's annoyance, "she is rather more tolerable to live with. Though I suppose I could take offense that your mother-in-law is doing what I could not, I shall be philosophical and appreciate her efforts instead."

Then whistling a jaunty tune, Mr. Bennet strode away toward the library. He was rarely removed from its confines when in residence at Pemberley, and more than once Elizabeth had caught William in there with him, avoiding the chaos the rest of her family sometimes caused. She supposed she could not be angry with him, for she knew he loved her despite her improper family.

With Mrs. Bennet's improvement, the rest of the girls should have been easy. Mary was no trouble, for she only needed a little guidance. By the time Elizabeth returned home from London, the changes in Mary had already been striking, for her father's attention and tutelage had taught her there was more to life than Fordyce, and as she was intelligent, her insights into the works Mr. Bennet had coaxed her to read were well considered and enjoyable. When she had been introduced to one of William's friends the year after Elizabeth's own season with Lady Anne, the man had been so taken by her that he had asked for a courtship within weeks of making her acquaintance.

"Well, that is a surprise," William had said upon hearing the news.

"Why so?" asked Elizabeth, curious as to his meaning. She knew he was not slighting Mary, for he had long found her the most tolerable of her sisters other than Jane,

"The night of our argument with Lady Catherine, Hardwick sought my promise to introduce him to your sisters. I agreed, but never thought he would marry one."

Elizabeth laughed. "It seems we Bennet girls are irresistible to men of society."

"Perhaps you are, Elizabeth," said Mr. Darcy catching her in his arms and silencing her with a kiss which made her breathless.

By contrast, Kitty had been only a little difficult. Kitty was not so ungovernable as Lydia and being removed from her sister's influence had done wonders for her temper. She had come out the year after Mary, meaning the coming season would be her second. Though she had no firm suitors during her season, she had informed Elizabeth that she was content for it to be that way, for she did not feel she was ready for marriage. Between Kitty and Georgiana, a firm friendship had been established—Kitty was visiting Georgiana's home at present and would meet them again when they descended on London for the season.

That left the final Bennet sister . . . . Elizabeth and Darcy's steps had led them to the music room, and Elizabeth could hear the discordant sound of the pianoforte being played very ill flowing from the room. At the same time, a bevy of complaints reached her ears from the girl who sat at the instrument. Sharing a grin with William—though his was more akin to a grimace—Elizabeth pushed open the door and entered the room.

"Lizzy!" exclaimed Lydia as soon as she caught sight of them. "I cannot imagine how you endured these lessons, for I have done nothing I hated more in the entirety of my life!"

"In fact," said Lady Anne before Elizabeth could respond, "if you had only a little more patience, you would do very well. I dare say you have almost as much talent as your elder sisters. It is your application of that talent which is an issue."

"I do not understand why I must learn to play anyway," groused Lydia. "It is not as if I am fit to be heard by anyone other than family."

Though Elizabeth had witnessed her mother-in-law losing her temper with the final Bennet daughter more than the other two combined, in this instance she remained calm. "No, I dare say you will not play in company at all after your coming out. It will take more practice before you are fit to do so."

"Lizzy," said Lydia, her voice nothing less than a whine. "Why must I do such silly exercises when they do me no good at all? I want to go to London and dance at parties and balls and see and be seen. This is all nonsense—I have been out in society for more than three years."

"Perhaps you would prefer to wait another year for your coming out?" asked Mrs. Bennet, who sat near to Lady Anne. "It would be no trouble to delay your coming out until you are nineteen and better qualified to control your outbursts."

Lydia cast a resentful glare at her mother as she always did when Mrs. Bennet spoke to her in such a manner. The girl had not taken her mother's defection well, for whereas Mrs. Bennet had indulged her in anything, her new outlook on life had made her determined her daughters would do her credit. At present, Mrs. Bennet was perhaps harsher with her daughter than the woman who was seeing to her education.

"I have already had to wait two years longer than Mary, and a year longer than Kitty!" was Lydia's petulant complaint.

"If we followed that schedule," said Mrs. Bennet, "you would wait *another* year, for Kitty is *two* years older than you. Perhaps that would be best, as I struggle to see any improvement in your manners."

"You should listen and obey, Lydia," said Mrs. Garret, the woman they had hired to help ready Lydia for her debut. "If you do not learn some manners, I am ready to advise your mother to do just that."

That silenced Lydia, and she turned back to the instrument, though not without muttering under her breath. Elizabeth shared an amused glance with her mother and mother-in-law and joined her sister on the bench.

"I know it is hard, Lydia, but this is how matters are done in London. You are accustomed to Meryton. London is a much more difficult place to pass yourself off with any credit—if you give those harpies any reason, they will tear you apart."

Lydia replied with an exaggerated sigh. "So you have told me, Lizzy. But it is just so *hard*."

"When you think it is hard, think of the delights which will come your way if you learn all you should. Then think of another year waiting. I am certain you will come to the proper conclusion."

Again Lydia sighed, but this time she sat up straight and squared her shoulders before beginning to play. Elizabeth listened for a moment, noting the girl's fingering and technique. Though she was uncertain Lady Anne's words concerning Lydia's talent were not embellished, she had some aptitude. It was only getting her to apply herself which was so difficult.

Squeezing her sister's shoulder, Elizabeth rose and moved away, making her way to her husband and sitting by his side. When she did so, he leaned toward her.

"Crisis averted?"

"Until the next one rears its ugly head," replied Elizabeth.

William shook his head. "Perhaps we should simply send her to Aunt Catherine. She would do anything, even behave herself, to escape before she had spent a fortnight at Rosings."

"And you would wish this on Anne and Anthony?"

A chuckle escaped William's lips, and he said: "It would serve him right for all the teasing I have endured over the years. In fact, I might find myself ahead of the game, should we give the responsibility of your sister to him."

Elizabeth swatted at her husband and turned back to her contemplation of her sister. As Lady Anne had averred, Lady Catherine had come around quickly—more so, in fact, than Elizabeth would have guessed. Though the lady was still no more than cordial to Elizabeth herself, she now doted on her daughter and new son-in-law and was often heard to crow about her daughter producing an heir, while Elizabeth's child had been a girl. As William and Elizabeth were deliriously happy with their daughter, they did not care a jot for the lady's opinion. In fact, Elizabeth hoped she would have something to share with her husband soon, and perhaps this time it would be the awaited Pemberley heir.

Thoughts of Lady Catherine often reminded her about Mr. Collins, as the gentleman still venerated her as his patroness, though the appellation now more properly belonged to her daughter. Mr. Collins, contrary to any expectation of Elizabeth's, had taken her father's words to heart. His failed proposal to Mary had seemed to teach him something, and when he found a young woman for whom he wished to offer, he took the time to court her. Mr. Collins too had produced a son and an heir for Longbourn. Her father, who had met the infant, had confided to Elizabeth that in looks, the child had taken after his mother. Elizabeth knew her father well enough to know that what he did not say was that he hoped the boy had also inherited his mother's temper and intelligence.

As for Elizabeth's favorite sister, Jane, who had married months before Elizabeth, was now the proud mother of two daughters. Though Mrs. Bennet had backslid a little and bemoaned the lack of an heir, Mr. Bingley had informed her his estate was not entailed and would be left to the eldest daughter, should they not be so fortunate as to have a son.

Mr. Bingley's sister had caught the gentleman who had accompanied her to the Academy and was now living in Bedfordshire with her husband. While Elizabeth could not call her a friend — and the former Miss Bingley seemed to have little desire to allow it — they were cordial enough in each other's company. Mr. Powell was not the same level of society as Mr. Darcy, and as such, their attendance at the same events was sporadic, a function of their connections to the Darcys through her brother. Elizabeth found she could cheerfully do without Mrs. Powell's company.

Regarding Elizabeth's Aunt and Uncle Gardiner, they still lived in London, and Mr. Gardiner's business grew more profitable every year. It was their hope the situation of Mr. Gardiner's business would allow them to purchase an estate within the next several years. Elizabeth wished for nothing more than to have her dearest relations situated nearby.

Of Mr. Wickham, Elizabeth had never again seen anything. His letters to her husband were frequent and pleading, and for a while, Mr. Darcy had ignored them, hoping his former friend was learning his lesson. In the end, though Mr. Wickham had pleaded to be allowed to go to the New World to make a new life for himself, Mr. Darcy had made good on his earlier determination and decided it was best to ship him off to Botany Bay.

"Do you think Lydia will be ready this year?" asked William, pulling Elizabeth from her thoughts.

"I believe she is desperate enough to do as she is told, so she is not held out of society," replied Elizabeth.

William nodded and returned to his contemplation of his sister by marriage. "I hope so, Elizabeth, for another year of this will be difficult to endure." Elizabeth smiled but did not reply, and after a moment William continued: "I have a friend who seems to enjoy the company of spirited ladies. Should we, perhaps, introduce them when we are in London?"

"You just want to be rid of her," accused Elizabeth, though not with any heat.

"Guilty," replied William with a smile. "But when I consider it, your sister will require a firm hand. Ramsay is a good man and has had the responsibility for three younger sisters for several years. I suspect he could be the making of her."

"As long as there is no overt matchmaking, Mr. Darcy," said Elizabeth. "I believe I have had enough of that for a lifetime."

William turned to look at her, laughter in his eyes. "My mother's actions were not improper, and you cannot argue with the results."

"Perhaps they were not," replied Elizabeth. "But Lydia differs from me and will not appreciate it if she thinks she is being directed."

"It is fortunate I agree with you, Mrs. Darcy," replied William, putting an arm around her and pulling her close. "We shall introduce them and step back to let nature take its course."

As Elizabeth leaned into her husband, she reflected that while she had found her mother-in-law's measures questionable, she was grateful to Lady Anne. To a large degree, she thought her happy situation at present was due to the lady's actions, and for that, she had no cause to repine.

The End

FOR READERS WHO LIKED *A MATCHMAKING MOTHER*

A Gift for Elizabeth
Sundered from her parents and sisters, a depressed Elizabeth Bennet lives with the Gardiners in London. When times seem most desperate, she makes a new acquaintance in Mr. Darcy, and the encounter changes her perspective entirely. With the spirit of Christmas burning within her, Elizabeth begins to recover from the hardships which have beset her life.

A Tale of Two Courtships
Two sisters, both in danger of losing their hearts. One experiences a courtship which ends quickly in an engagement, the other must struggle against the machinations of others. And one who will do anything to ensure her beloved sister achieves her heart's desire.

Mr. Bennet Takes Charge
When Elizabeth Bennet's journey to the lakes is canceled, Mr. Bingley, along with his elusive friend Mr. Darcy, return to Netherfield. Then Elizabeth learns her sister, Lydia, means to elope with a rake, and the very respectability of her family is at stake. Elizabeth takes heart when her father rises to the occasion; with Mr. Darcy's assistance, there may still be time to prevent calamity, and even find love.

The Challenge of Entail
Mr. Bennet ends the dreaded entail, leaving him free to leave Longbourn where he wishes. When the militia arrives in Meryton, they find a Bennet family much altered and Jane Bennet, a young woman destined to inherit a substantial property. Business in London delays the arrival of the Netherfield party to Hertfordshire, and when they do arrive, Mr. Darcy discovers the presence of a hated enemy and finds a woman he can admire.

The Impulse of the Moment
Mr. Darcy finds a young woman in Elizabeth Bennet who has matured from the girl he knew four years earlier. Elizabeth finds herself compelled by Mr. Darcy and attraction grows, a connection begins to be forged. But elements of Mr. Darcy's family, those who possess the power to exert great influence over his future, do not take kindly to his potential choice of a wife.

Whispers of the Heart
A different Bingley party arrives in Hertfordshire leading to a new suitor emerging for the worthiest of the Bennet sisters. As her sister has obtained her happiness, Elizabeth Bennet finds herself thrown into society far above any she might have otherwise expected, which leads her to a new understanding of the enigmatic Mr. Darcy.

For more details, visit

http://www.onegoodsonnet.com/genres/pride-and-prejudice-variations

About the Author

Jann Rowland is a Canadian, born and bred. Other than a two-year span in which he lived in Japan, he has been a resident of the Great White North his entire life, though he professes to still hate the winters.

Though Jann did not start writing until his mid-twenties, writing has grown from a hobby to an all-consuming passion. His interests as a child were almost exclusively centered on the exotic fantasy worlds of Tolkien and Eddings, among a host of others. As an adult, his interests have grown to include historical fiction and romance, with a particular focus on the works of Jane Austen.

When Jann is not writing, he enjoys rooting for his favorite sports teams. He is also a master musician (in his own mind) who enjoys playing piano and singing as well as moonlighting as the choir director in his church's congregation.

Jann lives in Alberta with his wife of more than twenty years, two grown sons, and one young daughter. He is convinced that whatever hair he has left will be entirely gone by the time his little girl hits her teenage years. Sadly, though he has told his daughter repeatedly that she is not allowed to grow up, she continues to ignore him.

Website: http://onegoodsonnet.com/
Facebook: https://facebook.com/OneGoodSonnetPublishing/
Twitter: @OneGoodSonnet
Mailing List: http://eepurl.com/bol2p9

Printed in Great Britain
by Amazon

57398999R00129